"Thought we'd squeeze fresh juice."

"Not if I get hold of your neck first." She advanced on him until they stood bare toe to bare toe on the tiled floor. "*Calder's Rose* was to be a joint effort—"

"As specified in our contract."

"Yet you—you—" She swatted his arm with the pages. "Snuck back into the living room after our argument yesterday and began the book without me."

He looked more confused than guilty. "What are you talking about?" Before she landed him a second blow, he snatched the pages and began to read.

Tongues jabbed hot and wild. Throbbing breasts aching for his touch. Pelvic bones grinding together. His hips jolted a dozen times. . . .

"I swear I never wrote a word of this."

She flicked a finger at the pages he held. "The plot's as coarse and crude as your gunslinger. You should be arrested—"

"I won't be signing a confession of guilt. I didn't write this!"

"There are only two of us sharing this cottage. You even left boot prints by my desk."

He tossed the papers on the kitchen counter, crossed over to the dusty outline of a boot near her desk. He frowned. "That's not mine. I may write Westerns, but I don't dress the part."

"What are you doing?"

"I'm going to draft a Wanted poster. Dead or alive, we'll have justice."

CALDER'S ROSE

KATE ANGELL

LOVE SPELL NEW YORK CITY

LOVE SPELL®

April 2003

Published by

Dorchester Publishing Co., Inc.
276 Fifth Avenue
New York, NY 10001

ISBN 0-505-52532-1

Printed in the United States of America.

Visit us on the web at www.dorchesterpub.com.

To family, and friends as close as family:

My mother, Marion Brown, and in memory of my father, Robert L.

Paul and Judy Brown, and my nieces and nephews—distance can never separate family.

Debbie and Ted Roome, Sunny and Jake—I have always appreciated your kindness, generosity, and holiday hospitality. You are the best.

Cindy and Sandy Smith—the unforgettable Twisted Sisters.

Madonna Knight—wonderful neighbor and typist-to-the-rescue. You are appreciated.

Those four-footed friends whose tails always wag: Senna and California Bonaventure.

And to Alicia Condon—gracious lady and editorial director extraordinaire. Thank you for "The Call" on my birthday.

CALDER'S ROSE

Chapter One

"You talking to yourself or to an imaginary friend?"

The man Devin James addressed looked over the top of his computer and stared her dead in the eye. "I'm stretching my imagination. You got a problem with that?"

She returned Shane McNamara's hard look. "You've begun answering yourself, when you should be consulting me."

His mouth thinned, the shift of his body revealing pure annoyance. "I'm not used to working with a writing partner."

"Neither am I." She picked up a bright yellow pencil with a green cactus eraser and twirled it between her fingers. "I'm enjoying it less by the minute."

Shane pushed his chair away from his solid mahogany desk, jumped to his feet, and turned to face her. Then, shoving his hands into the pockets of his worn black Levi's, he started his pacing once again. His muscles flexed restlessly beneath the tight stretch of a gray T-shirt that read, *Rattlesnake Kate's Saloon, Amarillo, Texas.* Moving from one end of the red Oriental carpet to the other, he filled the modestly furnished writer's cottage with charged tension.

Devin waited for him to produce a thought. Any thought. She clenched her teeth when he raked his fingers through his overlong black hair, then scrubbed his palm over his stubbled but angular jaw one more time.

"Since we can't write, let's eat." He patted his flat abdomen, as if to tame the growl of hunger. "I'm starved. Want to break for lunch?"

Devin glanced at the Art Deco wall clock. It was sky blue and shaped like a sun, its squiggly rays shooting high and spiraling low, dipping into an aquarium stocked with large aqua marbles and bright orange glass fish.

"It's ten o'clock," she noted. "Let's structure a schedule: work for two hours, dine closer to noon."

"My stomach thinks my throat's been slit." He glared down his nose at her.

She slid a cranberry-colored glass candy dish filled with gourmet jelly beans across the desk toward him. "Help yourself; these will take the edge off."

He scooped up a handful, popped them into his mouth, and began to chew. He immediately screwed up his face. "God-awful."

"It's best to sample one jelly bean at a time," Devin informed him.

"Now you tell me." Shane shifted his jaw left, then right, ground his teeth, and swallowed hard. "I tasted pear and apricot."

She drew the dish back to herself and sampled a

yellow jelly bean. "Mmm, pineapple, as fresh as sliced fruit."

He gazed toward the kitchen. "I'd rather eat the fruit."

"Later. We've work to do."

He scowled. "I hate schedules. Don't tie me to one."

She drew her lips inward, biting down on her irritation. "I write nine to five."

"I prefer midnight to six."

"Compromise—"

"Won't be reached," he said flatly. "I can't corral my creativity."

"Can't or won't?" she asked.

"I'm a law unto myself."

"You've no room for a writing partner?"

"Only one who abides by my rules."

Cocky son of a gun. "Don't fall off your high horse." Devin imagined him breaking his neck. "Our contract states that *Calder's Rose* must be a team effort. Team, as in two to write this book. You need me."

"About as much as I need a second head." He paused, then suggested, "We could write in shifts."

"We write together."

"For the moment . . ." He sauntered back toward his desk. Seated across the room he appeared less intimidating, focused on the book and not on her.

Devin flipped the pencil aside, blowing out an agitated breath. What had she been thinking when she'd agreed to do this project? Insanity didn't run in her family.

How had she allowed her editor, Angela Reims, to talk her into coauthoring a Western with Shane McNamara? Somehow terms such as *chance of a lifetime, six-figure advance, all-expense-paid book tour,* and *build a broader readership* had overshadowed the reality of the project. Under contract now, she and Shane had a ridiculously short time to produce a novel that would combine the lead characters from each of their best-selling series. Next year, the bookstore shelves would be stocked with *Calder's Rose*, a novel that blended romance with adventure, as Dare Calder of the *Texas West* series walked through the swinging saloon doors of Rose Coltraine's *Scarlet Garter* series.

The long-awaited Western would draw cheers from fans, smiles from editors, and a nervous breakdown from Devin James. They were only three days into the project, and already she wanted nothing more than to tear up their contract. Tear it to shreds. Let the batwing doors to the *Scarlet Garter* hit Dare Calder in the ass. She was beginning to dislike the gunslinger as much as she did his creator.

While Shane cleared a workspace, she took the opportunity to study him. The professional photograph that appeared on his novels blurred his sharp edges. McNamara looked as much a renegade as his character. The author's shaggy dark hair, unshaven jaw, and outlaw eyes would have looked perfect on a gunslinger like Dare Calder. From the moment she and Shane had been introduced, his steel-blue gaze had held her at gunpoint. She hadn't been able to slip his line of fire, no matter how hard she tried.

Press releases had tagged him a man's man and a woman's deepest desire. McNamara swaggered through life, writing near-pornographic Westerns that left the reader as hot as the Texas sun. Devin found him rough, arrogant, and distasteful. She'd love to chew him up and spit him out like a wad of tobacco.

The man brought new meaning to the word *tension.* She blamed the origin of her headache on Silver Star

Publishing; its continuous throbbing she attributed to Shane.

"Where shall we begin?" he finally asked.

She rolled her shoulders and suggested, "How about starting with a detailed outline?"

He shook his head. "I write intuitively."

Dread darkened her outlook on the project. "You never plot?"

"I thrive on gut instinct."

Devin rested her elbows on the marble desktop, her fingers steepled. She closed her eyes. Heaven help her.

"Are you praying?"

She blinked. Her thoughts had been anything but holy.

The ringing of the telephone saved her from responding. She leaned back in her chair as Shane reached across his desk and punched the speakerphone.

"Writer's block."

"Shane? Surely you jest?" The woman's voice held an impatient edge.

"Hello, Vic. And no, I'm not joking."

"Is Devin with you?"

"At my desk, Victoria." Devin welcomed a link to sanity.

Victoria Patton, the best public relations person in the business, cleared her throat. "Are you experiencing the same symptoms as Shane?"

"Not as much block as different writing styles."

Victoria's tone softened. "I see." There was silence, followed by, "Chances of compromise?"

"A long way off," Shane drawled.

"Listen, you two." Victoria's tone turned stern. "I just got off the phone with sales and marketing. They want us to start promoting the book with your first chapter."

"We haven't written a word," Devin confessed.

"Words, sentences, paragraphs. Put a few together. I need chapter one by Friday."

"Friday of what week?" asked Shane.

"This week," Victoria insisted.

Across the room, Shane's and Devin's gazes locked and held.

Devin shrugged a shoulder, then nodded her agreement.

Shane straightened, vigorously shaking his head.

"It will be ready," Devin promised.

Shane snorted, leaned back in his chair, and propped his feet on the desktop. "Incentive, Vic? Care to horsetrade?"

Victoria grumbled good-naturedly. "I have a bribe. The completed chapter will gain you two tickets to the Jamie Jensen concert a week from Saturday." A brief pause. "If Shane agrees?"

Why wouldn't he agree? Devin perked up and sat a little straighter. Glancing at Shane, she found him watching her. Intently.

He pursed his lips. "I had you pegged for classical or elevator music, not country-western."

"You're not much of a judge of character," Devin muttered.

Victoria's *tsk-tsk* drew his frown. "Know thy fellow writer. Truth be known, Devin also line dances. I've seen her tush-push and boot-scoot boogie. She draws more whistles than a train stop."

Heat slanted across Devin's cheekbones. She dipped her head to avoid McNamara's prying gaze. The last thing Devin wanted Shane to know was how she wound down after a day of writing.

Unaware she'd handed Shane a cartridge of ammunition, Victoria pressed, "Any objections to the concert, Mr. McNamara?"

"What's past is past," he said evasively, his tone low, cryptic.

Although Devin didn't understand his comment, it seemed crystal-clear to Victoria.

"Jamie's music's good, even if she is temperamental." Victoria sounded well acquainted with the singer.

"If it's convenient," their publicist continued. "I'll drop off the tickets when I pick up the rough draft."

"It's going to be real rough," Shane contended.

"You'll smooth it out," Victoria assured him. "I know it's not easy for either of you to write with a partner," she sympathized. "Your styles may vary, but once you mesh, the chapters will flow. This is going to be a best-seller."

There was a heartbeat of silence, which Shane broke. "Could you pack in a few board games, two decks of cards, several crossword-puzzle books, and a red Frisbee with those Jamie Jensen tickets?"

"*Games*?" The word stuck on Devin's tongue.

"Connect four, checkers, dominoes." Shane grew explicit.

Games designed for two players. Being the only other person at the cottage, Devin knew whom he'd choose as a partner.

"A boy and his toys." She groaned. "We'll never get any writing done."

"A man needs his entertainments," Shane said. "The creative process becomes easier the harder I play. Strip poker puts me in the mood to write all night."

Devin just bet it did. She rolled her eyes. She'd push for solitaire.

Victoria cleared her throat. "Anything more adult?"

He cast a glance at Devin and shook his head.

7

"You're leapfroggin' ahead, Vic. Old Devin's not ready for ForePlay. Store the erotic board games for a week or two."

Devin wanted to crawl beneath her desk.

Victoria, on the other hand, chuckled. "I was referring to *thinking* games, Shane. Trivial Pursuit, Scrabble, Rapid Recall."

"Only if you can find the kiddie knockoff."

"I'll shop around," Victoria said. "How about, Devin? Can I bring you a coloring book?"

Devin cringed. Another secret out of the bag.

"A coloring book?" Shane threw back his head and laughed out loud. "Are you a sixteen or ninety-six Crayola kid?"

"A box of eight will suffice," Devin said stiffly.

"I figured you for black, white, and gray."

He saw her as basic, bland, and boring.

"Do you ever scribble? Color outside the lines?"

She was about to color him out of her life.

"Enough teasing," Victoria said. "Everyone has his own way of relaxing. Behave and play nice."

"I'm always nice," Shane said.

"Get back to your writing, and I'll see you soon." After a hurried "Good-bye and good luck," Victoria Patton ended the call. The dial tone sounded.

Shane hung up, then, curving his hand like a gun, aimed his finger at Devin. "You promised more than we can produce, little lady."

It was midmorning of day three and *Calder's Rose* remained a blank page. If Shane were writing the book alone, he'd be well into the first chapter. But while he could control Dare Calder's actions, Rose Coltraine belonged to Devin James.

Even now, Devin sat stiff-backed and buttoned-down,

all prim, proper, and virginal. She looked like she lived her life with her legs crossed. A man would have to work to get her juices flowing. Shane never equated sex with work. He found it a labor of love.

Damn if she didn't remind him of a schoolmarm, ruler in hand, ready to strike. He liked his women casual, mussed, with hair loose, free to the wind and a man's hands. He liked sultry smiles, curved bodies, and spirits willing to gamble. Bustiers and garters turned him on—along with stiletto heels.

For all his imagination, Shane couldn't picture Devin with her wheaten braid unbound, her body relaxed, her aqua eyes promising sin and satisfaction. He'd bet his entire advance on *Calder's Rose* that cotton fibers, not imported silk, covered her feminine attributes. Pristine white and elastic. Maybe on rare occasions those date-night pastels.

He gritted his teeth. Only Devin could write Rose Coltraine into his gunslinger's arms, then into his bed. But one look at Devin told Shane he'd be doing a hell of a lot of replotting. He'd be writing around the clock.

Perhaps he should have pressed his editor to hire another writer besides Devin James. He'd had numerous authors clamoring for the honor of Dare Calder riding through their books. Three months prior, Candace Birch, whose plots roamed the Dakota Territory, had requested that Calder pass through the Black Hills and unite with Bess Daniels, the driver of her *Stagecoach* series. The thought of Bess and Dare having sex on the box of the Concord coach had proved as tempting as the offer from fellow writer Annie Wyatt, who boldly suggested Dare ride to New Mexico and lift the satin skirts of Ellen Travers, singer and dancer in the *Santa Fe Acting Troupe* series.

Both offers held more allure than Dare Calder's ride •

into Cutter's Bend and his eventual romance with Rose Coltraine, a sexually deprived saloonkeeper.

Stanley Remington, his editor, disagreed, however. Stan promoted the unique and the unusual. Prodded by mountains of fan mail, Stan favored Calder's involvement with Miss Rose. Shane could understand the appeal. To unite a lawbreaking gunslinger and a virtuous woman of the West had numerous possibilities. Unfortunately all angles led to the outlaw's willingness to court the prudish proprietress.

Women came to Dare easily, willingly. He'd never had to win their favor. The seduction of Miss Rose would take all of Dare Calder's energy and patience. It would be a true exercise of Shane's imagination. He wondered if Devin James was worth the trouble.

He glanced her way and caught her booting her computer. "Ready?" she called.

He thumped the switch on his computer with the palm of his hand. "Give me a second."

"Your seconds run into minutes, into hours—"

"Your point being?"

"Let's get down to writing." She rubbed her hands together. "I work well under pressure."

"I sure as hell don't."

She cast him a sideways look. "Not even for Jamie Jensen tickets?"

He shrugged. "You could have purchased her latest CD."

"I'd rather see her live."

"You along with thousands of other fans."

"Perhaps the next horsetrade will favor you."

He'd make damn sure it did. He watched as Devin inhaled deeply and exhaled slowly. She repeated the breathing exercise five times.

Shane wondered about her purpose. "Is that some kind of meditation?"

"I'm relaxing and focusing," she explained.

He followed suit: inhaled, exhaled, and coughed loudly. "I'm centered."

She flexed her fingers on the keyboard. "Where shall we start?"

"With Rose Coltraine in Dare Calder's bed."

Devin started, nearly tipping over her chair. "Not possible! Miss Rose is a saloon proprietress, not a whore. And I won't let you make her one."

"Come on," Shane pressed. "My books begin and end with an orgasm."

"I agree. Your books are steaming with sex. Not love. Just page after page where Calder is parking his boots under some big-breasted woman's bed, while his black heart beats with excitement."

He didn't take kindly to her potshot. *"Black heart?"*

Devin huffed. "Well, isn't he an arrogant maverick, hell-bent on lust and depravity? Or did I miss a tender scene somewhere?"

Shane's hackles rose. "Look, despite Calder's many flaws, my stories always end with him righting a wrong. He bares his soul. That should count for something."

"I've read every one of your books," Devin said, raising her chin, "and Calder bares a heck of a lot more than his soul."

"Calder's a virile guy. A western gunslinger with a high level of male hormones."

Devin's unladylike snort surprised him. "Miss Rose cares nothing about Calder's testosterone level. Holding on to her virginity is what she means to do!"

He drilled his fingers on the desktop. "I'm sure your readership admires her virtue," he said, trying to placate her.

"My readers' admiration extends to the men who have courted Rose, and kept their hands to themselves."

Shane laced his fingers and cracked his knuckles. "Now, don't you think the fact that she's dated cattlemen, sheriffs, and cowboys and is still chaste might wear thin after a while?"

"Rose does keep regular company with rancher Wayne Cutter. They're business partners. They've grown close over the years."

"Well, apparently not close enough. She's still a virgin!" Devin's stubbornness kicked like a mule. He was a damn good writer. She had no right to riddle his suggestions with bullet holes.

Agitation pushed him to his feet. He circled his desk, stalking Devin James. Flattening his palms on her marble desktop, he stared at her forehead, noting the tic at the corner of her right eye.

As seconds rounded into a full minute, she yanked a red pencil with a white cowboy-hat eraser from a souvenir mug and ground it in the electric sharpener. At half its original length, she removed it. Creating a row of heart-shaped doodles on her violet-edged blotter kept her gaze averted.

He continued to breathe down her neck. Intimidation sometimes got results.

Her pencil produced a garden of flowers, then a hillside of trees.

Stilling his need to strangle her, Shane crossed his arms and rested a lean hip on the corner of her desk. He cleared his throat and asked, "Tell me, how much of Miss Rose is, in fact, you? What parts? Your prissiness? Your holier-than-thou attitude? Or is it her ability to stay as cool as ice while the hero's pants are on fire?"

"Come on, McNamara—you don't believe that stuff,

do you?" Devin challenged. "Where did you learn how to write? One of those private pop-psychology-promoting arts colleges? Critics and journalists always ask that question, but you know as well as I do that there's not a whole lot to support that theory."

He studied her speculatively. "I disagree. All authors draw on their personalities to create."

"Some draw on their sex drive."

He caught her mutter and smiled lazily. "Be honest, Dev, what part of you is written into your saloon proprietress? Miss Rose is wide-eyed, innocent—"

"Whereas Dare Calder is blinded by big breasts." She lifted a brow. "Apparently your taste in women runs to the D cup."

His gaze lowered to her chest. "You shouldn't have a problem with voluptuous women."

Her hand fluttered to the front of her navy blazer. She pulled the lapels of her double-breasted jacket together. "I have no problem with the women of Calder's past." She spoke as if to a child—a very big child. "My problem lies with Calder bedding Miss Ross. The man's going to have to keep his fly buttoned."

"He's not going to like it," Shane said in a growl. "Chapter one begins with his arrival in Cutter's Bend. Chased for days by that damn bounty hunter Art Noble, Calder's dusty and dirty and his throat's parched."

"Saddle sores? Chafing?" She smiled sweetly.

"Hardly," he said. "Calder was born to the saddle."

"Do you ride?" she asked.

He grinned. "Save a horse, ride a cowboy. I prefer to be ridden."

"No doubt whipped and spurred."

Shane winced, and absently rubbed his lean flank.

Devin returned to the book. "Calder the gunslinger:

13

leather-skinned, squinty-eyed, as bowlegged as a horseshoe."

He cut her a sharp look. "Dare is sun-bronzed and eagle-eyed. He walks just fine. There's no hitch in his giddyap."

She wrinkled her nose. "Once he enters town?"

"He's in need of a cool drink, a warm bath, and a soft woman to ease the ache in his loins."

Devin shook her head. "Rose isn't relieving that ache."

"Then we'll find him a soiled dove. Is there a brothel in Cutter's Bend?"

"Several." She lifted her chin a notch. "You should know the layout. Victoria sent you my *Garter* series to review. There's a detailed map of the town on the inside cover of each book."

Shane fidgeted, uncomfortable over his delay in reading her work.

Her expression turned pained. "Still boxed and taped?"

And sitting in the hallway at his villa in West Palm Beach. Guilt swamped him. "Not enough hours in the day." Lame, even to his ears.

Her voice strained, Devin directed Shane to the brothel. "Eve's Garden is located on the outskirts of town."

"Belle . . ." He closed his eyes, creating. "She'll be the character to ease Calder's needs."

"Calder's always *in need*. Chapter one of *Texas Sunset* has Calder stabling his horse, then rolling in the hay with the stable mistress, after which he guns down the town sheriff, then returns for another tumble."

Shane's lips tightened. "A man needs sex before and after a good gunfight. If you'd bothered to read beyond the stable scene, you'd have discovered Dare did the town of Lariat a favor. He produced wanted posters that proved the sheriff had ridden with the Wesley Gang."

"Justifiable sex. Justifiable killing. Calder's code of honor leaves a lot to be desired."

"No one's complained thus far," Shane said. "Rose had best not squawk."

"Show me a redeeming quality," she insisted.

"Redeeming quality!" Shane jerked off the desk. He again took to wearing down the carpet with his long strides. His voice thundered through the room. "What is it with you women, always wanting to change men?"

He slammed his fist into the palm of his hand, then struck her desktop. The letter opener, a box of paper clips, and Devin all jumped. Shane looked directly at her, but instead of his writing partner he saw the image of a redhead with flashing amber eyes. Pain rose from his soul in haunting memory. "Man lent woman a rib and gave her life. But that didn't satisfy her. Hell, no. She wanted more. So much more. She demanded his heart and soul and a lifetime commitment." His heart pounded and his breathing caught. "She wanted him to be her man on her terms, not the man he was born to be."

Devin dropped her red pencil and clutched the leather armrests as she slid her chair away from the desk, away from him. The attentive tilt of her head and the flicker of concern in her aqua gaze stopped him cold. He'd said too much. Way too much. Hell, he'd ranted like a lunatic. He and Devin were temporary writing partners, not lifelong members of the Bleeding Hearts' Club.

His gaze lowered to her blotter, where she'd been doodling. She'd sketched small daggers, no doubt directed at him, along with a large red heart broken by a squiggly line down its middle.

A broken heart for a moonstruck fool.

The drawing pricked his anger. He hated women with insight. Women who analyzed. He'd never needed anyone to tell him how he was feeling, or why he felt that way. He couldn't allow Devin to get under his skin. She was far too perceptive.

"Am I out of character, Miss James?" he baited.

"I didn't mean to stare," she whispered. "You just became—"

"Long-winded? Only on subjects that push me to the edge."

"Change is never easy." She looked at him—thoughtfully, not critically. "Most mustangs kick and buck when they're first lassoed. Some never take to the saddle."

He breathed easier. "Enough on my life. Back to the book."

Devin rubbed the back of her neck and sighed. "Calder's riding into Cutter's Bend. Time of day? Miss Rose likes mornings. Crisp air. Awakening skies. How about dawn?"

"Dare Calder prefers dusk."

"A gunslinger who hides in the shadows?"

"Do not mistake caution for fear," Shane returned. "There's not a cowardly bone in Calder's body."

"Very well." Devin sighed. "He can ride into town at dusk, darkness concealing his identity."

"He'll remain in the shadows until he's certain Art Noble is still eating his dust."

"Noble has trailed Calder since book one," Devin said, recalling *Texas Shoot-out*. "The bounty hunter believes Calder gunned down his brother in cold blood."

"It was self-defense," Shane said. "Noble refused to

listen to the eyewitness accounts of the shooting."

She pursed her lips. "Wasn't Lester Noble caught cheating at poker?"

"Sure as hell was. Les was young and restless, and foolish to a fault," Shane recounted. "At a barrel bar in Southern Flats he produced four aces, only to discover that two other gamblers at the table each held one."

"Calder never took much to cheaters," Devin remembered. "He quit the game. Lester followed Calder and two other gamblers into the street, demanding the men return to the bar."

Shane nodded. "The men kept walking. Coward that he was, Les fired at Calder's back. Calder dived behind a horse trough, and the other two men took cover behind a prairie wagon. A round of bullets was fired, and when the smoke cleared, Lester lay dead in the street."

"Art Noble demanded Calder's arrest." Devin looked at Shane questioningly. "Yet the sheriff refused to bring him in."

"He was innocent, Dev."

"I'm sure he was." Her voice held anything but certainty. "Yet Noble sought revenge. Though he's gotten close to Calder, he's never gotten within firing range." She smiled and began to type. "Until now. Calder's about to take a bullet."

"Hold on a dang minute!" Shane circled her desk and twirled her chair around to face him. "I haven't agreed to Dare's injury."

Her gaze rested on his belt buckle. "Can you think of a more startling hook than your big, tough gunslinger being shot?"

Silence stretched between them, and as the stillness thickened with his indecision, he caught her gaze wandering from the flat of his belly across his lean hips and down his zipper. . . .

For no accountable reason, the corners of his eyes and mouth grew tight, along with the front of his jeans. He immediately shifted his stance.

And she swallowed hard.

He stroked a fingertip beneath her chin, drawing her gaze upward. "Are you thinking of a flesh wound or something more debilitating?"

The pulse at the base of her throat leaped. "Something . . . debilitating."

His hand dropped to his side. Widening his stance, he rested his hands on his hips, his fingers flexing. He was ready to gun her down. "Where has he taken the bullet? Upper chest cavity?"

"A bit . . . lower," she hedged.

"Abdomen? Hip? Thigh? Foot?"

Her eyelids fluttered and her gaze lowered, leveling on his zipper once again.

His thoughts turned black. *"Groin?"*

"Thereabouts."

"An impotent hero." He swore softly. "Why not have Rose just cut off his—"

"Emasculation is not her style," Devin said. "Rose could, however, nurse Calder back to health. She could sit by his bedside—"

"And hold his hand, bathe him . . . until he's healed?" Shane snorted. "Unless his wound is fatal, Calder will want more than his hand held if he's in bed."

She started to speak, but he stopped her with a jab of a finger near her nose. "I can hear your brain working, and a deathbed scene is also out of the question. Our editors would never agree to Calder's demise. I won't have you killing off my career."

She slowly swiveled her chair from side to side. "A mere bullet wound could—"

"Lay him up for quite some time." Shane leaned forward, menacingly close, snagging the armrests and stilling her motion. "How many pages did you plan to keep Calder out of the action?"

She contemplated a little too long.

His lips curled in disgust. "You're thinking chapters, aren't you?"

"Ten . . . or eleven." She folded her hands in her lap. "It was just a thought."

His voice turned cold and hard. "I'd call it a potshot darlin'. Snake-belly low."

This was his character, damn it. How could she? Anger vibrated from him, tangible and threatening. He wasn't sure he could control it.

Devin, however, refused to cower. She kicked out her penny-loafered foot and crossed her legs. "If you don't like my suggestion, come up with one of your own."

Shane moved back slightly. "As a matter of fact, I have an idea. A damn fine one, in fact. Let's open the book with a storm. Lots of lightning bolts and rolling thunder. That's when Calder rides into town and witnesses Miss Rose being trampled by a spooked team of horses hitched to a loaded dray. Better yet, a stampede of cattle. Calder could drag her from the muddy street piled with cow dung and swarming flies. Naturally Rose would be unconscious. And she'd remain so through chapter twelve."

He pushed himself away from her chair, straightened, and stomped back to his desk. Seated, he reclined, hands behind his head, feet propped on his desk and crossed at the ankles. His stare bored into the back of Devin's skull. He willed her to face him.

She whirled her chair around. "I . . . have another thought."

"Better than the first, I hope."

She nodded and her braid fell over her shoulder. She nervously fingered the end. "Calder rides into town. . . ." She paused until she received his slow nod of approval. "It's near midnight when he dismounts at the Scarlet Garter."

"Go on."

"The saloon is quiet for a Wednesday night and Miss Rose steps out on the boardwalk for a breath of fresh air. She looks at the sky; there are lots of stars, like sparkling diamonds—"

"Cut the romantic ambience."

"Very well. Calder needs a drink—"

"Don't make him sound like an alcoholic."

"Calder dismounts and climbs onto the porch, and that's where he and Rose first meet. They exchange glances, the long, lingering kind that promise—"

Shane shook his head. "He'd give her the once-over, nothing more."

"Not if he wants her in his bed."

He disagreed—vehemently. "If Rose doesn't give Dare a wink or a smile, he'll pass her by."

"Rose doesn't flirt."

Shane scowled. The starch in Rose's petticoats would soon turn Calder into a stuffed shirt. That he couldn't allow.

He slid his feet off the desk and straightened in his chair. "Rose Coltraine's mighty one-dimensional. A cookie-cutter character, with no real soul."

"No soul!" she sputtered, then lit into him. "What about Calder? He's no more than a cardboard cowboy."

The muscles in his face pulled tight. His gaze narrowed, and his words passed through compressed lips. "My gunslinger's tough, virile—"

"Like an anatomical pop-up!"

Silence separated them as Shane faced Devin's temper. Her glare now burned as hot as a fired bullet.

He held up his hands, palms forward. "Let's take a break."

"A break, isn't that what you do best?"

Her departing shot drew a groan from him. *Another day shot to hell.*

The writer's cottage shimmered with an unmistakable energy—formidable energy born of anger and frustration and creative passion.

"Quiet as a ghost town." Amid the shadows where dusk was becoming darkness, Dare Calder gained height and breadth. He palmed his six-shooter, his stance shifting as he looked around.

"You expected raucous and rowdy?" Rose Coltraine edged toward his voice, her crinolines rustling with her approach.

"Thought I'd be breakin' up a fight between Shane McNamara and Devin James." He holstered his gun. "Their standoff brought us here."

"The intensity of their emotions strengthened our reality," Rose mused wonderingly.

Calder patted his chest and thighs, then scuffed his boots. Dust powdered the carpet. "We're dang near human."

He strode forward and met her bold scrutiny. He knew what she saw: He stood six feet tall with a whipcord frame, a chiseled face, and gunsmoke eyes. A hunted outlaw, he wore his dark hair a little long around the ears, but that was because he seldom had time to sit for a barber. His tanned and windburned face showed he spent as much time outside as in. His dark clothing and gun belt, slung low on his hips, branded him as a hired gun—or worse, a gunslinger.

He knew the danger surrounding him heightened his appeal to women—an appeal no decent woman would acknowledge. Except, perhaps, in the privacy of her daydreams.

A shameless grin split his face, and his gaze lit with criminal challenge. "Care to kiss me?"

Rose gasped, and her face went pale. "How dare you insinuate—"

He tipped the brim of his black Stetson. "Guess I misread the look you gave me."

Her face regained a little color. "My curiosity breached propriety. I apologize, sir."

"Done gazin'?"

"I wish you gone." She dismissed him as she would manure scraped from a boot.

He wasn't moving a muscle. Golden blond with classic features, Rose Coltraine was a beautiful woman—far lovelier than the printed description of her character could convey. There was something about a really beautiful woman that could throw a man off, even a hardened drifter like himself. Such a woman could leave a man tongue-tied and foot-shufflin' if the man weren't careful.

Dare Calder planned to pick his steps, remain clear-witted. Wearing a rose-red dress the color of a prairie sunset, she held herself in a proud stance that said she wouldn't bend for beddin'. He wondered how many pages it would take for him to land her in his bedroll.

"I won't sleep with you." She dashed the speculative glint from his eyes.

Her sanctimonious tone rankled him. "You will, and you'll enjoy it."

Her eyes flared for the briefest of moments. "Don't bet your horse on it."

Her open dislike shortened his temper. "You're no more than a character."

"A character brought to life. I've personality and principles."

The pulse at the delicate base of her throat quickened. He rode her discomfort. "McNamara has a knack for turning hoity-toity into hanky-panky."

"Devin James won't allow such behavior!"

"Shane McNamara believes in sowin' one's oats."

Rose tossed her head. "I've no respect for dalliances."

Calder dipped his head, scuffed the heel of his boot, and pondered long and hard. "You a chuchgoin' woman, Miss Coltraine?"

She was slow to answer. "I attend both service and social."

"You're mighty right and proper." He nodded his approval.

"And fair-minded," she added.

He rubbed his knuckles along the dark shadow of his jawline. "Figured you'd be able to see the good side of a bad man. Thought you might have the patience to uncover my one true passion."

"A passion beyond your bed partners?" She sniffed.

"A secret lust for . . ." His voice trailed off.

She inclined her head, her expression as soft as her inquiry. "For what, sir? Or for whom?"

"Virgins." He tipped back his hat, and the slight twitch of his lips belied his seriousness. "I've always wanted to bed a virgin. I want to draw a touch of purity over my sordid past like a satin bedcover. I want to slide between her silken thighs and get lost in the takin' of a woman as if it were my first time."

Rose Coltraine was just such a virgin. Her blood heated and her cheeks burned. Flustered and fuming, she turned her back on him.

Unrepentant, he eyed the soft bun fashioned at the nape of her neck, held in place by bejeweled hairpins. He'd plucked countless hairpins, always taking pleasure in the slow fall of a woman's hair as he readied her for his loving.

His palms itched to touch Rose Coltraine, but he could tell she wanted to scratch his eyes out.

"I'll not share a paragraph with you!" she threw back over a stiff shoulder.

"We'll share pages. We've got a story to tell, darlin'." The corner of his mouth kicked into a knowing grin as he and his prediction swaggered back into the shadows. "Once we kiss, you'll pray the chapter never ends."

Miss Rose swore the devil wore cowboy boots.

Chapter Two

West Texas, 1896

Dusk, a time to end work and begin whoring. The sun fanned the horizon as Dare Calder rode toward Cutter's Bend. At trail's end he found that the town's excitement centered around Eve's Garden, a weather-scarred pleasure house noted for its stiff drinks and soft, sultry women.

Calder was in need of a little excitement. He was looking forward to two fingers of whiskey to wash the dust from his throat, a copper-tub bath, and a woman of imaginative appetites. A buxom redhead with great legs and a soft, sweet mouth. In that instant he decided he wanted to be pleasured by a pair of pouty lips and a slick, swirling tongue. Bounding from the saddle, he tied his black mustang to the hitching post. Raucous music mixed with liquor-charged voices blasted onto the street. A drunken cowboy stumbled out, reeled, then lurched back inside.

Resetting his black Stetson low on his forehead, Calder crossed the boot-worn porch and eased through the swinging doors. He evaluated the customers with one visual sweep of the room: cattlemen, card players, and soiled doves. There was no sign of Art Noble, the bounty hunter chasing his hide.

Relieved, he settled at the corner table against the west wall. A man had to protect his back. Shortly a redhead corseted in peach satin approached him. Interest shone in her eyes, and her smile welcomed conversation and a whole lot more.

"Name's Belle." Her lips curved invitingly.

"Calder," he replied.

"New to town?"

"Passin' through."

"Stayin' the night?"

"Depends on the hospitality."

Promised intimacy darkened her gaze as she leaned closer. The low-cut design of the bodice exposed the soft white tops of her breasts.

"Can I buy you a drink?" Calder offered.

She held out her hand. "I have whiskey in my room."

"How much for the bottle?"

"The shirt off your back."

He lifted a brow, and a lazy smile spread. "Pants and boots, too?"

She nodded, flicking the brim of his Stetson with her finger. "You can leave the hat on."

An agreement reached, Calder pushed from the table and stood. He took her hand, and she led him across the crowded saloon, up a flight of creaky stairs, and into a small room redolent of orange-blossom toilet water and sex. The door closed, and she leaned into him, all heaving bosom and trembling thighs.

In the flickering light of a single candle, she seduced him with her eager mouth and roaming hands.

"Give me a hard ride, Calder." She nipped his lower lip and sucked it into her mouth. Her tongue jabbed hot and wild, and she kissed him so hard his lips hurt.

Desire charged between them. He pulled her tightly against him, and as their kisses deepened his hardness grew.

Hot, willing, and aggressive, Belle stroked the long bulge under his pants, then undid the buttons on his fly.

"I want you." She moaned as her hand closed around him.

Skilled in seduction, Calder unbuttoned her bodice, revealing throbbing breasts aching for his touch. He fondled their fullness, laved the narrow areolas and nipples. He undid the rest of the fasteners. The peach satin slid down her body like a caress. She wore only short, tight silk underwear, which he skimmed from her body. Naked, she curved against him, divesting him of his shirt, then working on his gun belt, loosening it.

He helped her by undoing the gun belt and tossing it over the bedpost. Boots came next, followed by his pants. Then she threw her arms around him and pulled him onto the bed. The mattress was soft, with a few worn dips and lumps. Belle moaned as he worked one hand slowly up her inner thigh. She moaned louder when he touched her damp curls and found her ready for him.

"Now, Calder, I want you now," she said panting.

She lifted her knees and spread them, drawing him within the musky warmth of her body. Her eager hands directed him as he drove forward until their pelvic bones ground together.

He would have shown gentleness had she allowed him, but the woman beneath him lifted her hips and rocked wildly, taking him deeply, pressing him beyond control. She pounded harder and he worked faster until the whole world exploded. He nearly lost his Stetson. The climax scorched him, and his hips jolted a dozen times before he collapsed on her, driving her into the mattress with his weight.

They lay there for several minutes while he recuperated. Her eyes were wide, staring at him in wonder.

"Straight shootin', cowboy," she breathed against his neck. "I'm used to satisfyin' men, not bein' satisfied."

Calder raised himself on his elbows and tipped his hat. His lips curled in a slow, sexy smile. "Give me ten minutes, sweetheart, and we'll shoot for the moon."

They crossed the heavens several times that night.

My books begin and end with an orgasm.

As morning's first light touched the horizon, Shane McNamara's words echoed in Devin's mind. She decided he would eat those words for breakfast. All in one bite. She hoped he choked.

Fury whipped her soul. She wanted to shout at him until he went deaf. She settled for pounding on his bedroom door. Wincing, she rubbed her palm. She slapped several pages of recently printed manuscript against her thigh. Her dusky-purple velour robe shifted, then separated over her abdomen. She secured the panels and tightened the belt. "Get up, McNamara—"

"Before you huff and puff and blow the house down?"

She whirled to see Shane entering the kitchen

through the sliding glass doors, juggling an armful of fresh oranges and grapefruits against a navy–T-shirted chest emblazoned with a pirate galleon flying the skull and crossbones and the inscription *Smugglers' Pub, Madrid, Spain.* He laid his bounty on the butcher-block counter. "Thought we'd squeeze fresh juice."

"Not if I get hold of your neck first." She advanced on him until they stood bare toe to bare toe on the tiled floor. She held the pages between the tip of her forefinger and thumb, as if they were too hot to handle. "*Calder's Rose* was to be a joint effort—"

"As specified in our contract."

"Yet you . . . you . . ." She swatted his arm with the pages. "You sneaked into the living room after our argument yesterday and began the book without me."

He looked more confused than guilty. "What are you talking about?" He snatched the pages before she landed him a second blow. "Once we parted I never crossed the battle lines."

She waited for his nose to grow. "Then you got up ahead of me."

"Thirty minutes ago. I had just enough time to shower and dress. Pick some fruit." He squinted one eye, studying her closely. "While you rolled out of bed gunning for bear."

"I woke to the hum of the computer, the running of the printer. And . . . and this!" She pointed at the pages.

"Quite the light sleeper, I see. Sure you're not sleep-walking?"

"I'm a morning person."

"Then you woke up on the wrong side of the bed."

"I awakened in a great mood."

"Something sure as hell shifted."

"The story line shifted! How dare you—"

"Wind down, Dev." He glanced at the manuscript pages, then stiffened slightly. "What's this about?"

His puzzled expression didn't fool her, the low-down, underhanded sneak. "Don't play games with me, McNamara. I'm talking about that scene you dared to write while I was asleep." She leaned forward, jabbing the pages. "Eve's Garden, Calder and Belle."

He scanned the pages. The room closed in around her. Her throat went dry as she reread the scene along with Shane.

. . . tongue jabbed hot and wild . . .
. . . throbbing breasts aching for his touch . . .
. . . pelvic bones ground together . . .
His hips jolted a dozen times . . .

Devin's heartbeat quickened and she grew warm. Incredibly warm. She fingered the collar of her robe, fanning the velour over her collarbone.

Shane paused in his reading and looked at her. His eyes glinted with amusement. He'd obviously gained perverse satisfaction from her discomfort.

She crossed her arms over her chest and tapped one bare foot. "The initial scene revolves around Calder and Belle. It was supposed to be about Calder and Rose."

"Then why did you write it that way?"

His puzzlement irked her. She resisted the urge to slug him. "I didn't write it, you moron. Stop turning things around!"

He eyed her balled fist and eased back a step. "Decompress, Dev. It's easily fixed. We'll delete Belle, substitute Rose—"

"You're missing the point."

"I swear I never wrote a word of this."

She flicked a finger at the pages he held. "The plot's

as coarse and crude as your gunslinger. You should be arrested—"

"I won't be signing a confession of guilt. I didn't write this!"

"There are only two of us sharing this cottage. You even left boot prints by my desk."

He tossed the papers on the kitchen counter and crossed over to the dusty outline of a boot near her desk. He frowned. "That's not my print. I may write Westerns, but I don't dress the part."

"The boots belong to a man. They're too large to be a woman's."

"Check my bedroom closet. No boots, Sherlock." Shane headed for his own desk.

Devin dogged his steps. "Where are you going?"

He slid into his chair. "To draft a wanted poster. Dead or alive, we'll have justice."

"Great idea. Bounty hunter Art Noble could begin the tracking."

"I'm not liking your sarcasm, Dev."

"Well, I don't appreciate your blasé attitude." She stood near his chair, hands jammed in the pockets of her robe. The fabric parted, exposing her paisley silk chemise and matching tap pants in scarlet, plum, and peacock blue.

Shane paused, his gaze sweeping the swells of her breasts and the curves of her thighs, before she clutched the robe closed.

"Nice jammies." He cocked his head. "Thought you'd bed down in a high-collared granny gown."

Had he truly wondered about her sleepwear? Even a long cotton gown couldn't keep away the image he summoned. Her heart slammed, then stilled as a very naked McNamara pulled back the sheets in her mind's eye.

31

These physical cravings he inspired were so unlady-like, so unlike her. Only a scoundrel like Shane could make her tingle in places best left untouched. Shaken, she looped the belt into a knot never meant to be untied. "Concentrate on *Calder's Rose.*"

"Then stop distracting me."

She eyed him suspiciously. "Why don't you show some concern for the manuscript? How did this happen?"

He swirled on his chair. "I have no idea. I'm at my wit's end."

"A short journey, McNamara." She slammed her hands on his desktop, leaned toward him, ignoring his scowl. "This smacks of your imagination. I would never write this trash."

Trash! Shane was offended. Calder might be down and dirty, but Shane took pride in his creation. It was true he always began and ended his books with Calder's sexual release. The scene he'd just scanned was a surprisingly accurate imitation of his style.

Devin James must have burned the midnight oil to create these pages.

He pursed his lips, studying his writing partner. Perhaps her suppressed sexuality was revealed in this raunchy scene. Could it be that, suddenly embarrassed by her true self shining through, she'd gone on the offensive, blaming him at the top of her lungs?

He didn't know what was motivating her strange behavior, but one thing he was sure of: she was in for an awakening, by God. This glimpse of her latent sensuality pushed him to loosen her up just a little. Hell, maybe a lot. It was for her own good.

Even now she crowded his desk, all flushed and feminine, wrapped in anger and her gaping robe. Scarlet paisley caressed her breasts, while thin satin straps arced over her shoulders. Shane wished himself silken fabric, all clingy and molding and tucked in for the night.

"Shane!" Devin stomped her foot. "Are you listening?"

He hadn't been. Her stomp, however, drew him back to the boot print. It was physical evidence of a possible intruder. Devin James needed his protection. He would set the cottage alarm tonight.

"Calder's romp with Belle must be deleted."

He stared at her straight on. "Regardless of who wrote it, it's a good scene. Leave the romp. My gunslinger's sated."

Her eyes narrowed to aqua slits. "We know who wrote it, McNamara. And if Calder's sated in this scene, then he'll just have to remain sated—"

"For no more than a chapter. Calder lives hard and fast. He's entitled to his conquests."

"Dare Calder is a *character,* you dimwit!" Devin thumped the flat of her palm against his forehead, making him blink. "You're in control of the story. Temper his lust."

Shane grimaced. "You always so slaphappy?"

She laced her fingers over her abdomen, suddenly quite still. "Not until today."

"There are other ways to gain my attention. I suggest you find one."

She nodded, bit down on her lower lip, and squeezed her hands bloodless, seeming far more discomfited than the situation warranted.

Shane rested his elbows on the desktop, steepled his fingers, and blew on their tips. "We need to establish a working relationship. Cut the accusations, Dev. I'd never undermine *Calder's Rose.* You have my word."

"I guess I got a little carried away. I promise to keep my hands to myself."

He wouldn't mind having her hands on him if they were using a softer, gentler touch. He scratched his jaw. "I thought you were more reserved."

She blew out a frustrated breath. "You'd make a preacher swear."

"And less sarcastic. You're either home-tutored or went to private boarding school."

She stepped back from his desk. "Huddleston-Smythe, Minneapolis."

A highly reputable scholastic institution, open to the new generation of old money. "Where ivy walls protect good girls from bad boys." He could picture her in her uniform: navy blazer, starched white blouse, knee-length skirt. In some ways she was still wearing that uniform in her adult life.

"You're public school," she retorted. "I'll bet you spent as much time in the principal's office as you did in class. You're smart enough, so grades came easily, but you got bored quickly. You cut classes, pulled pranks, chased girls."

"Caught a few. My father battled more than one irate mother whose daughter kissed and told."

"Elementary lip locks?" she asked sweetly.

"Second base and stealing home on my twelfth birthday. No sweet young thing could resist the eldest Mc-Namara."

Her hand went to her heart. "There are more of you?"

"I have three younger brothers." He ignored her look of horror. "While you must be an only child. Born to overprotective parents, I'll bet, with imaginary siblings. That's why Rose Coltraine's as protected as family."

Their childhoods had been so different. He was suddenly sad. He could picture Devin, alone and lonely, fantasies her closest friends. His own sandbox playmates had led to schoolmates, then bedmates, but he wondered if Devin had ever embraced more than her imagination.

Not until she sighed did he breathe easier.

"Writing pays my bills," she explained. "I spend as much time with Rose as I do with anyone else."

"You need to get out more." He tapped the end of his nose with one finger. "No boyfriend? Fiancé?"

"I have a boyfriend—Skip Huddleston."

Shane raised a brow. "Huddleston, as in Huddleston-Smythe academics?"

Devin nodded. "A family of Einsteins."

"How's brain-boy in bed?"

She shifted uneasily, and couldn't meet his eyes. Shane blew out a disbelieving breath. Surely the staid, pretentious Huddleston delivered more than theory and thesis. Her expression, however, confirmed his worst suspicions. The man wore his socks to bed. No wonder Devin was wound tighter than Rose Coltraine's corset. There'd been no yip in Skip.

"Who's the love of your life?" she asked, drawing him from his reverie.

"I'm happily single by preference."

"There was a woman. . . ."

He prayed the memory would escape her.

"I seem to remember a picture and article in *Power* magazine that linked you with . . ."

He tensed. "I have no involvements, Dev. That's straight from the horse's mouth." He pushed his chair from the desk, then rose. "Toast? Juice? A pot of coffee?"

"A light breakfast with heavy plotting works best for me."

It didn't sit well with Shane. He wrote as he lived—undisciplined—and worked when the muse moved him, often at odd hours. Working with Devin forced him to format his thoughts and limited his freedom. To his chagrin, his muse yawned widely and closed its eyes. Shane prayed it wouldn't snore.

Their deadline loomed on the not-so-distant horizon. While due dates caused him nightmares, he'd met every one in the past. He was on a first-name basis with the Federal Express staff who overnighted his manuscripts. Several of the employees actually sent him Christmas cards.

Now, pressed to write, he felt an invisible noose tighten around his neck, choking his creativity. He'd rather swing from a big oak tree than adhere to Devin James's law and order.

Compromise. Victoria Patton's suggestion came back to him. Devin had conceded on Calder bedding Belle. Turnabout was fair play. He shrugged. "Breakfast. I can chew and chat at the same time."

She looked at him as if he ate from a dog dish. "I'd prefer you to chew with your mouth closed."

He curled his lip, debating whether to bark or growl. He'd dined with executives and politicians; his lovers fed him breakfast in bed. No one had ever complained about his table manners. Until Devin James.

Let her think he'd roll over and have his belly rubbed for a Milk-Bone. Her mistake would only help his plot to loosen her up.

They crossed to the kitchen. There Shane opened the stainless-steel refrigerator and scanned its contents. Their publicist had stocked food to his liking. "What's your pleasure?"

He turned and caught Devin on tiptoe, searching the bleached wood cabinets for dishes. The bottom of her velour robe skimmed high on her thighs—long, curvy, toned thighs. She had legs meant to capture a man's hips while she rode out her pleasure.

"Pleasure?" She peered deeper into the cupboard.

He grinned. "In food."

Her sidelong glance caught the hound dog sniffing. She dropped down hard on her heels, tugging her robe below her knees. Her glare was colder than the air escaping from the refrigerator. "Put your eyes back in their sockets, McNamara."

Prissy Miss James had backbone, all right. Bending slightly, he swung the door of the refrigerator wide and rattled off its contents like an auctioneer. "We've got blueberries, strawberries, raspberries, green grapes, cantaloupe, eggs, bacon, sausage, Poppin' Fresh biscuits—"

Devin waved him to silence. "Blueberries and strawberries."

He passed her the wire containers. She rinsed the fruit under the tap, then poured a mixture into a glass bowl. After removing a spoon from the cutlery drawer, she began to eat.

The woman definitely needed to unbend. "Haven't you ever heard of finger food?" Shane stole a plump strawberry from her bowl. He bit into the berry, and the juice trickled onto his forefinger. "Seduce our tastebuds." He licked the callused tip clean.

Her eyes widened, and an unexpected heat surged through his body. He again dipped into the bowl and offered her a sample. "Selected for your pleasure."

She frowned and tried to back away, but she was wedged between the corner of the refrigerator and the sink. Shane took advantage of the small, crowded space to crowd her even more. He teased her mouth with the ripe red berry until she parted her lips. He then slid both the fruit and his finger inside. The moist heat of her mouth slickened its tip. He withdrew it slowly, waited, and watched, wanting to part her lips a second time.

Devin barely took time to chew before she swallowed hard. "More?" he whispered near her ear.

Her hand shook as she placed it over his wrist and eased his hand away. "Thank you, no. I'm perfectly capable of feeding myself."

Shane, however, continued to eat from her bowl. He watched her pop a plump blueberry in her mouth, roll it around on her tongue, then bite down slowly. Her eyes closed for the briefest of moments while she savored its sweetness.

Her next selection was a dark red strawberry. Squeezing its stem, she nibbled toward its middle. Shane's abdomen pulled tight. He couldn't take his eyes off her parted lips and the juice that glossed their reddened fullness. He had the wildest urge to kiss her.

"Whoa, doggies." He shoved himself away from the counter and sought a bar stool across the kitchen.

"Are you ready to plot?" she asked between bites, apparently unaware of his physical reaction.

He blew out his breath. "Let's set a few ground rules: no debilitating injuries."

"And no steamy sex."

"How about a straightforward deflowering?"

"Not on Rose's life." She sighed defeatedly. "Goodbye, Jamie Jensen tickets."

"Not necessarily," he said placatingly while studying her. "Is the concert really that important to you?"

"I'm a big fan."

"Enough of a fan to allow Calder to kiss Miss Rose in chapter one?"

Devin stiffened. "A live concert and a storybook kiss are two completely different issues."

"Here's the trade-off." He rubbed his hands together, feeling utterly brilliant. "How about a case of mistaken identity? We could write a scene where Calder enters the Garter and gets involved in a poker game. Well into the game, Rose breaks up the players just as rancher Wayne Cutter is about to bet his half ownership in the saloon. Calder then leaves, and moments later Rose steps outside for a calming breath of fresh night air.

"Allow Dare to steal a few kisses, a few caresses, before he realizes Rose's true identity . . . and you will be dancing in the aisle at the Jamie Jensen concert."

Devin grew thoughtful. Selecting another strawberry, she tapped the tip against her lips. "Where, exactly, did you plan on Calder taking such liberties with Miss Rose?"

He grinned. "You mean copping a feel?"

"If that's how you must put it."

"How about an alleyway? We'll need a place where identities are blurred by shadows."

She bit down hard on the berry. "Rose isn't easy. She would fight his advances."

"Not if Calder's kisses were mind-numbing."

"Mind-numbing?" She choked on the strawberry.

"Not romantic enough for you? How about a toe-tingling, heart-throbbing kiss? One that's hot, wet, and penetrating. A kiss that's nearly orgasmic."

She scrunched up her nose. "I'll have to think about it."

"Care to think about it in the sunshine? We could take a short walk before getting down to business."

She hesitated. "I don't know. . . ."

He had the feeling she would rather walk alone. "Two's company."

Devin contemplated his suggestion longer than he liked. Eventually she shrugged. "It's a public beach."

"No, it's an isolated beach on private property," he corrected. "We could walk for miles in either direction and not come across another living soul."

He slipped off the bar stool and approached her. "Naples, Florida. Southern heaven." He scanned her upturned features. "Let the sun caress that pale, porcelain skin. Allow the sand to squeeze between your toes, the water to splash your ankles, and the breeze to ruffle that tight-ass braid."

Going anywhere with Shane was probably a bad idea. The man was arrogant and needed to be put in his place. However, fresh air and sunshine appealed more than writing just now. "You're quite the sweet talker, McNamara," she tossed over her shoulder as she returned the bowl of fruit to the refrigerator, then headed toward her bedroom. "Tight-ass braid, indeed! Your flattery turns my head."

Shane's deep chuckle reached her beyond the closed door. His amusement was at her expense, Devin well knew. Earlier his male heat and seductive teasing had cornered her in the kitchen. Desire had curled in her belly when he'd touched her lips with the strawberry. Skip Huddleston had never fed her anything but the occasional compliment. For one wild heartbeat she'd wanted to taste more of Shane than just the tip of his finger.

Strawberries had just become the forbidden fruit.

Dropping onto the bed, she slumped over and rested her head in her hands. She prayed a walk on the beach would revive her determination to write *Cal-*

der's Rose. Perhaps if she and Shane spent time talking, time getting to know each other, their views on the book would mesh and he'd stop his erotic taunting.

Wishful thinking, her creative muse snorted. *Shane McNamara and Dare Calder like their women breathless, brainless, and busty, while you and Miss Rose seek solid, decent relationships. From the moment you and Shane met, you've been circling and sniping, neither one of you willing to give an inch on the story line. Don't shoot yourself in the foot by believing a walk on the beach will uncover a mature man beneath his childish posturing.*

Devin chased away her muse. Straightening, she untied her robe, then slipped out of her pajamas and into a lacy bra and French cut panties. Standing before her closet, she selected a tangerine halter top and a pair of white walking shorts. A spritz of SunSplash behind each ear boosted her confidence. She told herself she had no wish to impress Shane McNamara. Comfort was her only concern in the Florida heat.

Barefoot, her so-called tight-ass braid swinging between her shoulder blades, Devin returned to the main room. She found Shane on the lanai off the kitchen, lounging in a rattan fan-back chair. The gurgle of an antiquated hot tub situated to his left muffled her arrival. As soon as he spotted her, he stood.

"Just listen to those jets." He motioned her toward the redwood tub. "Take a deep breath and inhale that steam."

Devin approached slowly. "Hmm. Very nice."

"Not just nice, Dev—hot, sweaty, pulsing."

Unwanted images formed in her mind, startling in their force and clarity: Shane nude, his lean body wet and slick with sweat, his muscles sleek and slippery, his arousal jutting—

Heat shot from the tips of her toes to her hairline.

She dipped her head and pressed three fingers to her throbbing temple. What in tarnation was the matter with her?

"That must have been some hot flash," Shane teased. "You're panting, Dev."

She squinted between two fingers and caught him checking her out. Not a casual look between friends, but definite male perusal. Her spine stiffened. "Eyes front and center, McNamara."

He took his sweet time meeting her gaze, then had the nerve to chuckle. "You remind me of a Dreamsicle: soft creamy orange ice cream with a stick up—"

She waved him to silence. So much for compliments. "I get the picture." Unable to help herself, she took him in. All of him.

Shane looked as if he'd been stranded on a desert island. A faded tropical-print shirt hung unbuttoned on his broad, hair-roughened chest, while frayed cutoff jeans hugged lean hips and muscular thighs. His feet were also bare, long and well formed. Tousled dark hair fell across his forehead, and the shadow of a beard darkened his jaw.

"Have I stepped out of character once again?" he asked.

The man was part chameleon. She shook her head. "You're not complex enough to have more than one character, McNamara."

He grinned. "Let's walk." He shoved open the sliding glass door and allowed her to pass before him. "Sand, surf, and salt air." He tilted his face to the sun. "Vic's spoiling us rotten."

She thought Shane was already rotten, but declined to mention the obvious. Together they crossed a lush expanse of saint augustine grass. As they headed toward the seawall, Devin breathed deeply, appreciative of the warmth that bathed her skin. She smiled to herself as she noted a shell-pink gazebo near the shoreline, along with a doublewide hammock stretched between two queen palms. A redbrick barbecue sat just beyond the hammock. Devin loved to barbecue.

Once they reached the embankment Devin touched Shane's arm. She motioned for him to sit beside her on the low-planked boat dock. After they were seated, she gathered her courage and said, "I want to take this time to get to know you better."

Shane lifted a brow, looking downright dubious. "Do you want to scratch my surface or glimpse my soul?"

"Please, no deep, dark secrets."

He rolled his eyes. "Then let's start with good old barroom pickup lines. What's your sign?"

She took the line and ran with it. "I'm a Libra."

The scales. Cautious, balanced, harmonious. A woman who played it safe. Definitely Devin James, Shane mused. He, on the other hand, rammed ahead. "I'm an Aries."

"The sign of passion and fire. You're known to be reckless and impatient."

The woman knew her astrology. "On the plus side, we have strong beliefs, and know what we want from life."

She met his gaze squarely. "What do you desire most?"

"Careful, now, you're going for my soul." He turned away from her, running his fingers along the weathered planks, unwilling to share his need to calm his restless spirit and eventually settle down. Devin saw him as a rogue author, as a man easily distracted and hard to confine. He decided to go with her first impression.

43

"I desire blondes, brunettes, and redheads. The more the merrier."

He could tell his response hadn't surprised her. "You're a man of immediate gratification and few future goals."

He wanted to deny her claim, but instead, pushed to see her blush. "Your favorite sexual position?"

Her cheeks flushed with color. "A little too personal."

"I like a woman to ride my thighs."

He caught her gaze flicking to his groin. "More than I need to know, McNamara."

She had looked, however. She'd stared right at his zipper. It was strange how her brief glance caused him to stir in an invitation for her to straddle his thighs.

Shane immediately shifted both his body and the conversation. "Your favorite food?"

"Spaghetti. I make a sauce that would knock your socks off."

A little Italian ran in her blood. Though he loved spaghetti, food had never knocked his socks off—only sex. "I love deli sandwiches."

The conversation lulled as Devin leaned back and rested her weight on her elbows. She raised her face to the sun. "This is paradise."

"In comparison to your Minnesota winters, it's heaven on earth."

She shrugged. "I've withstood the snow and ice for twenty-nine years. There's a real hominess in sitting before a fireplace, sipping hot chocolate topped with marshmallows—not the mini ones, but the big, puffy, campfire kind. I miss being inside, all warm and toasty."

"While Jack Frost nips everyone's nose?"

"I like the changes in season."

"So do I," Shane admitted, "but I travel to see them. There's nothing like fall in Vermont, a skiing weekend in Colorado, or seeing the cherry blossoms in Washington, D.C., in early May."

"But you always return to Florida."

"To West Palm, actually. Although the summers are hot and humid, I like it that way. Have liked it for thirty-three years."

"No doubt the hotter the better," she muttered. He smiled to himself. West Palm was home to the cultured and the monied. And to him, a man with a maverick mentality. He'd broken the boredom for numerous socialites, but he had yet to meet the woman who could hold his interest and claim his name.

He nodded toward the two Jet Skis tied to the end of the dock. "Do you Sea-Doo?"

She took her time looking over the turquoise and yellow sportscraft. "Can't say that I have."

"Too exciting, daring, fun for you?"

"Merely no opportunity," she said, a wistful look in her eye.

"Can you swim? Dog paddle?"

"Fairly well."

"I was a lifeguard one summer and could probably save your life if I had to." A little mouth-to-mouth might prove interesting. "If you like, we could ride the Jet Skis on one of our breaks."

"Breaks that are taking away from our writing time."

"Are you always so on task?" he asked.

"It's called dedication, McNamara. I believe in finishing what I start."

"So do I. We just have different means to an end, that's all."

Devin grew contemplative.

45

Shane squinted against the sun. "Do you still live with your parents?"

The corners of her mouth turned down. "Hardly. I own a lovely Victorian in constant need of repair. How about you?"

"Mediterranean villa, on the beach. Few maintenance hassles."

Devin yawned, then closed her eyes against the sun's glare, giving Shane the opportunity to sit in silence. He discovered he wanted to chat awhile longer.

"How long did it take you to get published?" he asked.

"Mmm, a while."

The dreaded rejection letter? A writer's nightmare. "How many declines, Dev?"

"Mmm, more than one." She remained evasive.

"Enough to wallpaper your office?"

"Only one wall." She cast him a sideways glance. "How about you?"

"I nailed a contract on my first submission."

"That figures. Sex sells."

He could have taken offense, but he didn't. He felt too calm and relaxed in her company. So relaxed, in fact, that he could almost take a nap. "What do you drive?"

"A Saturn."

"How does it run?"

"Olivia gets great mileage—"

"*Olivia*? You've named your car?"

"A lot of people do."

So had he, in high school. To this day his vintage Mustang—Magnet, as in Babe Magnet—held reserved parking next to his Porsche in the underground garage at his villa.

He nudged her with his shoulder. "Tell me, Dev,

have you ever driven over the speed limit? Have you ever seen a state trooper's lights flashing in your rear-view mirror?"

She opened her eyes and sat forward. Her shoulders hunched. "I got a ticket once."

Devin the speedster. "How fast were you going?"

"Actually it was for driving too slowly."

Shane coughed into his hand in an attempt not to laugh.

She ignored him. "It was right after I'd gotten my driver's license. I wasn't keeping up with traffic on the interstate."

Shane couldn't help it: He threw back his head and roared. "Your inner animal must be a snail."

"While yours is a lone wolf."

"I've howled at the moon on occasion." His thoughts turned to how loudly he'd howled. "Have you ever made it in the backseat of a car?"

She averted her gaze. "Can't say that I have."

"You've never been parking?" Some of his best memories were of fogging up the windows in his Mustang. "No midnight kisses? No starlight, star-bright sex?"

She peered at him from the corner of her eye. "You bring a whole new meaning to wishing on a lone star."

"My girlfriends found it romantic."

She took a deep breath. "Has life always been easy for you?"

Until I met you. "It's been my way or the highway."

"Your way for far too long."

She gave him no time to respond. Jumping off the boardwalk and onto the beach, Devin headed toward the tip of the peninsula.

Shane soon caught up with her. An easy silence stretched between them as seagulls shrieked overhead and egrets sprinted along the water's edge. Reaching the shoreline, Devin waded into the gulf. The water lapped against her calves, clear, cool, heavenly. A light breeze tossed her bangs as the sun kissed her face. Happiness tickled her ribs. She spread her arms wide, embracing the morning, and surprised herself by laughing out loud.

Her outlook suddenly as bright as the day, she cupped her hands and trickled water over her arms, then patted her cheeks with damp palms. The sun shimmered off the water, catching her in its halo. Partnered by low-cresting waves and shifting sand, she reveled in the ocean's dance.

Peace settled in her soul. She closed her eyes. . . .

"Watch out for the jellyfish!" Shane warned.

With a shriek and a wild splash she ran to shore.

His laughter stopped her on the damp sand.

She slugged him in the arm. "Not funny, McNamara. My heart's in my throat."

He traced the slender line of her neck, splaying his fingers against the pulse that pounded at its base. "You sure scare easily."

"You had no right—"

"To tease you?" He rubbed the soft spot with a slow circular motion. "Where's your sense of humor?"

"Lost . . ." He'd flattened his hand against her breastbone, kneading and stroking as two of his fingers traced the ribbed border at her neckline. Her heart no longer jumped. Instead the beat slowed to an erotic throb.

She absorbed his attention for the swift passing of a cloud. With the sun again on her face, she eased back a step. The man was potent—and dangerous. "I'm no longer afraid."

The heat from his fingers remained at her throat as she walked down the beach ahead of him. She was glad

Shane chose to keep several yards between them. His attentions frightened her more than the sting of any jellyfish.

He slowed and waited when she stopped to pick up and examine a shell. She didn't leave many unturned. Even the driftwood, dried seaweed, and crab paths caught her interest. She skirted the occasional dead fish, then sobered when she discovered a stranded starfish.

"Shane," she called, motioning him to her. "I need you."

He arrived in two heartbeats. "You need me?"

She looked down at the sand. "Help me with the starfish."

"Sure thing." He hunkered down and carefully dug out three of its five arms, releasing it from the compacted sand. When Devin bent down for a better look, he swung out his arm to stop her. "Watch it, Dev, if the starfish is hungry, it could bite."

As she stepped back, she caught his grin. She wanted to kick him. Hard. Did the man have a serious bone in his body? "I can see its sharp little teeth. You'd better be careful."

"Oh, I will." He lifted the starfish carefully, walked into the gulf, and released it.

He then returned to her side. "Better?"

"Much." She dipped her head. "Thank you."

"I'm sorry, I didn't hear you."

She looked up. "I appreciate your help."

"Better me get bitten than you."

"You're lucky the starfish didn't take off a finger." Glancing at her watch, she sighed. "I think we should get back to work. We've lost over an hour of writing time."

"The time hasn't been lost if you've enjoyed yourself," he said. "Look upon it as time needed to restore your creative muse."

He reached out and traced a finger down her nose, then over her cheekbone. "You're sunburned."

Devin wrinkled her nose. "I didn't think we'd be gone this long, otherwise I would have put on sunscreen."

He stared into her upturned face. She grew self-conscious, knowing she didn't present a glamorous picture. Wisps of her hair had escaped her braid, and her bangs lay damply on her forehead.

"Wide-eyed, sun-blushed. Amazingly mussed." He stepped nearer, bringing them nose-to-nose. His palm skimmed her cheek as he tucked the stray strands behind her ear.

The slap of the waves and the cry of the gulls faded beneath the pounding of her heart. Temptation was written in the sand. . . . She cleared her throat. "You're standing on my shadow."

He shifted his stance. "Me and my big feet."

His knowing grin strengthened her resolve. She would not allow this inexplicable attraction to draw her off the straight and narrow. Clapping her hands, she turned abruptly and broke into a jog. "Move it, Mc-Namara. We'll need to cleanup before we tackle the next segment."

Thirty minutes following their return to the cottage, Devin sat behind her desk and booted her computer. She'd showered, washed the sand from between her toes, and tightly plaited her hair. A black pantsuit reclaimed her professional edge.

Shane appeared shortly thereafter. From the look of him, he also had taken the time to shower. His hair was still damp, and the ends dripped onto a gray

T-shirt emblazoned with a sun-scorched skull and the words *Bone Ranger Bar, Death Valley*. He'd tucked the shirt into a pair of stonewashed Levi's. The soles of his expensive running shoes made soft sucking noises as he crossed the tiled floor and headed for the kitchen.

"I didn't eat much breakfast," he called to her. "Peanut butter and crackers feeds my muse."

With those words he proceeded to grab a paper plate, an enormous jar of creamy peanut butter, and a sleeve of Club crackers from the cupboard. He then swung open the refrigerator door and extracted a half-gallon of milk. Sidling up to her desk, he nudged aside her stapler and clipboard and laid out his snack.

To Devin's chagrin he pulled a rattan chair with a flowered cushion next to her desk and dropped into it.

"Uncross your legs."

Her knees jerked. "Whatever for?"

"I need legroom."

"Not between mine." She jabbed a finger across the room. "Stretch out behind your own desk, cowboy."

"I'm more comfortable here."

His proximity wrapped her in an unsettling intimacy. Devin struggled against the pull and tug of man and peanut butter.

"Care for a cracker?" Shane's forearm bulged as he twisted the lid off the jar. He then ripped open the crackers, plucked one out, and started to dip.

Devin slapped his hand aside. "Use a knife."

He cocked his head, narrowed his eyes, and said challengingly, "Fingers work best with snack food."

"Not when two people plan to eat from the same jar."

"My hands are clean. I just showered."

She sniffed and swiveled her chair to the left. "Sit

51

tight. I'll get the knife. Cracker crumbs—"

"Don't belong in bed, but add crunch to peanut butter." Shane spun her chair back to the right.

"Peanuts add the same crunch." She looked down her nose at him.

His brows slammed together.

Prude. Picky eater. She could read the accusations in his eyes.

She liked things clean and orderly. Two adjectives that obviously did not top Shane's priority list. He looked like the type who'd build a skyscraper sandwich, one so high he couldn't get his mouth around it.

"Ever bite into more than you can chew?" Plunging the cracker into the peanut butter, he scooped out a generous portion.

She'd thought that of him. "Certainly not. I'm quite selective—"

Shane stuffed the cracker between her parted lips.

Devin nearly choked.

He grinned, Cheshire wide. "Milk?" He held up the entire half gallon.

"A quss," she sputtered around the peanut butter that stuck to the roof of her mouth. She uncrossed her legs and attempted to stand.

Hair-trigger fast, Shane maneuvered his own chair directly in her path. He wedged one knee between her thighs. "No need for a glass," he countered as he peeled back the flaps on the carton and raised it to her lips. "I like a woman with a milk mustache."

Submission weakened her knees as his thigh bumped hers, the rough denim abrading her raw silk. Awareness tingled, speeding up her heartbeat. After chewing and swallowing hard, she grabbed a tissue and wiped her mouth, then lunged for the container.

"Into milk baths, McNamara?"

He held it just beyond her reach. "If you want to find out, then strip down and join me in the tub."

The images of their naked bodies, warm, wet, and milky, slippery from soap and steamy from sex, drew Devin up short. As no doubt Shane assumed it would. Appalled at how easily he'd pushed her to riot, she quickly recouped her dignity. Lowering herself onto her chair, she pulled the lapels of her blazer together and recrossed her legs—tightly.

"Finish your snack and let's get to work," she said stiffly.

She sat, her jaw locked, impatiently waiting while Shane McNamara devoured a full sleeve of crackers, along with half a jar of peanut butter. Each bite of cracker was over dramatized with a sweeping dip into the jar and a loud crunch. Raising the milk carton to his lips, he waited, catching her eye, then winked before sipping deeply. She watched his throat work, the contracting of those thick cords as he drained a goodly amount.

He then took what little remained to the kitchen. When he returned he settled onto his chair, crossing his ankle over his knee and his arms over his chest. "Prime creativity springs from a well-fed muse. Ready whenever you are."

He was as full of himself as his muse was of peanut butter.

Anxious to get started, Devin worked her lower lip. "The goal of the next segment is to introduce Dare Calder and Rose Coltraine. You suggested a case of mistaken identity."

"Start typing. I'll feed you the opening lines."

"I'm not your assistant, McNamara. I have thoughts to share."

"I'm listening."

"I want to describe the Garter before you move into the alley."

"A saloon's a saloon."

"This saloon is more than that," she insisted. "It's the setting for my series."

"Write your little heart out."

Devin began to type, reading out loud as the words appeared on the screen. "The saloon's bright lights beckoned drovers, drifters, and townspeople. The three-story building appeared more house than saloon. A bay window enhanced the front facing the street, and a porch ran the full length in grand style.

"The soft strains of 'Sweet Betsy from Pike' caught the attention of those passing by. Tied to the hitching rail, mustangs and geldings swished their tails and stomped restlessly. . . ."

Shane drummed his fingers on the marble desktop. "I can picture Calder walking through the door. Move ahead to the poker game."

"Don't rush me."

He slammed his palm flat. "Can't you type any faster? Your pacing is mule-team slow."

"Yours runs at a gallop."

"My books are definite page-turners, while yours tuck the reader in and put her to sleep."

"How can you say that?" she demanded. "You've never read one of my stories."

"But I'm working with you now, aren't I? And I can barely keep from yawning."

"I'm boring you?"

"Damn straight. My readers don't need all your description."

"My readers find it fascinating."

"Mine won't read beyond the first chapter."

Devin clamped her jaw against a retort. She hated

to argue. It always gave her a headache. Her temples throbbed even now.

Shane, on the other hand, had come alive during their heated exchange. Sarcasm had replaced his boredom. He sat on the edge of his seat with fire in his eyes and a sardonic lift to one brow.

"Well?" he baited.

"I need a breather."

"Then take five." He sank back in the chair and crossed his arms over his chest, his smug smile still in place.

Devin hated that smile. It was too self-assured for her liking. She wanted to wipe it off his face. Reaching across her desk, she selected several red jelly beans from the candy dish. She enjoyed them all in one bite, savoring the black-cherry flavor.

"Care for some?" she asked Shane.

"Sure, why not? My second taste test couldn't go as badly as my first."

Want to bet? She handed him a dozen light green jelly beans. "Enjoy."

He eyed them suspiciously. "What flavor?"

"I believe they're apple."

"Apple is good." He tossed them into his mouth, bit down, and made a face of pure distaste. "These aren't apple!"

She feigned surprise. "My mistake. Sour grapes, McNamara."

Shane looked as if he could strangle her. "A good way to get on my bad side," he grumbled as he swallowed hastily.

Devin quickly shut down her computer and stored the disk. She then rose and moved beyond his range. Entering her bedroom, she closed the door on any hope of compromise. Another writing session shot full of bullet holes.

"Holster your gun, Mr. Calder; we're the only two in the room." Rose Coltraine waved a lace hankie near her nose and sneezed. "Must you smoke?"

Calder holstered his gun, but took his time finishing his cigarette. A man didn't roll tobacco to have it stubbed out prematurely. He inhaled deeply, then swaggered across the carpet. "The room's dark as Devin's and Shane's moods. All that anger fleshed out the width of my shoulders."

Rose sighed in disgust. "Admiring yourself once again?"

"As well as your increased bustline."

She covered the dusty rose inset on her gown with a gloved hand. "Horse blinders, sir!"

"I'm focused on the storytellin'."

"Don't you mean tales of your sin and transgression?"

"And your highfalutin virtue." He flicked his cigarette butt, scuffed it beneath his heel, and scowled.

She sniffed. "Born to the Wild West, I've attempted to soothe its savage spirit. I've never encouraged rowdy and rough behavior."

"Nor raunchy sex."

"Propriety, Mr. Calder, closes the door on—"

"All but flat on your back." He grew smug, downright arrogant. "When we tuck in, you'll glimpse more than the ceiling."

She sounded as if she'd choked on a chicken bone.

He slapped her on the back, a solid thump between her shoulder blades. "Deep breaths. Don't give up the ghost—"

"You're knocking the air out of me!" She stumbled forward, hands pressed over her abdomen.

He snagged her arm, steadying her. "Catch your breath, Rose. I'm ready to ride herd on the story line."

Chapter Three

Scarlet Garter

Rose Coltraine strolled the second-floor balcony of the Scarlet Garter. Adorned in a dignified dress of petal pink, she skimmed gloved hands over a rail of polished mahogany that gleamed through twenty coats of varnish. Pausing at the top of the stairs, she caught her first glimpse of the crowd below. The candles on the chandelier cast a warm glow on the polished wooden floors. Rising cigarette and cigar smoke filtered through the three tiers of cut glass, turning the air blue. Along two walls, high-backed booths were built so the drinkers could seek privacy or partly hide themselves from other customers. A long stand-up bar with a footrail ran the full length of the third wall, and a rectangular-shaped mirror of smoky glass divided the kegs of beer from the bottled liquor.

Soft feminine laughter engaged with deeper male voices in a round of light flirtation. The roulette wheel was spinning, its red and black striped bands but a blur from the second floor. All the tables were filled with card players. One man, in particular, caught Rose's attention. Seen in profile, he sat as the fifth player in a game reserved for the town's prominent residents. Amid rancher Wayne Cutter and colleagues, the man looked dark and dangerous. Like a gunslinger. Rose witnessed him rake in the chips, hand after hand. While the other players tossed down their liquor, the stranger sipped, savoring both the whiskey and his winnings. He could own the town by morning.

Lifting her skirts, Rose took the stairs in search of her hired guns.

Dare Calder discarded one card and motioned for another. Wayne Cutter dealt him the king of spades. Calder leaned back in his chair, tipping his black Stetson low on his forehead. Four of a kind burned his fingertips. Lady Luck had kissed him full on the lips, had slipped him a little tongue.

Calder waited for the men to decide their fate. He'd won a small fortune between midnight and two. The stakes continued to mount. A small homestead north of town, two prize bulls, a horse and buggy, and partnership in the Scarlet Garter filled the pot.

Wealth and respectability clasped his shoulder. He was about to lay his cards down, to claim the goods, when the sounds of boots approached from behind.

" 'Bout time to break up the game, gents."

Calder turned toward the voices. Two men, obvious guns, stood there, hands resting casually on their holsters.

"Says who?" Calder challenged.

The younger one smirked. "Says Rose Coltraine. She's reclaiming the table for the house."

Calder's eyes narrowed. Rose Coltraine, the saloon proprietress. He'd heard of her. Gamblers revered her; the townspeople found her benevolent. He didn't hold her in the same high esteem at the moment.

Respect for the woman cleared the table of all but Calder. He sat there as disgust and disappointment claimed him. With his pockets full of gold pieces, and two promissory notes to cash once the bank opened the next morning, he scraped back his chair and took his leave through a side door.

Beyond the lights of the Garter, the heavens hovered black as sin over an alleyway reputed for its women of lost virtue. In need of a room, he headed toward the Landmark Hotel, around the corner on Bonanza Street.

He moved cautiously. Late-night drunks and young guns itching for a fight borrowed trouble from the darkness.

A rustle of crinolines stirred the silence. Moving on cat's feet, Calder approached the shadowed figure. No person of regard huddled in an alleyway at two in the morning. The female would either be awaiting a customer or a late-night lover.

"Nice night," Calder began.

"Quite peaceful," came the soft reply.

As Dare moved closer, he felt a stirring in his loins. "Care for some company?"

"I'm in need of fresh air, not company, sir."

"At this hour?"

"Sometimes the smoke and smell of whiskey is a mite much."

"So . . . you're a saloon girl?"

"I don't sing, dance, or serve drinks."

He breathed in her scent. Tea roses. She was definitely a high-priced whore. He snagged her hand and pressed it to his coin-filled pocket. "I'm in need of a woman."

Her hand spasmed near his button fly.

He swelled against her palm. Calder could hear the woman's heartbeat, the rasp of her indrawn breath.

"I've no need for man or money." Her shiver had become a tremble. "Release me, sir."

"After one kiss." His openmouthed onslaught caught the woman by surprise as he stopped her protest with his lips.

She shoved against his chest, once, twice, then hammered his shoulder with his fist. Just as he would have loosened his hold, she curled her fingers behind his neck and softened against his hardness.

Calder had never tasted lips so soft, so sweet, or a mouth so untried. Spurred by her low throaty moan, he growled his desire. Pushing her against the building, he pinned her with his wide shoulders, lean hips, and full arousal. The thrust of his knee between her thighs lifted her skirt and petticoats high. A flash of stocking-clad ankle, then silken calf, drove his hips against hers in a slow, even rhythm.

The thrust of his hand beneath her crinolines found her garter—

"Such liberties, sir!" She gasped, pushing away.

His heart fell as if thrown from a bronc. A final brush of his fingers over maiden-soft skin, and he eased down her skirts.

Indecently close, he cupped her chin in his wide palm. He ran the callused tip of his thumb over lips swollen from his passion. "I'll not take you against the wall," he breathed near her ear, "when you belong in my bed."

"Not tonight, not ever!" She brushed past him, her scent a lingering tease. "It's past closing time. I'd better get back inside."

"Will your employer have missed you?"

"I am the saloon proprietress."

Rose Coltraine. Younger than he'd expected. Lusher. Warmer. After their kiss, Calder forgave her for breaking up the poker game.

He sidestepped, then tipped his hat. "Accept my apology, Miss Rose, for takin' advantage."

"Who is offering this apology?" Her tone was as tight as her pursed lips.

"Calder, ma'am. Dare Calder."

She gave him a curt nod. "Good night, Mr. Calder."

He watched her gracefully move through the shifting shadows until she reached the side door. "When can I see you again?" he called.

The hair at the back of his neck prickled at her reply. "When you've flowers in your hand and courting in your heart."

Courting! Calder's lip curled. He'd sooner shoot himself in the foot.

"*Courtship.* This is Devin James's handiwork." Shane McNamara's temper built. Seated at his desk, he shuffled the pages she'd neatly stacked by his computer. The orange juice he'd swallowed turned bitter in his throat.

Their argument the day prior had wound him pretty tight. A rush of adrenaline had left him both agitated and surprisingly aroused. Never had a woman's anger left him so hard. It was pretty damn frightening. He'd planned to kiss and make up, but she'd left before he'd formulated an apology. He'd blown the kiss into thin air.

Though his agitation had faded within minutes of her departure, his arousal had lingered into late afternoon. He'd taken two cold showers before the heat finally faded. He swore he wouldn't let her get to him again. Sour grapes, his ass.

Following a restless night he'd awakened near dawn, only to discover how irate and irrational Devin could be. All his life he'd vented on the spot, allowed the air to clear and life to return to normal, while she, apparently, had let their words fester. Having blown their argument out of proportion, she'd decided to act. She had created a courtship.

Shane wouldn't allow it. His gunslinger would take a bullet before he'd put on a city suit and slick back his hair. He would tell Devin so, once she joined him.

Devin's bedroom door opened soon after. She breezed into the room wearing a sage-colored suit. Crossing to the kitchen, she drew a stoneware mug from the cupboard and poured herself a cup of French roast. "Coffee sure smells good."

Showered, powdered, and lightly perfumed, she possessed a freshness that beckoned like an invisible finger. Shane rose and crossed to where she stood. "It definitely smells better than cigarette smoke."

"Smoke?" She turned and sniffed, all innocence and concern.

"You left a discarded butt from your late-night writing session."

"I'm not a smoker," she defended, sneezing.

"Neither am I."

She looked at him over the rim of her mug. "I'm not sure what you're getting at. I didn't write last night. Once my head hit the pillow, I slept like the dead."

"So did I."

She blew on her coffee. "Is there a problem?"

"First chapter's almost completed. Strange, but neither of us claims to have written a word."

Her hand shook. Fearing she'd burn herself, he nodded toward her desk. "Have a seat; I'll get the pages."

Shane watched her closely as she reviewed the material. She sucked in a breath and shuddered. "The scene is not as I envisioned it. Calder trapped Rose in a dark alley."

"It was never a trap." He swung a rattan chair near her leather swivel and dropped down heavily. "It seems Rose needed fresh air."

"Which she chose to breathe alone." She turned a page. "It appears Calder planned to share more than air."

"He doesn't wish to share his life. An opening lip lock leads to fondling. Not hearts and flowers and a friggin' courtship."

"Live with it, since *you* wrote it that way."

"I didn't write it," he said in exasperation. "The courtship was *your* idea."

"Not entirely my idea. However, a show of kindness or a touch of consideration would definitely gain Rose's attention."

Shane gritted his teeth. "I won't have Calder pistol-whipped."

"He deserves to be beaten after he's molested my heroine."

"Dare didn't maul Miss Rose."

"He was repentant after he discovered her true identity," she conceded.

"So you apparently planned," Shane accused.

Her brows drew together. "If I'd written the scene, there would have been less tongue and touching."

No confession forthcoming. What type of game was she playing? Shane was beginning to believe more and more that Devin's late-night writing was a reflection of her suppressed desires. He planned to investigate that avenue further. But first he had to salvage his hero's dignity. "Calder's paying mighty heavily for a moment of pleasure."

"Perhaps pleasure for him, but punishment for Rose."

"Calder's kisses aren't that repulsive. Too bad he can't escape into the shadows, never to return."

"Kiss, grope, run?" She shook her head. "Think again."

"Calder's not going to like being roped into a courtship," Shane said, feeling as if he had a rope around his own neck.

Devin squared her shoulders. "He'd best come a-callin'."

"He'll need incentive. A sultry smile or a low-cut gown. In broad daylight, Calder wouldn't cross the street to pick up Rose's hankie."

"I'll motivate him." Devin smiled sweetly. "Rose Coltraine's mouth was swollen from Calder's brutal assault."

"It wasn't assault," Shane charged. "It was a stolen kiss, nothing more. Besides, Rose enjoyed it."

"She tolerated it. Realization of her identity should have struck him blind."

"Damn it, Dev, you're not taking his eyesight!" he exclaimed. "Change it to momentarily speechless."

"How about permanently mute?"

"Not on your life."

She crossed her arms over her chest. "Dare took liberties with one of the town's leading ladies. Liberties that could lead to a noose at sunrise."

"You're not hanging him." Shane leaned forward, itching to strangle Devin.

"The good citizenry of Cutter's Bend might take up arms if Rose were to bring charges against Calder."

He pounded the desk. "Trumped-up charges. That kiss wasn't grounds for a posse. Calder's never had to court sex. His women submit without question."

"Rose doesn't have air in her head or fire in her drawers."

Shane raked a hand through his hair. "You're going to make him sweat bullets, aren't you, Dev?"

She lifted her chin a stubborn notch. "Calder must respect Rose."

"He already admires her sweet mouth," Shane assured her. "And once she's lying beneath him, he'll respect every silken inch."

"You're despicable." Her gaze toasted him around the edges. "You make Rose's deflowering seem imminent. Yet nothing's been drafted to that end."

"Calder's kiss awakened a woman who's always been cinched in by her corset," Shane ground out. "He's about to loosen her laces."

The charged silence seemed suffocating to Devin. She pinched the bridge of her nose between thumb and forefinger. Never, in her wildest imagination, had she pictured her saloon proprietress wrapped in darkness and a gunslinger's arms. The image evoked a sensuality long denied her heroine. Deep down Devin knew that although Shane had written the scene, Rose Coltraine would fight any and all revisions. Devin must honor her character's racing heart.

Jealousy pricked her and Devin struggled with the emotion. How could she be envious of Rose's involvement? In a shadowy alleyway, her saloon proprietress had responded to a passion Devin herself might never experience.

Dare Calder had kissed her heroine senseless. Devin

couldn't claim that Skip Huddleston had ever done the same for her.

"Tell me, Miss James"—Shane leaned in alarmingly close—"have you ever had your lips licked and bitten? Bitten hard? Have you had a man thrust his tongue into your mouth with the rhythm of his mating?"

Devin pursed her lips, pressed her thighs together, and lowered her gaze. She hated Shane McNamara for the rush of excitement that drew her blush. Heat flooded her cheeks and pooled in her lower body. She wouldn't allow him to affect her this way. She swore she'd get the better of him, however long it took.

"From your silence, I gather you've never been kissed to the point of no return."

She ignored her erratic heartbeat. "I don't believe in getting lost in the moment."

Seductive mischief darkened his eyes. "Not even once?"

"I'm prone to—"

"Frigidity?"

"Restraint, McNamara!" she lashed back. His barb lodged painfully in her mind. Was she frigid? With Skip she'd never experienced the rush of desire Shane seemed to evoke.

"Personally," he confided in a whisper she wished she'd never heard, "I enjoy lust teasing my sensibilities."

Hot, wild, pulsing lust. She tried to stretch her imagination beyond Skip's missionary position, but failed miserably. Their lovemaking had always been tame, proper, predictable. This information she would not share with Shane. It was none of his business.

She booted her computer. "Time to write. Let's make it a joint effort today."

Shane scooted his chair closer. "I've an idea, let's

ditch the romance and cut to the heart of the story."

Devin eyed him suspiciously. "Which would be?"

"Mystery and adventure. Calder could witness a murder or crime as he heads back to his hotel. A plot point that could later involve Miss Rose."

"A crime committed by someone he'd recently seen or met . . . perhaps someone from the poker game." She contemplated his idea. "But because Calder's new to town, he wouldn't be believed."

"No one doubts Dare's word."

"Rose will believe him."

"Even if it's his word against that of a former suitor?"

"A former . . . I won't allow you to write Wayne Cutter out of the picture. He'd no more hurt Rose—"

"Unless he's being blackmailed."

"Who would have the power to blackmail Cutter? He's the most respected man in town outside of Marshal Dirk Morgan."

"*Dork* Morgan?"

She punched his upper arm. "Dirk, you imbecile."

He rubbed where she'd socked him. "Does the marshal have a missus?"

"The former Penelope Cambridge."

He whistled. "She sounds hoity-toity."

"She was born to high society," Devin explained. "In book three of my *Garter* series, Penelope and her father were traveling by stagecoach from Boston to San Francisco. Robbers attacked the stage near Cutter's Bend, and her father was killed. Her brother back in Boston inherited the family fortune."

"In other words, Penny was left without a cent."

"You're a laugh a minute, McNamara."

"How did Penelope survive?"

"Miss Rose offered her a job."

He rolled his eyes. "Doing what? Dealing faro?"

"Hardly. For a very short time Penelope helped with the cooking and cleaning. Which was so beneath her."

"Until Marshal Morgan proposed," he concluded.

"At which point Penelope walked out of the Garter and never looked back."

"So much for gratitude."

"Rose was glad to see her go," Devin confessed.

"Reason being?"

"Penelope had been flirting outrageously with Wayne Cutter."

Shane let out a war whoop. "The perfect setup! We'll give a little history, do a short scene on Dirk and Penelope arguing, perhaps over money. In walks Cutter, full of condolences. It becomes clear they've been carrying on an affair for some time. Penny informs him she's pregnant. When he refuses to run away with her, the blackmail begins."

"Cutter would never have to steal from Rose," Devin insisted. "He could buy the town ten times over."

"Cutter owns half the Garter," Shane pointed out. "His motivation: a grudge. He'd rob Rose blind for never puttin' out."

"A grudge against her virginity?"

"Strokin' without pokin' can really frustrate a man."

Devin nearly fell off her chair.

Shane caught her by the shoulder and helped secure her seat.

Her lips twitched left, then right. "How will you open the scene?"

"Right where the story left off, with Calder lingering in the alleyway, contemplating the courtship." Shane leaned across Devin and began to type.

She scanned the passage as he wrote. "Nothing that graphic."

"Only what Dare would like to do to Rose when next they meet."

Night hovered, as dark and perfumed as a woman's bosom. Rose Coltraine's bosom. Calder could almost hear her return, her steps as soft as twilight. He envisioned her again in his arms. Once he was holding her close, he would stroke her arms, her back, her—

"Get your hand off my thigh!" Devin demanded.

Shane jerked, the back of his hand red from her slap. "Sorry I didn't mean—"

"To stroke my thigh?"

She watched him fight the grin that threatened to spread. "I got carried away living the story."

"I suggest you let your mind, not your hands, do the telling."

Unrepentant humor rumbled in his chest. He coughed into his hand. Their shoulders bumped as they again crowded the monitor. Shane flexed a little muscle, holding his space.

Devin elbowed him low. Catching him in the ribs, she gained half the keyboard. She stretched across him, her shoulder grinding into his chest.

His thigh bumped hers.

She deleted the paragraph he'd just written. "Calder won't be stealing one of Rose's scarlet garters. Not now, not ever."

"Spoilsport."

Shane shifted, and Devin settled even closer—so close, her breast accidentally brushed his forearm. Twice. Her fingers froze on the keyboard as a warm tightness invaded her chest and left her nipples hard. Heat crept into her belly, and her abdomen pulled tight with need. Bowing her head, she gazed into his lap and prayed he would not find humor in her humiliation.

Apparently he had not, if the bulge beneath his zipper was any indication of his mood. Shane McNamara was as turned on as she.

"Dev, you're blocking the screen." His voice held an uneasy edge as he nudged her aside.

She straightened slowly, brushed her bangs out of her eyes, and ran the tip of her tongue over dry lips. "Sorry . . ."

Shane angled his chair to the right. He stretched out his long legs and rubbed his palms down his thighs.

Devin reached for her stoneware mug, cupping it between her hands. She sipped without testing the temperature. "Still h-hot!" Her hands shook as the French roast sloshed over the rim of her cup, splotching her silk skirt and Shane's blue-jeaned groin.

He shot off his chair as if scalded. "Do we need a first aid kit?"

She returned the mug to the desk. Then lifting the hem of her skirt, she shook it. "The kit won't be necessary. I burned a hole in my nylons, and there are a few red splotches on my knee. Nothing serious." She cast him a tentative look. "How about you?"

He unsnapped his jeans and unzipped them an inch. He tugged the denim off his skin. "No permanent damage."

A gym-toned abdomen and no tan lines. Her hand fluttered over her heart. "What can I do?"

"You could play doctor and administer a little salve."

She blushed hotter than his burn.

He shifted and cooled his teasing. "Let's change clothes and take a break."

"But we just got started," Devin protested. "How long a break were you planning to take?"

Shane shrugged. "I never promised nine to five."

"When shall we resume?"

"I can't pinpoint time to the second."

"How about to the hour?"

"Leave it at 'later.' "

"So much for team effort." She hit the escape key and closed down her computer. Rising from her chair, she found them toe-to-toe. "Until the muse moves you, what would you have me do?"

His gazed skimmed her, sinfully slow. "Try skinny-dipping or sunbathing in the nude."

"We need to continue writing. You're not help-ing. . . ."

"I'm doing the best I can," he said, cutting her off. "It's damn tough dealing with . . ."

"*What,* McNamara? And by all means, be specific."

There was no more than a heartbeat's hesitation be-fore he leaned forward and rested his brow against hers. "Dealing with a writing partner," he ground out. "A woman who's demanding of my time. It's not easy working with—"

"*Me?*" She clenched her teeth. "How do you think I feel?"

Shane leaned back a bit. "Exactly what I've been wondering. How do you feel, Dev?"

He was quick. Damn quick. Before she could react, he'd encircled her waist and pulled her flush against him. Her coffee-splotched skirt met his stained denim groin. She stiffened, her backbone as straight as a broomstick.

"Just as I thought." His teeth chattered, mocking her. "Cold. Ice-cold. The temperature drops ten de-grees when you enter a room."

Delving beneath her blazer, his wide-palmed hands stroked upward over the starched crispness of her blouse. Unbearably slowly he traced her ribs, each rise and indentation, then palmed the outer swells of her breasts before skimming her breastbone. Releasing her, he blew on his hands and rubbed them together. "Cold as a witch's—"

"Can it McNamara." She shot him a look of disgust.

He feigned a shiver. Reaching out once again, he aligned the lapels on her blazer. There was a fine tremor in those hard fingers as he fastened the large gold buttons that closed over her breasts. He fumbled with the second button. "Brr. Keep that cold air in."

Devin slapped his hands away.

Shane jammed them in his pockets and chuckled. "A lesson on men, Devin James. We like our women hot and responsive. Someone long on leg and—"

"Short on syllables?"

He ignored her. "Someone capable of firing our blood, not freezing our—"

Devin spun on her heel and headed for her bedroom. Her heart pounded in her ears, robbing her of his last word. She needed to be free of his presence, alone with her unsettling reaction to his teasing and taunting.

She would die of embarrassment if Shane McNamara ever discovered how she'd responded to his touch. Fortunately her button-down blazer had covered the rapid beat of her heart, the puckering of her nipples, the tightening of her abdomen. Had Shane not released her when he did, her knees would have buckled. She would have melted like sugar in the rain.

A most unthinkable response from a woman with a subzero libido. A woman with icicles hanging from her heart. A woman capable of spitting ice cubes.

A light tapping on the door gave her pause. "What is it?"

Shane cleared his throat. "I'm headed into town."

Devin pressed her forehead against the doorjamb. "How long will you be gone?"

"Not long enough for you to change the locks." He chuckled. "Can I bring you anything?"

"How about a new writing partner?"

"Ah, Dev, you strike deep. I thought we were made for each other."

"Get lost, McNamara."

He was halfway there. Shane took two steps, then stopped and glanced over his shoulder at the closed door. A door shut against him. He bowed his head and swore softly. He'd taken up the challenge of loosening her up. He'd crossed that line, invaded her personal space. Touched her—a touch intended to tease, not to kindle a response.

Her reaction had rocked him on his heels. The punch of desire had laid him low when her breasts had swelled and her nipples had hardened.

She'd been anything but cold.

The slight trembling that sliced through her had reflected his own inner tremor. Pleasure had spurred his taunts on, and she'd escaped to her bedroom, a safe haven against his insolence and bad manners.

The empty room seemed to close in around him. Usually he valued his privacy, but oddly he felt alone now. Over the years he'd carved numerous notches on his bedpost. Women came and women went. Only one had stayed too long. Although he couldn't deny his attraction to Devin James, neither could he act upon it. They were cast in a different mold. She was a forever kind of woman, and he was a gone-yesterday kind of man.

Needing to put a little distance between them, Shane snatched his car keys off the kitchen counter and headed for the door. A drive into Naples, windows down and radio blaring, would clear his head of a sanctimonious blonde on a short fuse.

Ninety minutes had crawled by when Shane returned to the writer's cottage. He'd driven into town with the sole purpose of ridding his thoughts of Devin James. He'd planned to do a little cruising, perhaps a little chatting should a major babe rev her car engine beside his at a red light.

Collaborating with Devin had put his brain cells through the ringer. He felt rung out mentally, yet physically edgy. He'd wanted—no, needed—to forget Miss Priss, if only for an hour or two.

He'd had no luck. With each mile that passed she'd crowded his conscience. He could almost feel her in the passenger seat beside him. He'd tried to lose her with each sharp turn, with each change of lanes. Eventually he'd accepted her presence. A small part of him almost wished he'd invited her along. A very small part.

After whipping around town, driving faster than the speed limit, expecting a ticket on every straightaway, Shane had grabbed a hamburger at a fast-food restaurant. The burger had settled as heavily in his stomach as Devin had settled in his life. He grew increasingly uncomfortable and restless and borderline ornery.

It was high noon when he parked his midnight-blue Porsche in front of the cottage. He stroked the imaginary hammer on his Colt .45. He was in the mood for a little gunplay. One shot, dead center.

"Shake it to the left, shake it to the right, what really turns me on is the shake."

Shane's gun never left its holster. Instead of firing, he stood just inside the doorway and blessed his good fortune. He'd caught Devin James exercising in the front room. Her back was to him, and he took complete advantage of his undisclosed presence. Propping a shoulder against the doorjamb, he pocketed his keys while admiring her workout gear. A sexy second-skin unitard in gold and plum swirls hugged a firm little body with dangerous curves. The skimpy attire allowed her full range of motion.

Lord, the woman could move. She combined a little line dancing with some aerobics, then added a whole lot of shaking. The shaking hit him the hardest. His heart picked up speed with each shimmy and gyration. Her tush-push did him in. His body stirred and throbbed. He began to sweat.

Perspiration glowed on Devin's skin. Her pigtails swung with the beat as she rotated her hips, whirled around, grabbed her towel off the back of a rattan chair . . . then froze. "H-how long . . ."

He pushed away from the doorjamb and sauntered into the room. "Long enough, Dev, to catch a whole lot of shakin' going on."

"I-I thought you'd be gone—"

"Longer?" He drew near enough to pull one of her pigtails.

She slapped his hand away. "At least through lunch."

Unaccountably, his only hunger had been for her.

"You could have said something!"

"And missed the show?" He took in the moist sheen of her shoulders, settled on the damp vee between her breasts, then skimmed the long length of her legs. He traced his lower lip with the tip of his tongue, then blew out a breath. "My timing couldn't have been better."

Hers couldn't have been worse. Embarrassment and indignation heated her already flushed skin. She'd been so engrossed in the music and her dance, she hadn't heard him enter. She damned him for not announcing himself, the peeping Tom. For just standing and staring and enjoying her uninhibited performance. Wrapping a fluffy gold towel about her waist, Devin moved to her desk, flicked off the tape player, and walked from the room with as much dignity as she could muster.

"Don't leave on my account." Shane's request rose on a plea and ended on a chuckle. "Another ten minutes of pivots and pelvic thrusts would be nice."

"They wouldn't burn as many calories as my anger," Devin shot over her shoulder.

"Have you had lunch?" he called.

"My appetite left with your arrival." She slammed the bedroom door, crossed the room, and collapsed on the bed.

The only sound came from the faint ticking of her alarm clock on the bedside table. She glanced at the time. Twelve-fifteen. Shane McNamara had returned not only early, but at a most inopportune time. When she'd compiled her afternoon's entertainment, she hadn't expected his return until late. Or so she'd hoped. Now, her enjoyment of an hour's worth of exercise, followed by an enormous bowl of popcorn and a marathon of Western movies on television, faded on a sigh of disappointment. As afternoon approached, she'd either have to hide out in her room or bite the bullet and face his unrepentant smirk.

She would never forget how he'd looked at her. His gaze had been hot and dangerous, coyote-hungry.

When he'd licked his lower lip, she'd sworn he'd tasted her. Her heart still raced from the aftereffects of that look. If she lived to be a hundred, she would never understand this turn of events. His sudden interest in her was unexplainable. Also unforgivable, given their circumstances.

She clenched her fists, more annoyed than unnerved. As writing partners, she and Shane must remain professional. Their collaborative efforts must remain focused on the book and not on each other. She hated this strange vulnerability that left her aware of him as a man.

Skip. Skip. Skip Huddleston. She mentally chanted her loyalty. Skip was her future. Six-week McNamara was just a short-term torment.

Control—she must regain her hold on the situation. Shane had said she was cold. He'd even gone so far as to demonstrate his point. Although he didn't realize how far opposite the truth was where he was concerned. Perhaps she could freeze him out of her life. At least make his teeth chatter so she could have the last word. He need never know her real reaction to him.

Determined to straighten out their working relationship, Devin rose, stripped off her unitard, and headed for the shower. Beneath the warm, relaxing spray, she let her mind wander. She wondered, under different circumstances, how it would feel to be chased and caught by a modern day gunslinger.

Shane had made popcorn. She could smell it, almost taste the butter. She could also hear the television. Indignation speared her. How dared he steal her plans for the afternoon? She hadn't invited him to join her. Worse yet, she was still gun shy of dealing with him.

Then there was the matter of a book that needed to be written. Time marched ahead without them.

The sanctuary of her bedroom enticed her. It would be so simple to climb into bed and curl up with a good book. It would be far more difficult to face Shane. She never knew what tactic to take with him. He was out of her league. His expertise ran beyond her experience.

But she'd never deserted under fire, even with both barrels leveled on her. She wouldn't run for cover now.

Sighing heavily, she dried and braided her hair, then carefully selected her clothes: a long-sleeved black pullover and matching tailored slacks, which she covered with a midcalf batik vest in peach and pearl. The less skin showing the better. A pair of low-heeled pumps completed her outfit.

She looked unapproachable. Beyond his reach. The full-length mirror reflected the desired effect. She couldn't have been more pleased.

Taking a deep breath, she opened the door and found Shane sprawled on the couch, a bowl of popcorn propped on his abdomen. Even in profile he was a ruggedly handsome man. Coal-black hair brushed a wide forehead; an early-afternoon beard cast sinful shadows over his cheek and jaw. The firm line of his mouth held her gaze, until he turned his head and lifted a brow. "Going out?"

"No, I'm in for the afternoon."

"So am I." He munched on a handful of popcorn, swallowed, then asked, "Do you always dress up to watch TV?"

Devin crossed to a rattan chair and sat down stiffly. "I'm not dressed up."

"You've got on a lot more clothes than you did earlier."

"I was exercising then."

He had the nerve to wink. "I know."

"I just felt—"

"The need to cover up?" He was all innocence now. "Hell, Dev, it wasn't like I saw you naked."

And he never would, she vowed. Distracted by a familiar theme song, she focused her full attention on the big screen color set. The Western marathon had begun. *"The Magnificent Seven?"*

"One of my favorite movies."

"One of mine . . . also."

Something in common. The idea that they shared a liking for the same classic Western relaxed her somewhat. Thank heavens she hadn't had to whine over what to watch or wrestle him for the remote control. They'd been in agreement. For once.

"Care for some popcorn?"

She started to rise. "I'll get a bowl."

He sat up, set the bowl on the center cushion to his left, dividing the couch. "We could share."

She didn't dare sit beside him. "I'd prefer my own bowl."

"In order to keep your distance?"

She wouldn't allow him the satisfaction of knowing how his closeness jarred her sensibilities. "I'm quite comfortable sitting over here."

Shane scratched his jaw. "You prefer straining your neck over watching the television straight-on?"

"On occasion." She proceeded to the kitchen, found a large mixing bowl in the cupboard, and took it down. She wanted her fair share of the popcorn. Returning, she held the bowl out to Shane.

He snorted. "This little piggy went to market."

"Just fill the bowl."

"We may have to pop a second bag." He shook half

the contents from his bowl into hers, then snagged her wrist when she would have returned to her chair. "Be honest, Dev"—a look of pure challenge darkened his gaze—"your true reason for not sitting on the couch is your inability to keep your hands off me."

She smothered her panic. "Don't be so cocksure." Setting her bowl beside him, she eased onto a cushion and smiled her sweetest smile. "I promise not to touch you—much."

His lips twitched. "Did you know this was a sofa bed?"

The cushions seemed to grow warm beneath her bottom. "We're not pulling it out."

"We'd be more comfortable watching TV in bed."

"I'm plenty comfy," she insisted.

"You're practically sitting on the armrest," he noted.

Devin settled in the corner of the couch. Beside her Shane slouched low, suddenly silent and as entranced as she, while the Magnificent Seven rid a Mexican village of outlaw bandits. The Western marathon continued with *Tombstone*, followed by *Unforgiven*.

Time passed far too quickly. It was early evening before she knew it. Once the credits began to roll on the third flick, Devin stood and stretched. "Can I get you a soda?"

Shane straightened. "I'd prefer a Samuel Adams."

"Sam who?"

"Beer, Dev. Grab me a longneck."

She returned with a Dr Pepper for herself and a beer for Shane.

He twisted the cap, took a long, cold swallow then tossed her the remote. "Your choice. Movie, sitcom, sports, news?"

Seated once again on the sofa, she glanced in his direction, staring a little too long.

"Enjoying my channel, Dev?"

Heat skimmed her cheekbones. "I-I was just about to switch."

"No need to hurry." He turned slightly. "I'm easy viewing all night long."

Shane McNamara might be easy on the eyes, but Devin saw only red. She pointed the remote control at the set and grated out, "You're nothing more than a click-by channel."

"If you say so . . ."

She'd said so, and she meant it. After flicking through a dozen channels, she paused on Prime Time Country. A new video was just beginning. To Devin's delight, the first chords of Jamie Jensen's guitar clashed with a roll of thunder. Heat lightning illuminated the sky, and a strong wind blew leaves across the veranda of a Southern plantation.

Ever so slowly the front door creaked open, and the sexy redhead strolled across the wide porch. The wind whipped her hair about her face, flattened her fringed white blouse against her full breasts, and lifted her short denim skirt high on her thighs. As the force subsided and the wild strands of her hair settled about her shoulders, the singer seduced the camera with her trademark golden gaze.

"It's 'Storm,' her latest video." Devin edged forward on the couch.

"Change the channel, Dev." Shane's voice sounded as ominous as the background weather.

"This is Jamie's premiere—"

He made a grab for the remote.

Devin, however, held it at arm's length. "You having a problem with my choice of stations?"

"Damn straight!" He dove for the channel changer. "Watch it another time."

Devin jerked backward, and Shane landed in her lap.

"Get off me, McNamara!"

"Switch it!"

"Give me a reason," she grated out.

"It's personal," was all he said.

Shane snagged her wrist, but Devin held tight.

Their wrestling ceased as Jamie's Southern ballad captured their attention.

"A storm rolled in one cold dark night in the form of a man achin' for a fight. His temper thundered over the force of the rain. Commitment be damned, along with my fame. Lightning flashed his departure, piercing my pain. Darkness closed around me, good-bye . . . Shane."

Good-bye Shane? Devin mouthed the words as she lowered the remote and turned down the sound. The photograph in *Power* magazine of Shane and a woman now flashed before her mind's eye in vivid focus. There was a skeleton rattling in his closet. A singing one, at that.

She narrowed her gaze on his wide shoulders stretched across her abdomen. "Anything you'd care to share?" she said in a hiss near his ear.

Shane eased up. He rubbed his side, down to his hipbone. "I think one of those popcorn bowls took out a rib."

Devin scooped up the bowls and set them on the coffee table. "Don't blame me; you dived for the remote."

"You didn't have to hold it so far out of my reach."

"It was a foolish move, and you know it."

The final faint strains of Jamie's song ended on a sigh.

"Forever in my heart, until my dyin' day. Come home . . . Shane."

Her heart in her eyes, the singer smiled sadly before turning back toward the house. The video faded on a clap of thunder and the sound of drizzling rain.

Devin's arm felt heavy as she raised the remote and clicked off the set. She tossed the device on the coffee table. Smoothing her hands along her thighs, she shifted positions, tucking her legs beneath her.

Shane's profile hardened, yet Devin proceeded as if he'd encouraged conversation. "*Where*, exactly is home?"

A dark scowl settled over his features. "Don't press, Dev."

The writer in her had to know more. She jabbed his sore side. "Answer me, McNamara."

Shane winced. "I don't want to talk about her."

"Well, I do. Where's home?" she repeated.

He released a short, sharp breath. "Charlotte, North Carolina."

"A long way from Palm Beach. How did you meet?"

He leaned forward, resting his elbows on his knees and his chin on his palms. "At a book signing."

"Jamie Jensen reads your Texas trash?"

A muscle jerked along his jawline. "It's not trash."

"Jamie waited in line for an autographed copy?"

"She was never in line."

Devin poked him a second time. "For an author, you sure are slow in recounting the story."

"Jab me again and you'll never hear the end."

She waited several heartbeats before prying further. "Where was your book signing?"

"At a large shopping mall in Nashville near J.J.'s recording studio."

She spread her hands wide. "Jamie just walked into your life?"

"She walked into a table where I was signing books."

"Details, McNamara. Details."

"Rein in, Dev." His eyes narrowed and his expression grew distant. "It was a Saturday, late afternoon. The bookstore had placed a table piled high with my latest books just outside the door. Within minutes of my sitting down, J.J. exited the neighboring western-wear store, arms laden with purchases. Unable to see over the top box, she collided with my table. Copies of *Texas Thunder* got mixed up with her rhinestone-studded vests, leather skirt, and turquoise boots."

Devin's heart turned over in her chest. "So you were hit by Cupid's arrow."

"The arrow would have been less painful." He glanced her way. "Ever been poked by the devil's pitchfork?"

She shook her head.

"One jab leaves you hot and horny."

Devin blushed clear to the roots of her hair. "How long were you together?"

"One year."

"When did you make the break?"

"Six weeks ago."

Devin's heart slowed. Shane McNamara, her writing partner, had been involved with one of country's lead vocalists. He'd parked his boots under her bed for an entire year. "Why did you leave?"

"I straddled the fence longer than she liked."

Devin gaped. "You couldn't commit?"

He dropped back against the couch, legs splayed, thumbs hooked in his front belt loops. "She wasn't the one."

Awareness swept her like a bad omen. She inched toward him. "Because she wasn't *the one*, you're holding up production on *Calder's Rose*."

"Come again?"

"Your procrastination. The concert. Victoria will withhold the tickets if we haven't finished chapter one." She lifted a brow. "But that's what you were hoping for, wasn't it? Not having to face your old flame."

"Lady, you're plumb *loco*."

"Then why are we only ten pages into the book? You're usually a fast writer, and I'm willing to work within your time frame."

Shane couldn't meet her eyes. "Ever think it's our character conflict that's slowing the pace? Your virtuous Miss Rose not meeting Calder's needs?"

"Don't use Rose and Dare to cover up the real reason—your sinister plot to avoid seeing Jamie Jensen."

"I was never plotting against you, Dev. I know how important the concert is to you."

"You have one hell of a way of showing your concern." She rose, her back stiff, an angry set to her shoulders. "Sweet dreams, McNamara."

Devin left the room without a backward glance. The click of the bedroom door closed her world to Shane.

He'd purposely forfeited the Jamie Jensen tickets. Which only proved he still had feelings for the singer—feelings he had neither confronted nor overcome.

The thought of him holding Jamie close to his heart left her own heart sad. That was a most disturbing observation, one she preferred to sleep on. As she slipped off her clothes, she wondered if Shane had also retired, and if Jamie Jensen slept over in his dreams.

Shane remained on the sofa, stretched out, yet uncomfortable, as he searched his conscience for a seed of truth to back Devin's accusations. Once burned, twice shy. Had his innermost psyche rebelled against facing his old flame? He rubbed a hand over his chest, tucked it beneath his armpit, grew reminiscent.

Jamie Jensen . . . a little bit wild and a whole lot demanding. While they'd heated the sheets, outside the bedroom they'd left each other cold. In the spotlight, adored by thousands, J.J. had never understood his need for privacy and solitude. She considered the time he'd spent writing as time away from her. She'd grown jealous of his career. So jealous, in fact, that during a fit of temper she'd deleted his entire rough draft of *Texas Gun.*

He'd quit the fight amid a storm of harsh words. There had been no closure.

The hour of reckoning was rapidly approaching. It was time to face his past. The future of *Calder's Rose* depended on it.

"Your boot tapping has become annoying, Mr. Calder. Any louder and you'll waken Shane McNamara," Rose Coltraine softly scolded.

Dare Calder stopped his tapping. He edged near the sofa where his creator now slept. He retreated when Shane stirred, rolling from one side to the other before sprawling once again on his back.

"The man's restless," Calder noted. "We've adjustments to make on the story line, and McNamara's sleeping with one eye open."

Rose tugged on his elbow. "Let us return once he's retired for the night."

"Could be a bit." He snagged her hand, pulling her snug against his side. The skirts of her blush-pink gown wrapped his black-denimed thigh. "I've ways to while away the time."

"By counting stars, Mr. Calder?"

"I'd sooner lie with you beneath them."

She pushed herself out of his hold. "On a bed of grass?"

"Unless you'd care to share my bedroll."

She gathered her skirts and swept past him. "In truth, sir, my feather tick holds far more appeal."

Chapter Four

"Dev? Wake up, Dev."

Shane McNamara flipped on the overhead lamp and flooded the bedroom with fluorescent light. "Rise and shine."

Devin buried deeper beneath the covers.

He crossed the room to her bed. Standing near the brass bars of her headboard, he prodded her shoulder. "Let's go, lazybones. I'm ready to write."

When she didn't stir, he took her by the shoulder and rocked her. "Cock-a-doodle-doo!"

"Leave the crowing to the roosters," she said with a yawn as she eased up on one elbow and came eye-level with the snarling Doberman depicted on the front of his red T-shirt. He scratched the words *Dog Breath Saloon, Cologne, Germany,* which stretched across his abdomen. He shifted his stance, and the untied drawstring on his black silk jogging shorts swung past her nose. Her gaze shifted right, left, then right again before she pushed herself to a sitting position.

Disheveled and drowsy, Devin James looked sexy as hell. Her golden hair curled about her sleep-flushed features, and her ivory poet's shirt had come unlaced, revealing a dangerous amount of breast. She looked soft and warm, desirable . . . bedable.

Something caught in his throat, something large and lustful that made him warm from the inside out. His blood thickened and his body stirred. He feared he would make a spectacle of himself.

Devin, however, had yet to notice his discomfort. Propped against the headboard, she rubbed her eyes with a balled fist. "Tell me I'm dreaming. That I'm in the middle of a nightmare."

"I'm not the bogeyman, Dev."

"That's debatable." She arched a brow. "Did I hear you correctly? You're ready to write?"

Shane nodded. "My muse woke me, all bright-eyed and bushy-tailed."

She glanced at her bedside clock. "It's two in the morning. Tuck your muse back into bed."

"Can't, Dev. I'm feeling expressive."

"I'm totally uninspired."

He reached out, took her by the arm, and tugged. "Give me one hour. Sixty short minutes."

She shook him off and rolled onto her side. "Does ten-thirty yesterday morning ring any bells?"

He blew out a breath. "I clocked out early on our writing session."

"Good memory." She punched her pillow.

Shane had no doubt she imagined it was his nose. "Come on, I'm wired to write."

"You've definitely short-circuited," she grumbled against her pillow. "Give me one good reason to get out of bed."

"A pair of Jamie Jensen tickets."

"A *pair*?" She turned back to face him. "You'll attend the concert with me?"

"Don't make it sound like a date, Dev."

"It's open seating, McNamara. I'll sit in the front near the stage, and you can grab a seat in the back."

He raked his hand through his hair. "That's pretty much how I'd envisioned it."

"Concert tickets for a writing session. You sure know how to horse-trade." Still not quite awake, Devin jerked back the covers, revealing a whole lot of leg. Slender, toned, tempting leg.

She nearly knocked him to his knees.

"I'll need to clean up first."

He rubbed his hands together. "Want me to draw your bath?"

"I'd planned to shower." She pointed toward the door. "Go start the coffee."

"Kamasutra Mandheling?" he asked.

"*Sumatra* Mandheling will be fine."

She closed the bathroom door, and Shane left her to her shower.

Once in the kitchen he paced from the step stool to the refrigerator, around the butcher-block counter, then back again. Restless as hell, he pilfered the cupboards, looking for something he couldn't define. Even the contents of the refrigerator held little interest. When his muse moved him, it moved fast, demanding he get to work immediately.

In this instance he had to wait for Devin James.

He moved to the living room and wore a path between the couch and the television. He stopped at Devin's desk, so neat and clean, not a speck of dust. He noted all the pencils had been sharpened to the same length. He removed one, snapped off the eraser and dulled the point. Childish but satisfying. He hated waiting.

He checked her stapler and found it stocked with staples. He hammered out six, then dropped them in the trash can. Her roll of Scotch tape had yet to be used. He tore off the paper tab. A bottle of Evian springwater and her dish of gourmet jelly beans stood at one corner of her desk. He traced the fluted rim on the cranberry-colored dish, then picked out one brown jelly bean. He did the sniff test. It smelled a little like honey, or maybe molasses. Surely a safe flavor. He popped it into his mouth.

"Prune!" It was utterly distasteful. He swallowed it whole.

The flavor lingered, subtle but sour. He decided coffee would kill the taste. He was on his second cup by the time Devin joined him. "Coffee's hot." He nodded toward the kitchen.

He liked the sound of her rummaging through the cupboards for the largest stoneware mug. It sounded downright homey. He heard her pour the Sumatra Mandheling, and smiled to himself as Devin sighed over her first sip. It was almost like playing house.

Almost, but not quite. He shrugged off his contentment. They were together to write, nothing more. She believed he'd sabotaged *Calder's Rose*, and he was about to prove her wrong. After considerable soul searching, Shane was ready to complete chapter one, then face Jamie Jensen. The book was his present, and Jamie was his past.

The thunder between him and J.J. would soon clash for the final time. And once the storm cleared . . .

"Where shall I sit?" Devin stood by his desk.

"Right here." He patted the fan-back chair next to

his own. "It's late, and I know you're tired. I'll even do most of the typing."

"How very considerate." She blew on her coffee as she settled beside him.

Shane glanced at her, then wished he hadn't. He liked what he saw—too damn much. Devin sat on the chair, legs curled beneath her, her hands cradling her mug. Floral bath gel scented her skin, and her damp hair was held in place by two barrettes, clipped high near her part. A coral jersey topped a pair of cream leggings. He like her dressed casually, in something other than those button-down suits. And minus that tight-ass braid.

Barefoot and freshly scrubbed, she looked soft and sexy. He shifted on his leather swivel chair, his concentration once again on his own desires and not on the project. He throbbed, ached, grew downright edgy. His jogging shorts suddenly seemed a size too small.

He turned his frustration on Devin. "Sit up, Dev. Try to look a little more interested."

"Sit up? Show interest?" She jerked forward, her eyes wide and her lips parted. "Don't press your luck, Mc-Namara. You're darn lucky I got out of bed."

He mulled over his supposed good fortune. He couldn't write the book without her, but having Devin so near had his hormones raging like that of a teenage boy with his first adult magazine. He berated his muse for prodding him from slumber.

He booted the computer with his fist on the switch. When the monitor lit with their efforts from the morning before, he summarized the last few lines.

"This next segment will cover Marshal Dirk Morgan and Penelope's argument." Shane laced his fingers together and cracked his knuckles. "Location for the shouting match?"

Devin settled back in the chair. "Cormet's General Store."

He liked the locale. He traced the edge of the keyboard, then began to type. "It's late afternoon. The day's been hotter than a mule's ass."

"A mule's—" she sputtered. "How about hotter than blazes? Better still, hot and humid, not a breath of air stirring."

"A mule's ass gets hot as asphalt in the sunshine," he contended. "My Western readers will get the picture."

"Mine will be offended."

"Your readers won't go blind over the word 'ass,'" he assured her before returning to the story. "Marshal Dirk Morgan rides into town, tired and dusty. Having been in search of cattle rustlers raiding Wayne Cutter's herd, he's spent two nights on the Triple C Range. As he guides his sorrel down Main Street he spots his wife on the boardwalk. She pauses in front of Cormet's General Store and presses her nose to the window."

He stopped typing. "You with me, Dev?"

"Hmm." She rested her head against the back of the chair, her eyes closed, her body relaxed. Her grip loosened on the stoneware mug . . .

"Devin!"

"Wh-what?" She started, nearly spilling her coffee.

"Eyes open—work with me."

One hand clutched the mug while the other covered her heart. She glared at him. "I was envisioning the scene, standing beside Penelope, right outside the store."

He swore he'd heard her snore. Turning back to their writing, he joined her on the boardwalk and peered through the window. "An enormous pickle barrel sits just inside the door. Bushel crates line the front of the counter, filled with onions, potatoes, and green apples. Tins of plug tobacco and jars of peppermint and licorice sticks are arranged high on the shelf beside the herbal medicine kits."

Devin nodded her approval. "Penelope enters the store. She walks down an aisle, past a glass case of chased gold watches and a carved ivory-handled Colt. Just beyond the hanging jeans, slickers, and sacks of flour, she stops beside a low table of fancy goods. She is immediately taken with a bar of ginger-scented milled soap and the new shipment of satin hair ribbons."

"Back on Main Street, Marshal Morgan reins in his sorrel before the telegraph office, one storefront south of Cormet's."

"That's not the lay of the land," Devin said. "The telegraph office is two storefronts north of Cormet's."

Shane made the correction. "Morgan wants to alert the sheriff of Backwater Junction to keep an eye out for any stolen cattle branded with the Triple C."

Devin sipped her coffee. "Once Dirk has sent his message, he heads toward the general store to see what supplies his wife might need. He nods at bespectacled store owner Calvin Cormet, who's sweeping behind the counter.

Tall and thin, clothed in sun-faded denim and dust, Dirk fingers the frayed ends of his cuffs. The telltale signs of hard times are etched around the marshal's mouth. He's been in need of a new shirt for months." Shane typed. "Penelope's heart is set on new hair ribbons. Frivolous satin ribbons. That ought to irk Dirk."

"Only mildly. He's got the patience of a saint."

Shane disagreed. "Penelope's got a twist in her pantaloons. She's got a guilty secret, but even though she's betrayed her husband, she still longs for the luxuries she once took for granted."

Devin ran with his thought. "The marshal finds his missus in the corner shadows admiring a lace handkerchief and the sapphire ribbons. She smiles and swishes her skirts at her husband's approach."

"A forced smile that doesn't make it to her eyes."

"Penelope touches Dirk's arm in greeting."

Shane snorted. "A light touch now, and a hearty slap later."

Devin set her empty mug on the corner of Shane's desk. "Penelope pats the dark ringlets near her left ear. It's been months since she's shown kindness to her husband, and he's leery of her intentions."

"She takes up a yard of sapphire ribbon and rubs it against her cheek," Shane said. "In a voice as sweet as a sugar plum, she asks her husband to buy her the ribbon. The item is pricey, and her request is downright petty. She's thinking only of herself. Dirk could buy two work shirts for the cost of the satin ribbon."

"With a heavy sigh, Dirk denies Penelope her purchase." Devin released a sigh of her own. "Penelope's lips pinch in an unattractive pout as she reminds Dirk of his wedding vows. He'd once promised to cherish her above all else."

"Penelope on a pedestal? Hard to believe," Shane said.

"In the early years of their marriage, the marshal adored her, and she tolerated him," Devin explained. "As time passed, so did his infatuation with his wife. He feels only a heartfelt regret for his poor taste in women. Slim and sharp-featured, Penelope turned bitter shortly after their marriage. Dirk knows from hard experience that the purchase of satin ribbons won't win either her gratitude or her kiss."

"So he stands his ground, and Penelope stamps her foot. She looks ready to bean him with a three-legged skillet," said Shane. "Grim-lipped, the lawman shifts uncomfortably. He's not prone to outbursts, but his wife is fussing, her tongue so sharp it could carve out a man's liver. Calvin Cormet stretches his neck, curious over the commotion."

"Calvin would never gossip," Devin said in defense of her store owner. "He's been privy to the town's worst scandals and always held his silence."

"Until now. Cal's tongue is about to wag."

Devin tapped her fingers on the armrest of her chair. "You're drawing my townspeople out of character. My readers won't recognize the good citizenry of Cutter's Bend."

"I've merely made your characters more interesting," Shane commented dryly. "I've added some excitement to their dreary little lives."

"Dreary?" Devin grew as angry as Penelope Morgan. "My characters attend barn dances, Sunday socials, and the annual Founders' Day Celebration."

"Hot times in the old town." He feigned a yawn. "Cutter's Bend can return to this side of sleepy once we've completed *Calder's Rose.*"

"I'm not happy—"

"I'm not overjoyed either, Dev," Shane said. "Not all your characters have changed traits. Rose Coltraine is still as prissy and virtuous as when the book opened."

"She'll remain that way when the book ends."

Shane envisioned a much different conclusion, one that involved lifted petticoats and a dropped holster. With that in mind, he returned to Cormet's General Store and the dilemma of the satin ribbons. "Her color high, Penelope Morgan insists Calvin Cormet will extend them credit. The more she sulks, the tighter Dirk locks his jaw. Marshal Morgan refuses to go into debt."

"His new shirt purchased and tucked under his arm, the lawman leaves his wife to stew," Devin continued. "Shortly thereafter, Wayne Cutter enters the store, impeccably attired in a flat-crowned white hat and tailored gray suit. The sound of Penelope's sniffling draws him to the back of the store. He finds her hidden behind an eight-drawer pine chest."

Shane slapped his thigh. "She cries on Cutter's shoulder, and takes solace in her lover's arms. Cutter purchases a lace handkerchief to dry Penelope's tears. He further purchases several yards of satin ribbon, but his generosity isn't enough for Penelope. She wants him to take her away from Cutter's Bend now that she's in the family way."

He grinned. "When old Wayne stalls for time, Penny demands money. He promises cash from the Scarlet Garter and sweet-talks her into sneaking out to his ranch again."

Devin scrunched up her nose. "There will be no graphic sex."

"It wouldn't be a pretty picture," Shane agreed. "Penelope's all skin and bones, and Cutter has a potbelly."

She cast him a dark look. "Cutter eats well—"

"Pot roast, potbelly."

"—but isn't round about the middle." She uncurled her legs, then stretched her arms. After several seconds she lowered her arms and rolled her shoulders. Her jersey shifted, baring one shoulder.

Shane stared at her shoulder. He clenched his fist, stilling the wild urge to track its soft curve.

Devin's shoulders rose and fell as she sighed. "Rose has lost a promising suitor, thanks to your story line."

"No big loss," he assured her. "My gunslinger's a better lover than the old farmboy."

She raised her chin a notch. "Cutter's a wealthy rancher. Rose is giving up a chance for security. Without Dare's courtship and commitment, there will be no further kisses."

Shane disagreed. "I predict sweaty bodies and love-tangled sheets by chapter three."

She stifled a yawn. "I predict abstinence."

He pitied his gunslinger. Somewhere within the next chapter Calder would need a willing woman. Perhaps he'd return to Eve's Garden and enjoy a second night with Belle.

From the corner of his eye he caught Devin sinking lower in the fan-back chair. Her head lolled onto her right shoulder, and her breathing slowed. "Care to work awhile longer?" he asked.

"Sure . . . I'm awake."

He took her word for it. He continued talking, typing, and pushing the envelope, all the while awaiting her comments and suggestions. None were forthcoming. He glanced her way. "Dev?"

She was dead to the world.

He flexed his fingers over the keyboard. Three A.M. wasn't her writing hour.

Pushing the chair away from his desk, Shane rose. Ever so gently he scooped Devin into his arms and lifted her high against his chest. She shifted, snuggled, then sighed contentedly.

The same contentment curled about his heart as he walked slowly, enjoying the task of putting her to bed. The light from the living area filtered into her room as he crossed to her bed, reached down, and tossed aside the lilac spread. He lowered Devin onto the matching sheets. On impulse he pressed a kiss to her forehead, then to her bare shoulder. Her skin was cool and soft, and he wanted to feel it grow hot beneath his palm.

His heart slammed with the wild desire to slip into bed beside her. He backed up a step before he did anything so foolish. In the shadowed room he watched her sleep. For several seconds she lay exactly as he'd placed her. Then stretching languorously, she curled onto her side and cuddled her pillow close.

For the first time in his life Shane wished he were filled with feathers and covered with a case. Just to be in bed with her . . .

Get back to work, his muse clamored. *The book's not going to write itself while you watch Devin James sleep.*

Male curiosity held him where he stood. Devin wouldn't allow him in her bedroom in broad daylight. However, amid the shadows he could seek clues that gave insight into his collaborator not only as a writer, but also as a woman.

He soon discovered she was a believer of the saying, "A place for everything and everything in its place." All the items on her dresser were arranged according to size and shape. Decorative frosted vintage wine bottles in white, olive, and green stood over an assortment of vitamins, creams, and lotions and a small bottle of perfume. Plain barrettes and designer hair clips formed a perfect row. A rose-colored bowl of fragrant potpourri nudged a packet of scented stationery.

It appeared Devin planned to stay in touch with the outside world while Shane roamed Cutter's Bend.

Farther down the dresser a boar bristle hairbrush was so clean, it looked as if it had never been used. Thoughts of replacing the two glossy women's magazines with a copy of *Playgirl* gave him a charge, but he doubted Devin would be amused.

A tiny snow globe next caught his eye. He picked it

up and shook it. Fake snow settled around a miniaturized Minneapolis skyline. Never far from home, Devin traveled with her city.

A small framed picture of a man with short brown hair and teeth as white as Chiclets drew Shane's frown. *Yippee Skippy?* He turned the photo facedown.

The night is passing, his muse warned. Shane retreated to his computer.

The chapter was still flowing as the clock ticked away the minutes and he and Mr. Coffee welcomed the morning hours. By five A.M. he'd expanded the dialogue and fleshed out the scene at Cormet's General Store. He'd made clear Penelope Morgan's manipulations with both men.

Shane grinned. This subplot would definitely enhance the story line. The book had taken a turn for the better. Wayne Cutter was no longer in the running to court Rose Coltraine. By pairing Cutter with Penelope Morgan, Shane had legitimately eliminated Dare Calder's competition.

What time was it? Devin James awoke to a room filled with sunshine. She stared at the ceiling and recalled the early-morning writing session with Shane. She must have dozed off . . . and he must have put her to bed. She vaguely remembered him talking out the plot, wanting her approval, before she drifted off.

She glanced at the bedside clock. Nine-fifteen. She'd slept away a good portion of the morning. She rolled out of bed with a yawn and a big stretch. She still wore her jersey and leggings. At least Shane had had the decency not to tuck her in naked. She swallowed hard at an image of his hands slowly stripping off her clothes, leaving her bare to his gaze and the inevitable intimacy of his body.

She shook her head, embarrassed by her thoughts. She would change her own clothes, then go find her writing partner.

"McNamara?" After dressing in a champagne linen jacket, wide-legged pants, and leather huaraches, Devin strolled into the main room. No sign of her writing partner. She cautiously crossed the floor until she faced his bedroom. The thought of him sleeping, sprawled across his bed naked, no doubt, both intimidated and intrigued her.

She knocked and waited. Then she knocked a little louder. When no answer came she pressed her ear to the door. It opened on its own. Devin peeked around the frame.

"Shane the rooster has crowed." Still nothing.

An overwhelming curiosity pressed her forward, and she tiptoed into his deserted sanctuary. Absolute discord. She shook her head over his drop-kick, wherever-it-lands lifestyle. His king-size bed remained unmade, the burgundy satin cover sheet and spread rumpled at its foot. Devin glanced about and found the man had brought little to nothing of his personal effects to their six-week writing session. He definitely traveled light. At any give moment he could pack up and move on. As he once had with Jamie Jensen.

She circled the bed and advanced on the nightstand. A CD Walkman and a toppled assortment of discs were spread over the top. He favored country-western singers. A can of mixed nuts, several packets of cheese crackers, and a bag of Bavarian pretzels had all been opened. Shane McNamara snacked in bed. Behind the mixed nuts, an unopened box of extra-large neon condoms flashed the world.

Neon! Devin's cheeks burned. The man had no shame. Sheathed in Tangerine Tango, Lemon Lick, or

Strawberry Sin, he would glow in the dark like a human nightlight. He snuffed out all need for candles. Devin equated candles with romance. The scent, the flickering shadows, set the mood for making love.

Neon condoms would bring no more than a quick heat to the sheets.

Burn 'em up, Shane.

Devin suddenly needed air. She hightailed it out of his room as if her drawers were on fire. And in truth, she couldn't deny the heat now spreading up her thighs.

Once in the kitchen she pulled open the refrigerator door and found relief in the cold air. A note from Shane had been scribbled on a napkin and stuck beneath a pitcher of freshly squeezed orange juice: *Sun's up, and so am I. Join me, I'm catching some rays.*

A glass of juice in one hand and a rye bagel in the other, Devin slid open the sliding glass doors off the lanai with one foot and went in search of Shane.

"Looking for me?" he called from the double rope hammock hitched beneath two queen palms.

She slowly walked his way, the image of the neon condoms still fresh in her mind. "You're up early."

"I never went to bed."

She stared disbelievingly. "How can you function without sleep?"

He scratched his stubbled chin. "I'll let you be the judge of that after you've read chapter one."

She started, nearly dropping the glass and bagel. "You finished without me?"

"You weren't much good to me after three A.M."

Devin couldn't control her gaze. It traveled his length, from the top of his mussed dark hair, along his whiskered jaw, and over broad shoulders and a thick chest encased in a fresh T-shirt printed with a gray donkey, haunches high, and the words, *Kick-Ass Cantina, Matamoros, Mexico.* A pair of khaki shorts rode low on his hips.

He was as handsome as original sin. And just as tempting.

"I'm not much of a night owl," she confessed.

He studied her longer than she liked. "Nice morning-after glow."

Morning-after . . . He made it sound as sexual as his neon condoms. She turned toward the beach so he wouldn't catch her blush. "I-I appreciate your putting me to bed." The words caught in her throat. "I would have had cricks in my neck after a night on the fan-back chair."

"You tuck in mighty nicely."

Once again heat rose from her toes.

"Care to join me?" Shane inched over on the hammock.

Devin glanced his way. He looked so comfortable. So relaxed. So dangerously male. She curled her toes in her huaraches. "It doesn't look strong enough to hold two people," she hedged.

"Bears four hundred pounds." He patted the empty portion. "I'm a solid two hundred, and you're light as air."

"I weigh one-twenty—"

"Dressed like an Eskimo. Come on, Dev," he coaxed. "Take a load off. Just test your weight on the edge."

Devin was no fool. The edge would quickly lead to the middle, where Shane now lay. "Hammocks have always been like canoes to me," she informed him uneasily. "Whenever I've gotten in one, it's flipped."

"Ever come close to drowning?"

She shook her head.

"Then what's the problem?"

This time her heart flipped as Shane rose unexpectedly. Both the glass of juice and the bagel bit the dust as he snagged her wrist and pulled her down beside him. Devin shrieked, and the warmth of Shane's laughter heated the air by ten degrees.

The hammock swayed and threw her sideways, as she knew it would. She rolled and collided with muscle, sinew, and body heat. His scent was pure and virile, hot and vibrant, and tantalizingly Shane.

Devin forgot to breathe. She lifted her hand in a small, helpless gesture, and Shane laced his fingers with hers. "Lie still, Dev, or we'll both take a nosedive." His warm whisper fanned her ear.

She stilled instantly.

Shane eased onto his elbow. He could see the awareness of their closeness in her gaze. As he watched her, her aqua eyes became so pale they seemed to generate a light of their own. He leaned in, intimately close, never touching, yet all the while enjoying her conflict and uncertainty. He could tell she was as unsure of herself as she was of him. He savored her blush. They lay so near, he could feel the wild flight of her heart.

She was as fearful as she was fascinated by what was to come.

Lowering his gaze to her lips, he imagined their taste: moist, warm, and incredibly sweet. He breathed in her scent; light, fresh, and all that was Devin James.

Faced with the opportunity of unbuttoning both her blouse and her inhibitions, he felt his palms itch. Would she warm to his touch as the sun now warmed her skin?

Shane inched closer. "I want to kiss you, Dev."

She pressed back. "I want to get a jump on chapter two."

He wanted to jump her bones. "Care to horse-trade?"

She lifted a brow. "What do you have that I might want?"

Definitely a loaded question. "How about a productive writing session?"

She wasn't impressed. "We had one last night."

"I'm offering daylight hours."

He had her full attention now. "How many hours?"

He knew his limitations. "Two, maybe three."

"Make it four."

Four hours. Half a day. The woman was brutal in her bargaining. Dread seeped into his bones. He'd be a fidgeting fool in two.

He sought her gaze, and she returned his stare. She visually challenged him to corral his creativity and work within her timeframe.

He needed to think. His best thoughts came while touching her. Light as the ocean breeze he traced her brow, then one high cheekbone. He ran the back of his hand along the sweet curve of her chin.

She curled her slim fingers into his cotton shirt, just above his heart. One manicured nail scraped his nipple. His heartbeat doubled in tempo.

Interest in him as a man had darkened her gaze. The flick of her tongue to the corner of her lush mouth suddenly left him winded.

Was a sixty-second kiss worth a four-hour writing session?

"I'm all yours."

Her breathing quickened against his neck, and her fingers tightened in his T-shirt.

Had she realized she'd pulled him closer?

Liquid anticipation flowed in his veins, hot and heavy. On a hammock beneath the Florida sun, he felt time seem to slow and still like a frame in a movie. A primal, wordless desire drew him to Devin, and he marveled at how her mouth alone could be such a turn on. He kissed her with a tenderness he hadn't known he possessed, and with a gentleness born just for her. He experienced the kiss as if it were his very first, and there had been no other woman before her.

Something deep inside him wanted her to remember this moment. Wanted her memories to last long beyond their short time together.

He wanted her to take his kiss to her grave.

As the tip of his tongue tasted, laved, and parted her lips, Devin moved against him. She stroked his side, his waist, then worked her hand under the back of his shirt, where she traced the warm flesh along his spine. For several heartbeats he stopped seducing and began savoring, and soon became lost in her softness, her sweetness. Her surrender.

Sucking her lower lip against the hard edges of his teeth, he bit the soft inner flesh. Devin responded in kind. She nipped him on a low, sexy moan. Blood rushed through his body while temptation, hot and dangerous, curled in his belly. He felt an unmistakable jolt in his groin. This was moving too fast. He'd soon reach the point of no return. He'd never met anyone who could leave him so hard with the mere softness of her kiss.

With great effort he rose from the deepening intimacy. Relinquishing her lips, Shane took a mind-clearing breath. He pressed a kiss to her forehead, the tip of her nose, the fragile arc of each cheekbone, before pulling her close. He held her until their hearts slowed.

A warmth greater than the sun stole into his soul, followed by a sudden need to hold Devin forever.

Their kiss had stirred soft, tender thoughts—not all of them sex-driven. He couldn't put his finger on what it was about her that got to him, but affect him she did, and in such a way that his instincts warned him to keep his distance. Otherwise he'd be picking out china patterns and a best man. Sharing vows and wedding cake. Chauffeuring children to ballet and soccer practice.

Permanence. Rootin'-tootin' commitment.

His attempt to loosen her up had left his backbone like Jell-O. His world rocked and his body jerked and shifted. He needed to stand, and walk around, get some circulation above his waist as quickly as possible.

In his attempt to bolt, the hammock swayed wildly. . . .

The serenity that had filled Devin's body took flight. She made a mad grab for Shane, but snatched only air. Her cry mixed with the twisting rope, and, upended, she folded into a heap on the ground.

Flat on his back, Shane sprawled beside her left hip. Devin stared, disbelieving, at his suddenly transformed face. No longer heated by inner passion, he looked cold, distant. His bullet-hard gaze dared her to speak.

She blew her bangs out of her eyes and rubbed her tailbone. "You sure know how to bring a girl down to earth, McNamara."

"Are you hurt?" he asked in a growl.

Devin lifted a brow. "Does a bruised ego count?"

"Not unless it requires stitches." His gaze was level, unapproachable, until is drifted to her mouth. There it darkened to smoke.

A response curled in her belly, leaving her warmer than the day and extremely light-headed. He still wanted her, Devin realized, even if he had flipped the hammock and let her down hard. Butt-jarring hard. His abrupt change of heart both deflated and mystified

107

her. Shane had been aroused; she'd felt his need. His extra-large need. But then without warning, he'd landed them facedown in the dirt.

His sudden break for freedom filled her with a strange sense of loss.

Come home . . . Shane. Jamie Jensen wanted him back. Devin could understand the singer's plea. The man swaggered through life, living it large and on his own terms. He had the look of a loner, which only drew women to soothe his loneliness. His kisses were lethal. His slow, stroking hands were experienced. His seductive gaze made a woman believe he would change, just for her.

Devin's writer's eye told her different. Shane McNamara and Dare Calder were two of a kind. Creator and character were both motivated by fear of commitment.

But Shane had lit a fire in her heart. A fire that was rapidly singeing Skip Huddleston's memory. She needed to douse her desire before the slow burn consumed her. Shane was dangerous and unpredictable. He would never offer stability. Skip, however, could give her the security she needed in life.

Tugging on the hem of her jacket, Devin got to her knees, then slowly rose. Without looking at Shane, she straightened the ropes on the hammock, then retrieved her empty glass.

"Looks like the ants have started on your bagel," Shane noted.

Devin kept her back to him. "They still have their appetite."

He was behind her before she'd heard him move. Catching her by the shoulders, he turned her to face him. She tried to shrug off his hands, but his hold only tightened.

"What happened in the hammock . . . the kisses . . . I won't apologize for those moments of—"

"Major indiscretion?"

"I'd have gone with pleasure." He squeezed her upper arms. "Admit it, Dev, we burned as hot as the sun on that hammock."

"Until it conveniently capsized."

He scowled. "You said hammocks weren't good to you."

She scrunched up her face and imitated his flinty glare. "Strain your brain, McNamara. I wasn't the one who set it in motion."

He tossed his dark head. "You're blaming me?"

"If the shoe fits."

"I'm barefooted."

She stepped on his toes as she edged around him. "Let me know when you want to begin our four-hour writing session," she tossed over her shoulder as she headed toward the cottage.

Shane watched her go. An odd tightness crept into his chest as the boundaries he'd set around himself no longer seemed defined. Devin James was knocking down fences faster than he could build them, and he didn't like that one dang bit.

He'd always been able to read women; hell, he could write a book on them. But Devin was different from the other women he'd dated. Something about her had him over a barrel.

He'd stared a hole in her back as she'd crossed the yard and entered the lanai. Yet she hadn't even glanced back once to see if he'd been watching her. It was better that she hadn't; otherwise she might have seen her continued effect on him. He'd become a walking erection. If that pain didn't give him writer's block, the pressure of their collaboration soon would.

Blowing out his breath, he followed her inside.

He found her leaning against her desk, listening to the speakerphone.

". . . around noon?" he caught Victoria Patton's question.

Devin explained. "Vic wants to drop off the board games and concert tickets. Is noon good for you?"

Shane shook his head. "Make it dinnertime instead. I need to shop SunBake Boardwalk this morning. We won't continue writing until after lunch."

"You owe me four hours," Devin said, holding up four fingers as a further reminder.

"I know," he returned.

"Glad to hear you're working."

Shane could hear the relief in their publicist's voice. "When haven't I come through for you, Vic?"

An audible sigh. "You ride your deadlines to the wire."

"But I always cross the finish line."

"This time you're riding double," Victoria reminded him.

She was right. Devin James slowed his pace. "We won't need an extension on our contract."

"I'll hold you to that, Shane. Later, you two," Victoria concluded.

With the disconnection, Devin turned on Shane. "*Shopping*? Are you insane?"

She made him a little crazy. "What's wrong with that? I want a new T-shirt."

"Can't it wait until I've reviewed chapter one?"

"Read it after lunch." He motioned her toward the door.

She held back. "I want your promise we'll write as soon as we return."

He held up his hands to show her he hadn't crossed his fingers. "Word of honor."

He could tell she didn't believe him for a second. He held out his hand. "Come with me. I'll buy you something special."

She took his hand. "I could use a new pair of shoes."

He'd hoped to buy her lingerie.

"Let's hit the road. My Porsche seats two."

Rose Coltraine stepped cautiously into the sitting room. She cleared her throat and spoke her mind. "I rather like what Shane McNamara has written."

"Well, I sure as hell don't." Dare Calder fingered his six-shooter. "The scene at Cormet's General Store runs eight pages. That's seven pages too long."

Rose twisted her gloved hands. "Must you always be the center of attention?"

"Self-preservation. It's my book."

"Believe what you will."

Calder ground his teeth as he immersed himself in the scene. "Marshal Morgan's cut trail and Wayne Cutter's slithered into the general store." Calder hooted. "See that smarmy expression written on Penelope's face? She believes she's got both her husband and her lover under her thumb."

"I wouldn't have believed Wayne could fall for her if I hadn't seen it myself," Rose said softly.

"Well, Cutter's anticipation of their lovemaking showed quite clearly in his face . . . and lower." He curled his lip.

"I-I hadn't noticed."

"The man's a handful of thumbs," Calder scoffed. "He fumbled their embrace, held Penelope like a sack of potatoes. And his kiss was all wet and slobbery. The rancher gnawed on her mouth as if chewing on a bone."

Rose squared her shoulders. "I've kissed Wayne, and he's not a dog, Mr. Calder."

"I'd call him a big old hound for trespassin' on another man's wife."

He heard her breath catch. She fingered the pearl buttons on the bodice of her antique rose gown. "You believe in fidelity?"

He shifted his stance. "I avoid married women."

"A man with a conscience?" A soft smile edged her lips.

He tipped back his Stetson and looked her dead-on. "There's enough single women to keep my fires burnin'."

Her lower lip quivered. "You're not a one-woman man."

"Glad to see we're on the same page, Miss Coltraine. I've too much tumbleweed in my blood to ever settle down."

Silence distanced them until Calder drew his gun and fired at the manuscript pages stacked on the corner of Shane McNamara's desk. The sheets fluttered, several falling to the floor. "It's time to write about me."

"Us." She covered her ears. "Must you shoot off your suggestions?"

"Must you be so damn priggish?"

"Manners and gentlemanly conduct—"

"Won't get me anywhere with you. I know what works and I'm stickin' to it." He snagged Rose around her trim waist and drew her tightly against him. She sputtered. He silenced her the best way he knew how— with a stolen kiss.

Chapter Five

Scarlet Garter

Dare Calder returned to the alleyway for three nights in hopes of catching Rose Coltraine unescorted by her hired guns. Prior to midnight on the fourth night, he'd become involved in several games of poker and roulette. He'd won a little, and lost a whole lot more, all for a glimpse of the saloon proprietress.

Only once had she taken the stairs, slowly, one at a time, her gloved hand in a death grip on the polished banister. Her gaze had skittered over the customers, soon locating him at the poker tables. She'd retreated on a swish of petal-pink skirts and matching high-button shoes.

Calder had felt like a discarded joker.

He'd folded on a full house, and taken to the alley, anticipating her need for fresh air. It was long after closing when the back door finally creaked open. Calder's expectations rose, and his body stirred. He pushed away from the wall and straightened. Miss Rose would face both him and his desires before rooster's first crow.

The person leaving the saloon was disguised by the darkness, but there was nothing feminine about the shadowed form. The broad hunched shoulders and thick middle belonged to a large man. The man grunted as he stumbled on the rickety stairs. Calder caught the flash of a burlap bag and the jingle of coins.

Tracking like an Indian, Dare followed the man as he sneaked around corners and down alleys. He was acting like a low-down thief.

Once reaching the livery stable, the man scanned the horses tied to the hitching post. "Damn 'loosa, never hitched where I left him."

Calder recognized the deep, nasal drawl and white Stetson of rancher Wayne Cutter. He heard the rancher give a low whistle, then watched him pace a full circle in the street. When Cutter's wandering Appaloosa appeared, he stepped into the saddle. He tied the burlap bag to the horn.

"Must get away," Cutter muttered as he kicked the horse into a canter. On the early morning air, the sound of clinking coins blended with the 'loosa's pounding hooves.

Calder stepped from behind the corral of half-tamed horses. He scrubbed his knuckles against his stubbled jaw. Cutter was as shifty as the shadows, and definitely up to no good.

Perhaps Rose Coltraine could shed light on the rancher's late-night dealings. The man's strange behavior gave Dare a surefire excuse to question Miss Rose.

* * *

The town yawned, awakening slowly as dawn lit the deserted streets. Bold as brass, Dare Calder entered the Scarlet Garter through the front door. Shafts of gold bordered by deep shadow spilled over his boots as he crossed the polished planks of the bar floor and ascended the thickly carpeted staircase in search of Rose's bedroom.

A beefy-faced man with thin blond hair dozed in a chair outside a thick oak door with a glass knob. The guard was Dawson McKay, one of Miss Coltraine's hired guns.

Conversation would prove tiresome.

Confrontation would force his gun.

On cat's feet, Calder flattened himself against the wall and eased toward the door. His hand outstretched, he turned the knob and prayed for a well-oiled hinge. A soft click granted him entrance.

"This should stave off the cavalry," he murmured, setting the dead bolt from inside.

Through lace curtains, sunlight and shadows battled for the same territory. At the borderline between darkness and light, Calder located Rose Coltraine's bed. He approached it slowly.

He found her wrapped in a pristine sheet and a slumberous blush.

As she turned onto her side the sheet slipped free, revealing the curve of her bottom, the sleek lines of her hips, and a scarlet garter worn high on her alabaster thigh.

Dare Calder's stomach twisted. The need to touch her was strong. The sun was rising, and so was he.

Restraint buffered his need. There would be no cock-crowing sex. Miss Rose was a lady, and Calder understood the consequence of impropriety. A lynch mob was not to his liking. As a result Dare kept his hands off Rose. When he heard her indrawn breath, he was surprised she didn't scream.

Tension tightened the cords in Rose Coltraine's throat. She could barely swallow, much less scream. Though the gunslinger hadn't touched her, she felt surrounded by him. His black Stetson rode low on his brow, casting his eyes in shadow. High cheekbones surmounted the unshaven hollows of a face born to haunt a woman's dreams. His physical presence both disturbed and intrigued her.

Rose rolled onto her hip and straightened the sheet, covering her nakedness. "I don't remember inviting you to my bed."

"You didn't." Calder shifted his stance. "I came to talk, nothin' more."

"You're trespassing, Mr. Calder." She clutched the sheet tighter. "My chambers are private. Off-limits."

"You keep your door closed to men like me." He moved to the foot of her bed, snagged the end of the sheet, and tugged. The linen slid off one shoulder and dipped between her breasts. "I'll not trample your privacy, nor take undue liberties." His tone was dark and determined. "I'm here to trap a varmint."

She started. "Varmint."

He wrapped his hand about the carved pine bedpost and leaned toward her. "A thief, Rose."

"Someone's stealing?"

"From the Scarlet Garter."

She frowned. "My hired guns protect the saloon from drunks, rowdies, and robberies."

He cocked a brow. "But what if the thief was one of your own?"

"My men are plainspoken, dependable. Both Sony and Dawson worked Wayne Cutter's ranch before hiring on with the saloon. Cutter only enlists—"

"Bootlickers."

"You're mistaken, sir," she said, defending her men. "They answer only to me."

"They answer to you given Cutter's consent."

"You defy belief!" She stiffened and pointed to the door. "Take your leave."

He took a bold step forward and rested his thigh against the bed frame. "Hear me out." He stroked the butt of his six-gun.

She eyed his gun as she drew the sheet to her chin and settled more deeply into the feather tick. "Speak quickly, sir."

Calder's jaw grew as tight as her hand on the sheet. "I caught Wayne Cutter leavin' the Garter this morning, long after midnight."

Rose shrugged. "He's half owner of the saloon. His hours are his own."

"Is he known for sneakin' out the back door?"

She waved one hand in dismissal. "Sneaking or leaving at will? Surly, sir, I haven't concerns—"

"You damn well should. Cutter was carrying a bulgin' burlap bag."

Her breathing slowed. "You're sure it was Wayne?"

"No one else in town wears a white Stetson."

She pressed her fingers to her eyes. "How did you gain your information, Mr. Calder?"

He shifted his stance. "I spotted him in the alley and tracked him to the livery."

"Your purpose for such late-night spying?"

"Happened to be in the alley seekin' your company."

"I haven't returned to the alleyway since—"

"We kissed," he finished for her. "I've stood there in the shadows for three nights runnin'."

She licked her lips. "You wish to court me, sir?"

He shook his head. "Thought to steal another kiss."

His honesty made her blush. "And you call Wayne Cutter a thief."

He looked her dead on. "You need my protection, Rose."

"Protection against Wayne Cutter? Certainly not. He's honest, respected—"

"Light-fingered," Calder said. "Cutter's been twirlin' numbers on your safe."

"Wayne's a devoted business partner," she insisted.

"Dedicated to skimmin' the profits."

"Your accusations damn the man who built this town—the man who financed most of our businesses." She took a deep breath. "Your story's no more than a tall tale. A tale that won't gain my favor."

A muscle jumped along his jawline. "In offerin' my assistance, I sought only to keep you safe." He turned to leave. "Take a fair accountin' of last night's profits. Should you come up short and decide to take me up on my offer, I'll be stayin' at Eve's Garden."

The house of ill repute, where fallen women with painted lips, rouged nipples, and perfumed inner thighs welcomed customers with bottles of whiskey and silky sighs. "Always hankering after a bunch of petticoats." She spoke to his back. "You've never assisted a woman with anything more than helping her out of her clothes. I could no more trust you than I could—"

"Trust Wayne Cutter." He ended her tirade near the door. "I ain't no saint, Miss Coltraine, never tracked the straight and narrow. But I ride with truth and self-respect. Can your rancher say the same?"

Dare ended their conversation by slipping out the door as silently as he had entered.

"Are we having fun yet?" Shane McNamara asked on the drive into town.

Devin James glared at him. "I'd be blown out the window if I weren't wearing my seat belt."

Shane couldn't help grinning. The trip had been swift and breezy with the Porsche's windows down and the sunroof cranked wide. Her tight-ass braid had been blown to pieces and now the blond strands whooped it up, avoiding her fussing fingers.

Shane liked her disheveled. The flash of frustration in her aqua eyes, the agitated color that tinted her cheeks, her soft groans of irritation when her hair refused to cooperate only heightened her appeal. It all combined to make her look like a woman who experienced life, instead of just writing about it.

He parked the car close to SunBake Boardwalk and exited. Devin didn't wait for his assistance. By the time he'd locked the car door, he caught no more than her pantsuited back and her tangled braid. The woman could power-walk. She'd cross the sandy lot, climbed eight steps, and entered If the Shoe Fits before he'd slipped the keys into his khaki pocket.

Shane scanned the colorful storefronts and absorbed the Bohemian ambience. The lively steel-drum music being piped along the wooden planks lifted his spirits. He smiled for no reason at all. He located Three Shirts to the Wind at the far end of SunBake, near the boat dock. He strode the distance.

He dodged windbreakers swinging in the doorway as he entered T-shirt heaven. Sleek, sexy, twenty-something Suzie, wearing her identification badge low on her left breast, spotted him immediately. She jammed the box of suntan lotion she'd been ticketing beneath a display table and sashayed his way. Her white-blond hair skimmed sun-bronzed shoulders exposed above a cherry-red tube top. She wore white short-shorts secured with a thin silver belt. Sparkling crystal ties laced between her toes and around her ankles, leaving the bottoms of her feet bare. She smelled of coconut oil.

Suzie advertised fun in the sun.

"Can I help you?" Her voice had the breathy little catch of a babe on the make. She stood so close they were nearly rubbing belt buckles.

Bold was not always beautiful. He edged back a step and surveyed the shop. "Mind if I browse?"

"Not at all."

His idea of browsing differed greatly from hers. Suzie was joined to him at the hip. She held T-shirts up to his chest, then directed him to the dressing room. There her reflection joined his in the mirror. She became more of a hindrance than a help.

As quickly as was humanly possible, Shane narrowed down his choice. He tossed a black T-shirt on the counter near the register. He'd chosen it strictly for its blushing power. Devin would turn crimson when she read its slogan.

He lifted his wallet from his back pocket and extracted a Ulysses S. Grant. Suzie took her sweet time ringing up his sale. She plucked the fifty from between his fingers, then counted back his change. After slipping the shirt into a plastic bag, she held it just beyond his reach. "My shift ends in thirty minutes—care to take me to lunch?"

"I have a prior commitment," he answered, knowing he didn't sound sufficiently regretful.

Suzie passed him his purchase. "Lucky lady." She sighed as he turned to leave.

"Lady?" Shane came to a dead stop.

"The one you're off to meet."

Devin James. He swallowed his chuckle. His writing partner would never claim to be fortunate in their acquaintance. She barely tolerated his existence. Their kiss, however, had stirred awareness into attraction. Next time he planned to knock her sensible shoes off.

Bag in hand, he strolled past Giggle Moon, a bright orange storefront filled with stuffed animals and wooden toys. He gazed in the front window of The Bookie, and found his latest release, *Texas Justice*, displayed on the dump, a collapsible cardboard showcase. Three rows below was Devin James's *Scoundrel's Kiss*. Noting the title, he wondered which of her male characters had been smoochin' with Rose.

On a whim he entered the store and purchased a copy of her book.

"I didn't take you for a romance reader." The middle-aged lady behind the counter looked at him over her bifocals.

"I know the author," he returned.

"Devin James?" The cashier fanned the pages of the paperback. "I've never read her work, but my sister loves her novels. Evelyn swears they're keepers."

"A keeper, huh?" Shane paid for the book, then dropped it in the bag with his T-shirt.

"Can you tell me what she's like?" The clerk looked hopeful. "My sister would love to know."

"Isn't there a picture of the author on the inside of the back cover?" he asked.

She shook her head. "Never has been. And her biography is as generic as Jane Doe's."

Shane scratched his chin. Perhaps Devin valued her privacy. "The author is blond and blue-eyed." His description could fit half the women in America.

"Thanks, I'll tell my sister." The clerk moved down the counter to assist another customer with a stack of gardening books.

Returning to the boardwalk, he dragged his feet past

The Fudge Factory. Memories assailed him, not all of them pleasant. Jamie Jensen had been obsessed with white-chocolate and hot-fudge body paints.

Shane, however, had never developed a sweet tooth.

Two doors down, Gossamer Whisper tickled his fancy. In the display window sheerest lace and finest silk lingerie draped a brass headboard suggestively. The window dressing stimulated his imagination. He looked deeper into the store, beyond a diaphanous chemise and an ivory satin bustier, and straight into Jamie Jensen's trademark golden stare.

Her wide-eyed surprise punched him square in the gut.

Shane blinked rapidly, expecting Jamie to disappear. Instead of vanishing she came into vivid focus, from her tumble of red hair to her stunning figure.

Lace and satin slipped from her fingers as she ya-hooed and dashed toward the door.

Shane's heart slammed so violently, he swore he'd broken a rib. He thought about running, but had no place to hide. Certain she'd chase him to the ends of the Earth, he planted his feet and braced himself for her welcome.

"Shane! Darling! I heard you were in town. I knew you'd find me." Jamie Jensen flung the door wide and, with a hop and a skip, leaped high into his arms.

The wind was momentarily knocked from his lungs as Shane dropped his package and cupped the singer's leather-clad bottom in his large hands.

He shook back his hair and tried to extricate himself from the redhead's embrace. "Still not one for hand-shakes, I see."

"I want to touch you all over," she breathed against his mouth.

"Not in front of innocent shoppers." He patted her

bottom, then released her. Jamie tightened her thighs about his hips. She stuck like human Velcro.

"J.J." His warning fell on deaf, triple-pierced ears.

Her gold hoops winged his hard jaw as she swooped in and took possession of his mouth.

A fire lit, spreading a little heat. The flick of her tongue and the crush of her breast wound him around her finger. For all of thirty seconds. Her too-obvious desire turned him off faster than a bad book review.

Their tongues battled, as much for his freedom as her gratification. He bit down on her lower lip—forcibly. She moaned, then popped off him like a pulled soda tab. He did not release her lip until her stilettos hit the boardwalk.

She wobbled back a step. The whimsical beaded trim on the cuffs of her low-slung chartreuse leather pants swayed wildly. She straightened her amethyst bandeau top. Her attire belonged on the stage, not on a shopping spree.

"I thought you'd be glad to see me." She pouted. "Destiny brought us together."

Fate had kicked him in the groin—damn hard. "I'd like to see more than your face in mine," he returned flatly.

"How much of me would you like to see?" She held out her hand in invitation. "Come check out my purchases."

Lingerie purchases. "I haven't the time."

She stroked his forearm. "Make time, Shane."

He pulled back. "I'm no longer on your clock, J.J."

She tossed her hair. "Ten minutes is all I'm asking."

He didn't want to give her sixty seconds. "I'm in a hurry—"

"As much of a hurry as on the night you left me?"

Her eyes narrowed to dangerous slits, the early signs of a royal snit.

Several bystanders eyed them with interest. If he didn't play his cards right, things could turn ugly. He was in no mood for a public spectacle. Shane nodded toward the store. "Ten minutes, J.J."

She was all smiles and swaying hips as she reentered Gossamer Whisper. The sensation of someone watching him stopped Shane cold as he bent to retrieve his package. He scanned the boardwalk, which was relatively clear. He looked toward the shoe store where Devin had been shopping. Eerily, the store's peacock-blue entry seemed to sizzle with more than sunshine.

Was his imagination playing tricks on him? Shane wondered. Or had Devin James witnessed his and Jamie's reunion from amid the spiked heels and flats.

Guilt settled in his bones and whittled at his conscience. It shouldn't have mattered, but, strangely, it did. He felt as if he'd cheated on his wife. He'd never felt so unfaithful. He forced himself to remember that Devin was no more than a six-week writing partner. He had pledged no vows.

On an agitated sigh, he trailed after Jamie's exotic perfume. He entered a hot-pink fantasy of transparent chiffon and obvious seduction.

"I'll model my negligees." Jamie scooped up wisps of lace and satin and glided toward a dressing room.

"Morning, McNamara." A brick wall of a man with sandy hair and hazel eyes pushed away from a display case of edible panties and crossed to Shane.

"Ross Hunter." Shane clasped the band manager's right hand, then slapped him on the back with his left. "Buying or just browsing?" he teased his old friend.

"Nothing in my size," Ross returned easily. "I'm here on a bribe. J.J. has promised that however long we shop, her band will extend practice second for second."

Shane lifted a brow. "And you believed her?"

Ross jammed his hands into the pockets of his charcoal-gray slacks. "She's written a new song that makes her sound like a braying ass."

Shane fought his laughter, but lost to a deep chuckle. "That bad?"

"I call it like I hear it." Ross pursed his lips. "J.J. hasn't sung on-key since you walked out of her life. She shouted her voice raw that night."

"She'll recover. She always does," Shane assured him.

"It's been six weeks, man." Ross cut him a sharp look. "In the interest of all concerned, smoke a peace pipe."

Shane expelled his breath slowly. "I can't do that, Ross. J.J.'s high-maintenance. She'd never take second place to my writing."

"Then make her a priority," Ross said.

"Those days have passed."

Jamie, however, did her best to reclaim Shane's interest.

When she appeared, neither man could find his voice. Beneath a hand-crocheted gown of gray mist, her naked curves promised no sleep tonight, or any night. She circled Shane in a mating ritual, brushing her body against his, then raking her inch-long fingernails down his chest. Curving her hands about his waist, she pulled him flush against her. Their bodies locked like two pieces to a puzzle.

Jamie Jensen was definitely warm and willing. She wanted him.

Red-faced, Ross Hunter faded from view, returning to his post by the melt-in-your-mouth panties.

"You feel so good." Jamie's sex appeal wrapped around Shane like the snake from the Garden of Eden. Temptation squeezed the sanity right out of him.

"You feel—" *Ouch!* The swift kick of an invisible foot struck with tangible force. He jumped back and rubbed his left buttock, thankful the store stood empty of all but the salesclerk.

Stunned and bewildered, Shane shook his head. There was no one behind him, but he hadn't imagined that kick. "I'm out of here," he declared.

Jamie blocked his path, confused and pouty. "You can't leave."

"Fashion show is over," he said firmly.

"You promised me ten minutes. I have five to go." She dashed back to the dressing room.

"I should cut trail," Shane muttered, itching to walk.

"J.J. would waltz down the boardwalk after you," Ross warned, serious as a judge. "You wrote her out of your life once; she won't let you do it again."

Resentment or regret? Shane had heard something in the manager's voice that had him looking at Ross, really looking at him for the first time. Tight lines bracketed the man's mouth, and his eyes had gone dark with concern and . . . caring. A whole lot of caring.

Realization slapped Shane on the back of the head. Twice in one day he'd been brought to his senses by invisible, yet tangible forces. He wanted to slap his thigh and whoop out loud. If looks didn't deceive, Ross Hunter had it bad for Jamie Jensen. So bad it appeared almost painful.

The evidence, however, faded with the manager's harsh order. "I want her happy, McNamara."

"We'd only make each other miserable," Shane said.

Ross blew out a tired breath. "She'll do her best to convince you otherwise."

Jamie certainly did try. She reappeared in a slither of peach satin designed to tease, but not reveal. Halfway across the store she slowed, then stopped just beyond Shane's reach. Her hot amber gaze locked with his while she waited for any small sign that he still wanted her.

Shane sensed he had only to smile, nod, or flex the tiniest muscle to encourage her. For several long minutes he held his breath and prayed she would accept his rejection gracefully.

"Sleep tight, J.J., but sleep alone."

She took the final step that separated them. She traced his jaw, then his mouth. "One night, Shane. A dusk-to-dawn."

Her reference to their sexual marathons only brought back memories of the mornings after. The bedroom of hard knocks had taught him sex wasn't a path to permanent happiness. At dawn he and J.J. had broken their embrace, separated by their differences.

There was no going back. "I'm ready to ride."

"Ride out of my life forever?" The tightness in her voice matched the tightness of her features. "Aren't you coming to my concert? I've written a new song just for you."

"Ross mentioned your song." Shane caught sight of the manager lurking around the counter by a rack of crotchless red teddies.

Ross dipped his head and retreated further.

Shane covered his smile by clearing his throat. "Pack up your purchases, J.J.; you've promised Ross a long rehearsal."

"Come hear us practice," she urged. "We could catch up on old times between sets."

What was past was past. "I'm collaborating on a book, and my partner's a workhorse." He spread his hands wide in hopes of evoking sympathy. "I'm tied to the computer with no free time."

His white lie turned Jamie's mood black. Putting her hands on her hips, she glared at him. "You used to make time for me."

He wouldn't repeat his mistakes. "It's late. I need to leave."

"I will see you again."

There was no such handwriting on his wall. He prayed fate wouldn't bring them together again. "Good-bye, Jamie."

With a nod to Ross Hunter, Shane departed.

Blinded by the sunlight he stood on the boardwalk, facing If the Shoe Fits. Devin. Excitement elbowed him in the ribs. He tried to ignore his anticipation as he walked toward the shop's French doors.

Peering inside, he spotted her just beyond a display of sequined evening bags, pivoting before a full-length mirror. A glimpse of her trim ankle above a plain brown shoe scrambled his senses. The Pied Piper of leather pumps lured him inside. He was suddenly seduced by footwear. Strappy sandals, suede loafers, and saddle shoes were strewn all around. It appeared she'd tried on every style and color. An unlaced pair of sneakers stuck its tongue out at him. He was glad she'd discarded the denim canvas.

More than that, he was glad to see her.

Shane McNamara had arrived. Devin knew the moment he entered the store: his presence filled the room, then stormed her soul. She nearly twisted her ankle when his reflection appeared behind her own in the full-length mirror.

close she felt the tightness of his every muscle. The man was definitely solid.

The steady force of his heartbeat against her ear drummed some sense into her. She realized how silly she'd been, how stupid she must appear. Clicking her champagne-glass heels would not turn her into Jamie Jensen. She was plain and boringly conservative. She'd never be flashy enough for Shane. Before his arrival she'd pretty much decided on the black-and-white saddle shoes, taupe Mary Janes, and mocha-brown flats. They matched her wardrobe—and her staid lifestyle.

"I'm steady," she whispered against his chest.

His arms flexed, and he released her. "Be practical, Dev. You're not the stiletto type. You're more a—"

"Comfortable shoe?" She swatted him with a shoe-box lid.

He stepped back and looked down at her. "Don't try to be someone you're not." His voice was deep and dark and as hypnotic as his gaze. "Comfortable is good."

The man could make an old shoe sound sexy.

He was also going to pay. "Get out your credit card, McNamara. You promised me a new pair of shoes, and I'm holding you to it."

"I'll buy you two pairs and take you to lunch, if you're interested," he invited.

Devin nodded. "I saw an advertisement for Sheckie's. Salads and sandwiches. We can discuss the book we're not writing over lunch."

While Shane paid for her shoes, Devin waited by the door. Out of earshot he motioned to Lillian. "Substitute the rhinestone pumps for the brown flats."

Lillian read him like a book. "Might I also suggest a pair of thigh-high stockings with rhinestone-studded back seams for the lady?"

"You surely might," he agreed, imagining staid Devin James playing dress-up just for him.

"Our return policy requires the sales receipt," Lillian informed him as she added the pumps and nylons to the paper bag.

"Ye of little faith," Shane quoted, and Lillian crossed her fingers, wishing him luck.

Carrying the shopping bag, he followed Devin through the door and onto the boardwalk. She power-walked, and he poked along, never losing sight of her trim ankles.

Sheckie's served plain food at fancy prices. The customers didn't seem to mind. A toy train chugged along a track above their heads, and model airplanes circled on wire hangers.

The food arrived in a child's lunch box. Devin ate from a vintage Garfield, and Shane from Scooby-Doo. Five minutes into the meal, Shane was tied into knots. His roast-beef sandwich sat untouched beside a small unopened bag of barbecue potato chips while Devin sipped and nibbled. There was nothing sexually suppressed about her now. The way she ate bordered on the orgasmic.

"I have a wonderful idea for the next chapter," she was saying. "Calder and Miss Rose enjoy a buggy ride and picnic down by Bent Tree Creek. Cold chicken, boiled eggs . . ."

Distracted Shane caught only bits and pieces of the story as she reached for her glass of soda. The erotic play of her slender fingers from base to rim played on his imagination. He could almost feel her touching him as she wrapped her fingers about the middle of the glass and squeezed.

Shane scooted forward on the vinyl café chair. He

tucked his lap beneath the pub table to hide the tent in his khakis.

". . . a walk by the creek . . . a field of flowers . . . Calder picks bluebells and buttercups for Rose . . ." Devin drew the glass of soda level with her chin and nuzzled the rim.

A wicked shiver shot through Shane's abdomen. He could almost feel the warmth of her breath, the moistness of her mouth.

"After he pledges his intentions for a very long courtship, Rose might let Calder hold her hand. . . ."

Courtship? Surely he'd heard incorrectly. His heart slammed as Devin took her first sip of soda. Damn but the woman could sip. The soft pull of her smile left Shane as light-headed as the bubbles rising in her glass. He hadn't a clue as to why she was so damn happy.

"Calder arrives, wearing a city suit, his hair slicked back, and carrying a book of poetry. . . ."

Devin's tongue darted over the light spray of carbonation on her lips. Her pleasure curved in a generous grin.

"Seated in the parlor. Calder promises Rose his sunset years. . . ."

Sunset years? Shane had no plans for his gunslinger to age—ever. He expelled an agitated breath. Stretching out his legs, he kicked Devin's shin. She jerked and lifted a brow.

"Sorry." He didn't sound all that sincere.

She set her glass on the table and noted his untouched sandwich. "Roast beef too rare?"

"I'm not as hungry as I thought."

She eyed him strangely. "You were the one who suggested we eat." She reached across the table. "Mind if I sample?"

"Be my guest."

Devin traced a short nail along the foil seal of his chips before slowly tearing the bag open. The scent of hickory rose like an outdoor barbecue. She inhaled deeply.

Shane's chest tightened as she slipped two fingers into the bag, selected a chip, and brought it to her slightly parted lips. Flicking the pink tip of her tongue to its flat side, she licked, nibbled the edge, then relished its full flavor on a crisp crunch.

"I love that outdoorsy taste." She sucked the hickory seasoning from the pad of one finger before enjoying a second chip.

For a split second Shane wished himself the largest, saltiest barbecue chip in the bag. He could imagine— almost feel—her sweet, moist tongue savoring his taste. A taste not of hickory smoke, but of hot male need.

He settled even farther under the table.

"I've other thoughts on the story line," she continued, oblivious to his discomfort.

While Devin plotted, Shane sweated bullets. He tried to glance away, but his gaze returned to her mouth time and again as she consumed her turkey sandwich.

Perspiration broke out on his forehead and at the base of his throat, where his pulse ran wild. He made a grab for his lemonade and downed half the glass. The aftertaste was as sour as sucking on a fresh lemon. He puckered his lips, frowned, and struggled with his lust.

Devin met his gaze between bites. His scowl forced her sandwich back onto its plate.

"Care for some sugar?" She nudged the condiment tray toward him.

"I'm sweet enough."

She swallowed her comeback with a sip of soda.

"Are you almost finished?" He was ready to leave the restaurant.

"I'm a slow eater."

Slow and sensual. An absolute torture. He tapped the face of his watch with one finger. "Gobble down or leave it. Time's ticking away."

"You're that anxious to write?"

A four-hour writing session seemed like a picnic compared to the torment of watching her eat. "I'll get you a doggy bag."

"I'd rather have this lunch box."

Andrew Jackson paid for their lunch. The vintage Garfield lunch box cost him an extra ten bucks. But he counted it money well spent just to be on their way. The growl of his stomach broke the silence on their stroll to the parking lot.

They reached the cottage a few minutes after three. Shane threw his head back against the headrest of the driver's seat and scowled. "We've killed half a day."

"*Who* needed a new T-shirt?" Devin asked.

"*Who* knew there'd be construction on the return trip?" He thumped his palm against the steering wheel.

"Our writing session awaits." She pushed open the car door and stepped out. "Head 'em up, move 'em out, McNamara."

He remained in the car for a good long time, Devin noted. She'd stored her bag of new shoes in the closet, boxes unopened, and returned to her desk before Shane finally appeared. When he did, he looked downright haggard.

He raised a hand and waved off her question as he crossed to his bedroom. "I'm stiff from sitting in the car so long."

Stiff he was. In profile, she caught the thick bulge beneath his zipper. Her heart slowed and sank to her toes. Shane and Jamie's boardwalk reunion had turned him on, and his body was still reacting to her memory. "A shower might help."

"Appreciate the suggestion." He paused at the bedroom door. "While I'm showering, why don't you read what I wrote last night?"

"Definitely a good idea." She headed for his desk. Once there, she found the manuscript pages scattered across the top, several having fallen to the floor.

As Devin collected the pages, she found several with burned holes around the edges the size of a dime. The faint scents of old leather, roses, and gunsmoke clung to the paper. Definitely not cologne, but perhaps Shane had burned a candle to set the mood for his writing. He didn't seem the type. She fanned the pages to clear the air.

After placing them in order, she dropped onto his chair and began to read. Within seconds she closed her eyes and massaged her temples. Shane McNamara threatened her sanity.

"Problem, Dev?"

Angry, she stood to face him, only to be struck speechless by the slogan on his new T-shirt: *Shuck Me, Suck Me, Eat Me Raw, Ollie's Oyster Bar*. Devin felt her jaw drop and her cheeks heat.

"Nice shade of red." Shane's grin was slow and knowing as he tucked his hands into the back pockets of his snug, faded jeans. "Into oysters, Dev?"

Oysters? Possibly. Into Shane, most definitely. The man was a major distraction. His wide shoulders and solid chest could make any T-shirt sexy, no matter what it said. He was too good-looking for his own good. He knew his power over women. For several seconds she'd lost her rage and reason.

Strengthening her resolve, she cornered him by the coffee table.

He cocked a brow. "Circling the wagons?"

"Mmm-hmm."

"Must be serious."

"Last night after you tucked me in, you sneaked Dare Calder into Rose Coltraine's bedroom."

He stilled. "What happened in her bedroom?"

Devin's jaw worked. She was tired of his games. "Calder saw Rose naked."

"Did he get an eyeful?"

She had a strong urge to punch him. "You're as crude as your gunslinger."

"What, exactly, did Calder see?"

"The curve of Rose's backside."

"That's it?"

"That's far more than he should have seen." She glared at him and he glared back. "You couldn't just wrap up the scene at Cormet's General Store; you had to take it to the bedroom."

His expression tightened. "Still skinning me alive?"

"With a dull, rusty blade."

"Mind if I review the damage before you take my scalp?"

"As if you don't already know what's been written."

"Maybe I don't."

She sighed, wondering why he kept up the pretense. Confession was good for the soul. He needed to spill his guts.

She handed him the pages. "Read fast."

He dropped onto the couch and fingered several of the pages. "Where did these burn marks come from? They almost look like . . . bullet holes."

"You tell me," she said.

He shook his head, shrugged, then started to read.

Devin watched him review the material. Strangely enough he appeared as taken aback as she.

Shane frowned. His gunslinger had seen more of Miss Rose than Shane had seen of Devin James. It hardly seemed fair, he silently mused. He wasn't about to take exception, however. Not when his writing partner had blood in her eyes. Unfortunately he hadn't written these pages. Not by a long shot. Although he liked the setup, Shane couldn't take credit for Rose's wake-up call.

He clenched his teeth. When had Devin found time to write the bedroom scene? Perhaps she'd returned to the keyboard between dawn and sunrise, when he'd taken to the hammock, and the cottage stood empty to all but her sensual awakening of Rose Coltraine.

The end of the scene irked him royally. Rose had ignored Calder's warning about Cutter's thievery. That definitely pointed to Devin's authorship.

Shane stood up. He faced Devin from across the coffee table. "Calder offered Rose protection, and she shot him down cold."

"You forgot to provide proof—"

"Proof! Calder caught Cutter robbing the Garter. White Stetson and burlap bag. How much more evidence does Rose need?"

"Just like that"—Devin snapped her fingers beneath his nose—"Rose is supposed to believe an ogling gunslinger over a respected rancher?"

Shane's gaze narrowed. "Calder doesn't ogle."

"Oh, please, he roves the range with those eyes."

He'd had enough. "Calder and his gaze are about to travel twenty miles east to Horse Collar Junction, where a hot little dance-hall girl will welcome him with open arms."

Devin bit down on her lower lip until it turned white.

"He can't do that. The dance-hall girl isn't Miss Rose."

"And for that he'll thank his lucky stars!" Shane crossed his arms over his chest. His temper was hot, but he kept his tone cool. "Next time you decide to add a scene, discuss it with me first."

"I never added this scene!"

Contrary woman. She was stubborn to a fault. Why didn't she realize her own latent sensuality was driving her to flash Rose's white thigh and sinful red garter? And why the hell couldn't he stop thinking about Devin's latent sensuality?

He took a deep breath and returned to the scene. "Most men like to watch women sleep. Most women look sexy as hell with their hair in disarray, their bodies soft and warm. Unfortunately you misjudged Calder's reaction to your saloon proprietress. One look at snoozin' Rose won't make his heart go pit-a-pat. Calder needs more than a hint of nudity to spin his spurs. He needs ample breasts and pebbled nipples, a triangle of soft curls—"

"If that's the case, perhaps Calder should leave town." Devin's mouth thinned with schoolmarm pique. "He's worn out his welcome."

Worn out his welcome? Calder had been in town less than a week, and Rose had yet to be cordial to him. "You get rid of Calder and you get rid of me."

She had the nerve to wave. "Happy trails."

Shane scowled. She was really ticking him off. "You'd write Calder out of Rose Coltraine's life?"

"In a heartbeat."

"Calder stays." Whether she liked it or not. "He'll saddle up when he's damn good and ready. One town's the same as the next. Rose isn't anyone special. Dare's pretty much seen and done it all."

"Physically he's done it all, but emotionally he's still a virgin."

"A virgin!" Shane jerked as if he'd been shot in the back. "Calder shows emotion. My gunslinger feels—"

"Satiated, but never satisfied," Devin snapped. "He acts on urges, on a level with most animals."

Shane clenched his teeth so tightly he was sure he would crack his jaw. "If you'd stayed awake last night, we wouldn't be arguing now."

"I'm not used to midnight howls."

"Rooster blood doesn't run in my veins."

"Yet whenever we separate, strange scenes pop up on the computer."

"Very strange indeed." He scratched his jaw. "I've a solution."

"I'm listening."

"We sleep together."

She paled. "Not one of your better ideas."

"But a logical one, nonetheless. By sharing a bed, we'd know where the other person was all night long." Some spooning might be fun. So might a little kissing and a lot of touching. And if that went well . . .

"I will not sleep with you for the sake of the book," Devin said firmly, her color returning. "I could no more trust you than Rose could trust Calder."

"What's to trust? Their courtship is dying a rapid death."

Devin was close to hitting him; Shane could see it in her eyes. She'd balled her fists until her knuckles turned white. "Calder needs to have more evidence before he accuses Cutter of further wrongdoing," she said.

"Rose needs to be more trusting. Once she sees Calder's on the mark, she'll eat crow. A stringy old crow."

She made a face, then unclenched her fingers slowly,

almost painfully. She shook out her wrist, and her right hand spasmed. "Cramp," she said through her teeth.

"How bad?"

"Almost as bad as our argument."

"That bad, huh?" He felt guilty at the thought of hurting her.

"It was clench my fist or clobber you," she admitted on a sigh.

Such restraint. Shane blew out a breath. His passion had curled women's toes. Never had a woman's fingers cramped to avoid knocking him silly.

"Next time, swing away," he said.

She cradled her right hand in her left and massaged her palm. "I agreed to no more hitting."

"Give me your hand." He reached for her, and she pulled back, rotating her wrist just beyond his fingertips.

"Trust me; I'm fine. The circulation is returning."

He could make it return a lot faster. Snatching her hand, he pulled her down on the sofa, right beside him. Circling her wrist, he lowered her hand onto his thigh. He then massaged the soft flesh of her palm and stroked between her fingers, very slowly.

Devin wiggled her fingers, and Shane nearly rose off the couch. Pinpricks of pleasure shot toward his groin. He closed his eyes against the warm, teasing sensations that slid across his abdomen, and forced his concentration back to the delicate palm and spread fingers that could stroke a man into forgetting his name and address.

Devin flexed her hand once again, this time raking her nails over his thigh. He opened his eyes. If she extended her fingers fully, the tips would touch the base of his zipper. He exhaled slowly. So very, very close.

"I'm much better, thanks."

Better for her, but worse for him. The ache in his groin surpassed any old hand cramp.

"I'm ready to work," she informed him.

"I'm getting there."

"This month? This calendar year?"

"Pushy broad." He stood slowly, stretched, then reached for Devin. He pulled her up beside him. They brushed hips, just enough for him to feel her softness. Such nice curves. "Your computer or mine."

"We can start with mine."

He followed her to her desk. He pulled up a fan-back chair while she booted her computer. He sat down heavily. "Four hours?"

"You promised."

So he had. A promise based on a kiss. He studied her profile and the sweet curve of her mouth. He remembered her taste, and wanted more. He leaned in as Devin turned his way.

"Where were we?" she asked, her lips now pursed, her expression pure workaholic.

A bit of a turnoff. "Rose needs to discover Cutter's true character."

"Which has always been upstanding until now."

"So he's slipped a little. And he's got reason— Penelope Morgan's blackmail."

Devin ran her hands along the armrests of her chair. "Rose must first discover Cutter's theft."

"Then she'll eat humble pie."

"You're obsessed with her admission of Cutter's guilt," she accused.

There was nothing wrong with a little obsession. "Her realization of Cutter's guilt will come with a visit to his ranch."

"Where she'll find the burlap bag?"

"Exactly," he grinned. "We're finally on the same page, Devin James."

A rather blank page, Devin noted, since she hadn't written a word. She started to type. "Let's begin with Rose pulling the cash box from the safe and counting the night's take."

"The tally comes up short," Shane added. "No matter how many times she adjusts the column of figures, she can no longer deny the truth."

"She's been robbed."

"The gunslinger had told her as much." He looked smug. "Calder had gone so far as to name the thief."

"Rose is troubled, and unable to understand why the wealthiest man in town would rob his own business." Devin typed on. "She decides to make a surprise visit to Wayne Cutter's ranch. She has her buggy hitched and, escorted by her barkeep, Willis Eldridge, travels four miles south to the Triple C spread."

"The air is dry, the road dusty," Shane said.

"Rose will need her handkerchief." Devin quickly described one with lace and intricate embroidery.

"Eldridge had better have a bandanna," Shane said. "There's been a drought, and a dust storm's blowing in from the west."

Devin glanced his way. "A drought?"

"I'm the weatherman on this book."

"A drought would kill Cutter's longhorns."

"I'll forecast rain for tomorrow."

"I'm writing storm clouds on the horizon today."

"Good idea," he agreed. "The advancing storm can turn Rose and Eldridge into drowned rats on their return trip to town."

"I won't have her new gown ruined by rain," Devin said firmly.

"Afraid she'd melt?"

"She's not a witch."

"Calder might call you on that."

Devin hated his gunslinger. "Have a jelly bean, McNamara," she suggested, just to shut him up.

Shane eyed the candy dish with disdain. "I haven't developed a taste—"

"For the finer things in life?"

"Gourmet jelly beans—"

"Come in twenty flavors. Surely there's one to your liking."

He looked skeptical. "None thus far."

Shane seemed to bring out the dark side of Devin. "The big man's scared of a little jelly bean?" she taunted.

"Who are you?" He leaned closer and looked her in the eye. "When did you split personalities?"

"When I started working with you." She nodded toward the candy dish. "Eat one."

"Snacking takes time from our writing."

Not a plausible excuse. "I'll knock five minutes off the clock for each jelly bean you eat."

"Knock off ten."

"Fifteen if you eat two."

His gaze shifted from her to the candy dish and back again. "Bargaining time. Two jelly beans for a thunderstorm."

Watching him eat the jelly beans would be well worth the damage to Rose's gown. "Make it a gentle rain and you've got a deal."

"Rain is rain," he finally agreed as he reached for the candy dish. "I want Rose wet."

Straight-faced, Devin watched as he selected first a pink, then a black candy. He rolled the jelly beans on his palm, taking a full minute before popping them into his mouth.

His expression—pinched nose and lips and watery eyes—was priceless.

"Chokecherry and . . . *fig*, nasty little suckers." He reached across the desk for her bottle of springwater. Twisting the cap, he took a good long swallow. "Snack's over, and a storm's brewing."

Devin returned to her typing. "Rose arrives at the Triple C and enters the ranch house through the kitchen. She knows Cutter always hangs his rawhide range jacket and hat on two wooden pegs near the back door."

"Today the seam of a burlap bag peeks from beneath the brim of his trademark white Stetson," Shane inserted. "Her presence as yet undetected, Rose slips the bag from the peg and peers inside. She finds several coins along with a promissory note from gambler Lawrence Whitt."

"Rose places the bag back on the peg under his Stetson just as Wayne Cutter enters the kitchen," Devin said. "He's as surprised to see her as she is to learn he's the thief."

"Cutter the thief," Shane said with great satisfaction.

She glared at him. "Calder the tattletale."

"Calder never tattled," he said in defense of his character. "It was his civic duty to inform Rose of the rancher's theft."

"The information could send Cutter to prison for life."

"Or he could hang."

Devin jumped out of her chair and stood over Shane. "I will not kill off Cutter."

He was slow to answer. His gaze was level with her chest now. Time stopped as he stared openly and appreciatively at her breasts, three inches from his face. "Prison's good."

Her own face heated as her nipples tightened and her breath caught in her throat. How easily he could throw her off balance. She clutched the armrests as she eased back into her chair. Shane's gaze lowered right along with her.

She cleared her throat and concentrated on the computer screen. "Over a midday meal of beef stew, buttermilk biscuits, and strong black coffee, Rose makes small talk, until—"

"Cutter's wide girth bends the legs of the chair as he tilts back, relaxed. The chair squeaks, splits—"

"I will not have Cutter falling off his chair for your amusement," Devin said.

"My readers would have laughed."

"Your readers have a warped sense of humor."

"At least they have a sense of humor."

"My readers laugh," she returned, indignant.

"There's a big difference between a soft chuckle and a belly laugh," Shane said.

"This book isn't based on ha-has."

Shane shrugged. "A little comic relief never hurts."

"Not at Cutter's expense."

"The man's already lost his dignity," Shane muttered before moving on. "Back to the meal . . . Wayne Cutter has begun to go bald, his handlebar mustache thicker than the hair combed over his forehead."

Devin drilled her fingers on the desktop. "Cutter has a full head of hair, and he has never worn a mustache."

Shane stretched out his legs. "Sin has altered his appearance. Adultery has caused him to lose his hair. The mustache is part of his midnight disguise."

Shane flexed his left ankle, and it brushed her calf. Twice. She pulled her feet under her chair and sat a little straighter. "Adultery and thievery. Cutter has broken two of the Ten Commandments in a—"

"Bible-toting community?"

Shane's smile irritated her. "My characters attend church every Sunday."

"The remaining six days they silently lust and covet their neighbors."

She jabbed two fingers at his left shoulder. "Until Dare Calder rode into town, Cutter's Bend had little crime and no dalliances."

Shane snagged her hand. "No jabbing. If you want to touch me, touch me nice."

Touch him . . . all over. Had she just sighed?

His expression told her she had.

She pulled her hand free, hating Shane and his maverick mentality. He'd introduced lust and theft to her God-fearing town. Before the book ended Devin swore she'd sweep the streets clean of Dare Calder. "Let's get Rose and Wayne through their meal, shall we?"

Shane leaned forward on his chair. His wrist grazed her forearm as he rested his elbows on his knees and his chin on his palms. He was sitting way too close. "Cutter puffs out his chest with enormous pride," Shane continued. "He brags about how the Triple C is thriving, how he runs prime beef all the way to Kansas now. He's also expanded the ranch house by a full wing."

"The ranch house was already enormous," Devin said. "Why would he add on further?"

The corners of Shane's mouth twitched. "He's aiming to marry. He's hoping to fill the rooms with a passel of young'uns."

"A passel?"

"Seven or eight little Cutters."

Devin rubbed the bridge of her nose. "Who's the lucky lady?"

147

"Rose, of course. She'd make a mighty fine brood mare."

Shane was a horse's ass if he thought Rose was ready to have children. "Rose fingers the French lace on the high collar of her coral-pink dress. In her kind, gentle manner, she refuses to stand with Cutter before Judge Wentworth when he next passes though town."

"Rose reminds Cutter that their partnership lies solely in the Garter," Shane added. "Cutter then scowls, his jowls sagging. His feelings for Rose go deep."

Resigned, Devin sighed. "Rose can no longer return those feelings."

"Cutter then grows irritable and a little rash. What if he wants a further return on his investment?" Shane asked.

"Rose would be forced to sell her half of the saloon. Cutter's next partner might not be so amiable. A part of Rose wishes—"

"He'd kept it in his pants?"

"That too, but more important, that Wayne would sell her his share in the Garter."

Shane's eyes narrowed. "Rose wishes to be sole owner?"

"Her character growth would dictate as much."

"She's older and wiser now?"

She looked pointedly at Shane. "Your plot development has forced her hand."

And so it had. The way *Calder's Rose* had taken shape, the story line placed Rose Coltraine in a precarious position. If Devin would abide by his suggestions, Shane could fix the outcome of the book and secure Rose's future. Dare Calder wasn't the bastard Devin thought him to be. She'd yet to see the good side of his gunslinger. Every time Dare approached Rose, Devin got the wary look of a mother protecting her child.

Calder wasn't out to steal her child. He was, however, out to make Rose Coltraine a woman. Calder wanted Rose in his bed.

Before Rose moaned beneath his gunslinger, Shane had to write Cutter behind bars. "Over slices of apple pie Rose brings up the missing money," he suggested, glancing at the Art Deco clock on the far wall.

"Stop clock-watching," Devin scolded.

"The hands aren't even moving." He started to rise. "Bet the batteries are low. I'll check them."

"Sit down," she ordered, and he complied.

She then began to type with a speed that forced Shane's full attention to the plot. "Rose mentions to Cutter that until recently the Scarlet Garter has never lost money. The saloon has been fortunate—no shortages, no robberies."

"Cutter's hand shakes as he stabs at his pie, the apple slices sliding off his fork. He reminds Rose that two of his best men protect their investment." Shane's smile broke. "Two men Rose is about to replace."

Devin slapped her palms against the sides of the keyboard. "Why would Rose replace Sony and Dawson? Cutter did her a favor sending them to her."

"Their loyalties remain with the rancher," Shane said. "She's about to select someone new to guard her back."

Devin closed her eyes and waited. "Who might that be?"

"Dare Calder, of course. He's chosen to stay in town and will soon be taking a room at the Garter."

"A fine turn of events," she said, rubbing her eyelids.

Shane wrapped up the scene. "Rose folds her napkin on the table and rises to leave. Cutter's sputtered swearing fades beneath the swish of her petticoats as

Rose Coltraine skirts the table and finds her own way to the door. After handing her into the buggy, Willis Eldridge urges the team of matching bays into a serious trot." Shane rolled his shoulders. "I'll need to stretch before we write the storm."

"I'll work on the storm while you stretch."

The soreness in his back forced him to trust her. He wasn't used to sitting for this length of time, and his body hated him for it. When writing alone he'd do several paragraphs, maybe a page, then throw a few darts at the board hanging on his office door or toss a basketball through his indoor hoop before returning to work. Breaks were good. He hated tedium.

Standing now, he reached for the ceiling. "Bring on the thunder and lightning. I want Rose's hair wringing wet. I want the bodice of her dress plastered to her breasts, her petticoats limp and her shoes soggy. I want—"

Devin waved him off. "I get the picture."

Moving away from her desk, Shane circled the coffee table. He glanced once again at the Art Deco clock. Two hours to go. Wandering toward the kitchen, he thought about grabbing a quick snack. As he swung open the refrigerator door, he silently prayed Victoria Patton would arrive early. He'd sell his soul for a little divine intervention.

The sound of Devin's typing turned him back to her desk. She appeared to be in a hurry. He didn't know fingers could move that fast. Her shoulders were hunched, her face mere inches from the screen. He caught her lips moving as she read what she'd just written. A minute passed and her slow smile spread. She seemed satisfied with the passage. Perhaps a little too satisfied.

He grabbed a yellow apple, then returned to her

desk to check on the scene. He took a bite as he read over her shoulder. His chewing slowed. "Where in the hell did Rose find an umbrella?"

Devin looked at him, her expression one of pure innocence. "On the floor of the buggy."

"It wasn't there when the scene began."

"Of course it was; you just didn't see it."

He finished his bite of apple, then swallowed. "Rose stayed dry?"

"The hem of her dress and the toes of her shoes got damp."

Devin had not played fair. He took a second bite of his apple, munched for a moment, then said, "I see Rose forgot her handkerchief at the Triple C."

Devin narrowed her eyes. "She did, did she?"

"Sure did. That pretty little handkerchief with the lace and embroidery. Her very favorite. Rose presses Eldridge to turn the buggy around and head back to the ranch."

"Since the storm's diminished, she could return," Devin agreed.

"How do you know the storm's passed?"

"I see nothing but blue sky ahead."

The thunderheads Shane saw were as dark as his mood. "I see a second bank of storm clouds rolling in."

"They are too far off in the distance to soak Rose and Willis."

"I'm the weatherman," Shane insisted. "The clouds are moving in fast."

"Not fast enough."

Shane cupped his ear. "Listen, I hear thunder."

Devin looked around him. "You're mistaken. It's a car in the driveway, and it looks like Victoria's Lexus."

"Vic?" Someone in heaven had smiled upon him. He set his apple on the corner of Devin's desk, then crossed the room and met Victoria at the door. "You're early."

"You look mighty happy that I am." Their publicist breezed into the cottage, a breath of fresh air in a lilac print dress and her favorite jade jewelry.

"Try ecstatic." Shane caught the blue athletic bag she tossed his way.

"Games and toys," Vic indicated before she crossed to Devin with a stack of coloring books and a small bouquet of pink carnations. "Disney Classics, your favorite. The flowers were delivered this morning."

Shane had a gut feeling he knew who'd sent the bouquet, but he waited for Devin to open the card—which she procrastinated in doing.

Victoria, it appeared, was in a hurry. "I've an emergency appointment in Atlanta tomorrow," she informed them. "My plane leaves in two hours."

"An emergency?" Shane dropped the bag by his desk. "Anything we can do to help?"

"Not unless you want to deal with a reluctant author who can't face a radio interview and book signing on her own."

"Victoria the hand-holder," Devin said. "You're good at your job."

"How long will you be gone?" Shane asked.

"Two days, maybe three," Victoria said on a sigh. "Silver Star wants the author in the public eye, while the author prefers anonymity."

Shane lifted a brow. "First book jitters?"

Vic shook her head. "Tenth book, and the author still bites her nails."

"I can understand her reluctance," Devin said softly.

Her tone set him back. "Devin the recluse?"

"To a degree," she replied, her voice even softer and

Join the Love Spell Romance Book Club
and **GET 2 FREE* BOOKS NOW–
An $11.98 value!**
Mail the Free* Book Certificate
Today!

Yes! I want to subscribe to the Love Spell Romance Book Club.

Please send me my **2 FREE* BOOKS**. I have enclosed $2.00 for shipping/handling. Every other month I'll receive the four newest Love Spell Romance selections to preview for 10 days. If I decide to keep them, I will pay the Special Members Only discounted price of just $4.49 each, a total of $17.96, plus $2.00 shipping/handling ($23.55 US in Canada). This is a **SAVINGS OF $6.00** off the bookstore price. There is no minimum number of books I must buy and I may cancel the program at any time. In any case, the **2 FREE* BOOKS** are mine to keep.

*In Canada, add $5.00 shipping and handling per order
for the first shipment.For all future shipments to Canada,
the cost of membership is $23.55 US, which
includes shipping and handling.
(All payments must be made in US dollars.)

NAME: _____

ADDRESS: _____

CITY: _____ **STATE:** _____

COUNTRY: _____ **ZIP:** _____

TELEPHONE: _____

E-MAIL: _____

SIGNATURE: _____

If under 18, Parent or Guardian must sign. Terms, prices, and conditions subject to change. Subscription subject
to acceptance. Dorchester Publishing reserves the right to reject any order or cancel any subscription.

more reserved. "I've never allowed my picture on any of my books. My bio is short."

And uninformative. He'd scanned her bio: a graduate of Brown and a Minnesota resident. Shane had wondered over her missing photo when he'd purchased *Scoundrel's Kiss* at The Bookie.

Victoria looked from Shane to Devin. "Some authors need fireworks and fanfare, while others prefer solitude and seclusion."

Shane knew which class he fell into: he was a Fourth of July bottle rocket. He was a good writer, and fan appreciation meant a lot to him.

He jammed his hands into the back pockets of his jeans. Even though Dev drove him nuts, he wondered how the promotion of their joint venture would affect her. If Silver Star publicized the hell out of *Calder's Rose*, would Devin survive the book tour? If he had any white hat cowboy in him, he would make the interviews and book signings easy on her. A slow grin spread. There just might be some hand-holding in his future, after all.

"What are you smiling about, Shane?" Victoria asked.

He shook his head. "Nothing worth sharing." He looked directly at the bouquet on Devin's desk. "Care to share the card?"

"Sure, why not?" She plucked the card from amid a spray of baby's breath and opened it. "The flowers are from Skip Huddleston."

"Yippee Skippy?"

"Mmm-hmm." He could barely hear her reply.

"His wishes?" Shane pressed, needing to know what old Skip had written.

Devin folded the card in half and traced one edge. " 'Have a good day.' "

Have a good day? What kind of message was that?

Didn't she merit a *Thinking of you* or *Missing you madly*? And carnations! She deserved more flower power. Perhaps the richness of champagne roses instead of a cluster of pink blooms no larger than a high school prom corsage. He had the urge to break a few stems.

"A true Hallmark moment," he muttered.

"Bite a bullet," Devin shot back at him.

"The chapter?" Victoria reminded them of the purpose behind her visit.

"Right here." Devin scooped the pages off her desk and presented them to their publicist. "And we have the overview you requested. The plot is strong and fast-paced."

Shane's gaze locked with Devin's. "You could almost say the book's writing itself."

"You certainly could," she agreed.

Victoria thumbed the pages, scanning the content. "Nice flow. How are the characters developing?"

"Miss Rose is fighting the inevitable," Shane mumbled.

Victoria apparently understood. "Rose hasn't fallen for Calder's charm?"

"Not entirely," he admitted. "Rose enjoyed their first kiss, however."

"Not as much as Calder did," Devin retorted. "A case of mistaken identity—"

"Branded her his," Shane finished for her.

"Sounds serious," Vic mused.

"Not church-wedding serious," he quickly corrected. "It's more sexual—"

"Sensual," Devin said. "Romantic."

Shane's nostrils flared. "Calder's his own man. He won't be led around like a bull with a ring in his nose."

Victoria winked at Devin. "Surely the swish of Rose's skirts has Calder sweating."

"My gunslinger's attraction is neither emasculating nor life-altering," Shane said flatly.

"Won't the romance element bring Calder to his knees?" Vic asked.

"It's too early in the book for Calder to propose," Devin said.

"Bended knees belong on a mattress not pleading for a woman's hand." Shane brushed passed Devin and headed for the kitchen.

Devin stuck out her tongue at his back, then turned at Victoria's chuckle. "Childish, I know."

"Shane rubs off on us all."

Devin sighed. "And he accuses me of split personalities."

"Are you in need of a mediator?" Victoria asked, concerned. "I'd be happy to hire a secretary for the duration of the book."

"Someone to do the typing? Someone to store the disks?" Not a bad idea. A secretary would keep Shane away from the computer. No scenes would be secretly written. She could sleep at night.

She glanced his way and caught him leaning against the counter, sipping from a carton of orange juice. "Use a glass!"

"Tastes better straight up," he retorted.

She waited for him to finish. Once he'd returned the juice to the refrigerator, she asked, "How do you feel about a secretary typing our book?"

"What's she look like?"

"Professional," Victoria said. "I've someone in mind, if she's available."

"Available day or night?" Shane asked.

"Preferably days, but nights as needed," Vic agreed.

His gaze narrowed on Devin. "So there would be just one person on the computer?"

"There would be a lot less confusion."

"A secretary would certainly keep us honest."

"Nothing would be written outside of our writing sessions."

Shane came to the same conclusion she'd reached earlier. "Works for me."

Devin breathed a sigh of relief. "Me too."

"Glad you're on the same page for once," Victoria said. "I'll have a secretary hired before I leave town." She then plucked two tickets from the side skirt pocket of her dress and laid them on the corner of Devin's desk near Shane's discarded apple. "Enjoy the concert, and keep writing."

"You heard Vic," Devin directed once the Lexus cleared the driveway. "Back to work, McNamara."

"Priorities, Dev." He returned to his desk, hunkered down, and unzipped the athletic bag. She watched him rummage through the assortment of games. Several minutes passed before he glanced her way. His gaze was hot and his smile sexy. "Play with me, Dev."

"Games, Mr. Calder, do you play?" Rose Coltraine tiptoed within the circle of moonbeams streaming through the front window. She stopped and softly shook the box of checkers.

"Mostly cards." Dare Calder moved, dark and deep as a shadow. A bottle of whiskey hung from his right hand.

"Horseshoes?" she asked.

"Pitched a few. Dead ringers."

"Do you owe your success to talent or intimidation?"

Calder almost smiled. "Pretty hard to coerce iron around a peg."

"Then you have some talent—"

"At drinking, whoring, and gunning down men." He

uncapped the whiskey. "I could use a drink right about now."

She touched one finger to her lips. "Speak softly, sir. Both their bedroom doors stand ajar."

"They're both asleep. Had Devin played with Shane like he'd asked, he would have returned to the book in time."

Rose sighed. *Calder's Rose* is gathering dust."

"With our help it will get written." He took a swig of the whiskey, then held up the bottle. "Join me?"

She shook her head. "No libation for me." She sniffed, took a step back, then clipped two fingers on her nose like a clothespin. "You appear to have been ridden hard and put out wet."

"You sayin' I stink?" Insulted, Calder eased even closer, towering over her.

Rose plucked an ecru lace handkerchief from the pleated sash on her pale pink gown. The scent of fragrant garden roses filled the air. She held the hankie beneath her nose. There was no kind way to put it. "You smell like something that might delight a buzzard."

Calder swept off his Stetson and wiped the sweat from his brow. "Kept company with the sun today. Walkin', thinkin', plottin' my story line."

"Surely you noticed the ocean?"

"Damn salty, Rose. Downright itchy to the skin."

"Perhaps the small pond—"

He slapped his Stetson against his thigh. Dust puffed from the brim. "I'll bathe before sunrise. Your ablutions come first, darlin."

The hankie slipped through her fingers, landing on the toe of her pointed shoe. Her hand fluttered over her heart. "Excuse me, sir?"

His grin widened with promise. "Ready yourself for a copper tub, Rose Coltraine."

Chapter Six

Scarlet Garter

Humble pie. Rose Coltraine poked her fork into a thick slice. It tasted as stale as her outlook on life. When she finished the first piece she was due a second slice. Maybe she'd eat the whole pie.

Wayne Cutter had proved a thief, and she was now in need of Dare Calder's protection. The thought of Calder settling in at the Garter settled as heavily as the pie.

Prior to the sun's full descent, she'd swallowed her pride and penned a short note to the gunslinger. Her barkeep delivered the missive to Eve's Garden. In her message she'd requested a meeting with him. She waited, but received no immediate response. The evening wore on. Disappointed, Rose assumed Calder had withdrawn his offer. She left the lights and laughter of the Garter and retired to her room.

The Seth Thomas clock on the bedside table was chiming ten o'clock, the hour for her ablutions. Crossing the room she secured the dead bolt on the door before stepping behind a four-paneled floral-covered screen. Once hidden, she slipped out of her honey-pink gown. Her hands followed the satin down her body, over her soft curves and silken skin.

Rose smiled in appreciation. The bath had been drawn perfectly. Three buckets of water had been heated on the stove and hauled from the kitchen, then added to two of cold, along with a lavish amount of rose oil. Enveloped in privacy and the fragrance of wild roses, she lowered herself into the copper tub. Heat stroked between her thighs like a man's caress, and the steam hovered over her breasts like a lover's breath.

She reached for the scented soap, closed her eyes, and imagined Dare Calder's touch. She slid the soap over her skin, as slick and moist as the gunslinger's tongue. After slowly lathering the creamy swells of her breasts, the concave dip of her abdomen, she parted her thighs. . . .

The rich aroma of an expensive cigar tickled her nose. A man in her suite? Her breasts heaved as she struggled to catch her breath. The bathing cloth lay within arm's reach. She made a grab and came up short. Snagged by a wide-palmed hand, the linen cloth dangled just beyond her fingertips.

Turning, Rose encountered a black-denimed thigh and a thick leather gun belt. Her gaze lifted over an earth-brown shirt stretched across a thick chest and broad shoulders. Gazing higher still, she discovered an outlaw mouth and gray eyes, hot and dark with male interest.

Dare Calder. She gasped and slid deeper into her bath.

"Evenin', Rose." His chuckle was low and husky. Trimmed sideburns, his boots polished, Calder pressed a lean hip against the copper tub. "I like my woman naked and scrubbed clean, and awaitin' me to towel her off."

His woman? Never! She held out her hand, a faint tremble in her fingers. "Please, sir, my linen cloth."

His gaze held hers as he slowly lowered the cloth within her reach.

"How did you get in?" She grabbed the linen cloth and spread it from one edge of the tub to the other in an attempt to cover her nudity.

A sly grin spread around the cigar clamped in the corner of his mouth. "The door adjoinin' your room wasn't locked."

"It will be after today."

"A locked door will never stop my entry."

She straightened the sagging and slightly damp cloth. "You could at least knock, Mr. Calder."

"I prefer to arrive unannounced."

That way he caught people unaware and at their most vulnerable. Exactly as she was now. "Why are you here, sir?"

Calder snuffed his cigar in a tin ashtray on a nearby table. "I received your note."

"You chose this precise moment to respond?"

"Seemed as good a time as any." His gaze swept the tub, the sagging cloth, and her exposed flesh.

Rose watched, horrified, as the wet linen dipped, then molded itself over her breasts and the tops of her thighs. She shivered, as aware of the man as of the water cooling in the tub. "I'm chilled. It's difficult to think or talk—" She sneezed.

A second sneeze, and Calder had bent, clasped her upper arms, and lifted her free of the copper tub. Her scream died against the gunslinger's solid chest.

"I'm not lookin', just warmin'," he said thickly as one hand anchored itself in her lower back and the other rubbed her from soft shoulder to pale buttock.

She squirmed, slapped his hands, and scratched his wrists.

Calder swelled against her. "Damn it, Rose, hold still . . . unless you want to aggrevate the situation even more."

"Release me!" She said in a hiss.

His grip tightened. "As soon as you calm yourself."

Rose fell instantly still. The moment his hold loosened she slipped free. Then, wrapped in the linen cloth, she crossed the room and ducked behind the paneled screen.

His deep chuckle and her ragged breathing faded into silence. Calder moved to the window. The evening breeze swept away all impure thoughts. Rose Coltraine had summoned him with an apology and a request for his assistance.

He would not put her in harm's way by taking her into his embrace. He could best protect her by keeping her at arm's length.

He would not touch her again. He'd remain celibate until he caught Wayne Cutter. Then he'd return to Eve's Garden and his bed of sin.

Gowned in blushing pink satin, Rose joined him within a very short time. Wisps of blond hair escaped her makeshift bun and curled damply about her ears and neck. A single strand of pearls lay upon her breast. She looked as soft as Texas twilight, and as unreachable as the North Star.

His gut clenched as he cleared his throat and announced, "I've a surefire way to trap Cutter."

She sighed, resigned. "I'm interested in your plan."

"Saturday-night poker." He scrubbed his knuckles

over his jaw. "Smooth sour mash should loosen the rancher's tongue. His reason for robbing you may surface. As the pot builds, his losses will mount."

Rose fingered her pearls. "You guarantee his loss?"

"A loss so great only theft will recoup his misfortune."

She hesitated. "You'll attempt to catch him?"

"I'll succeed in bringin' him down."

"Without harm?" she asked, the tone of her voice making it a plea.

"I'll do my best to deliver him whole."

"Your *very* best, Mr. Calder?"

He was slow to nod his agreement. A lowlife like Cutter was best put six feet under. But Rose didn't want him dead.

She clutched her hands before her. "Who besides Cutter will be dealt a hand at the poker game?"

"You plannin' a formal invite?" he asked.

"I'm seating witnesses to Cutter's crime."

"Make them well-heeled, but in Cutter's debt. Include the town marshal."

"Dirk Morgan?" she gasped in surprise.

"He's a lawman and jailer."

Her delicate hands fluttered over blushing pink satin. "I had thought to question Wayne myself."

His expression hardened. "You plannin' to be judge and jury."

"If necessary."

"It won't be. The man will be caught red-handed."

She straightened her shoulders. "He will have much to answer for, and a chance to plead his case."

Calder snorted. "You're a bleedin' heart, Rose." He tipped his Stetson and turned to leave.

"Mr. Calder?" Her tone brought him back around.

"Ma'am?" He slowed.

"I had hoped you would move out of Eve's and into the Garter," she said in a rush.

His gaze flicked over her room. "We'd share a bed?"

"Merely live beneath the same roof," she corrected.

He scuffed his boot, disappointment riding him hard. "I'll see the room."

She directed him to a room no larger than a closet at the far end of the hallway. He'd be forced to shove his saddlebags under the narrow bed, hang his Stetson on the doorknob. His reluctance must have shown.

"You'll have fresh linen," she said temptingly. "A handmade quilt and feather pillow."

"My feet will dangle over the end of the bed," he said.

She sweetened the pot. "Cook will feed you three squares a day."

He hadn't eaten regular meals since he'd arrived in Cutter's Bend. "Flapjacks with maple syrup?"

She nodded, hopeful. "A dozen eggs and a rasher of bacon."

"Coffee?"

"Made on a stove, not over a campfire."

"Steak?" he prodded, his mouth already watering.

"An inch thick served with three sides of vegetables."

He sobered, tipped his hat, and pretended cold feet. "I'll give it some thought."

Her hope dispersed on a ragged sigh. She trailed him down the hall. "I-I can pay you, Mr. Calder."

"Money's not what I'm after, Miss Coltraine."

He wanted her. In his bed.

Hang the man! She would give her body only in exchange for respect, honor, and marriage vows.

Dare Calder snubbed society. Damned propriety. Tongues would wag with his appearance at the Garter. The town would talk itself hoarse.

163

She stomped her foot. "I won't sleep with you."

He shrugged. "I've someone who will."

"You'll return to Eve's Garden?"

"Damn straight." He moved on.

And she followed. He could almost hear her mind working. "One kiss, no more."

"One kiss for bringin' in a man I'd just as soon kill?" He'd reached the top of the stairs.

"Perhaps . . . two."

He took the first step, then the second. The sound of boot heels muffled by carpet marked his retreat.

Her voice reached him on the bottom stair. "I need you, Mr. Calder."

She damn sure did. He turned to look at her over his shoulder, one hand on the polished banister. "I knew you'd come 'round, Rose. I'll stable my horse and return within the hour." Then tipping the brim of his Stetson, he shot her a smug smile and confessed, "In truth, darlin', I'd bunked in at three squares."

Devin James came out of a dead sleep, sat up and covered her ears. Outside her bedroom window lightning lit the midnight sky as bright as day, and thunder pounded so loudly it shook the windowpanes. The ivory metal blinds clanked like skeleton bones, and the curtains billowed like ghosts.

She wasn't fond of storms, especially those packing high howling winds. The bedroom walls echoed Mother Nature's wrath as the cottage creaked and groaned. Every sound in it was magnified bigger than life. Even the rushing of the rainwater down the drainpipe sounded like Niagara Falls.

She tried the lamp on her nightstand. No electricity. The numbers on her alarm clock were also dark, as was the shell-shaped nightlight plugged into the wall outlet.

She didn't want to be alone. Slipping from her bed she collected her lilac comforter and headed for the kitchen in search of a flashlight or candles. The beat of her heart echoed in her ears as she felt along the butcher-block counter. She stopped before the sink and inhaled deeply, to steady her nerves. The scent of whiskey and human sweat assailed her, as if someone had not bathed in days. The smell was eerie, almost haunting, as if the cottage pulsed with a third presence. . . .

Her heart skittered when a large shadow loomed over her.

"Dev, are you okay?" Shane's voice came to her through the darkness.

She turned and faced his bare chest, so close, so solid, so comforting. She breathed him in, so clean. "I'm all right now."

He tipped back her chin with one finger. "Surely you're not afraid of a little thunder and lightning?"

Lightning flashed, illuminating the room briefly. The belly of the storm rumbled as thunder rolled up and down the coastline.

"I'm as afraid of storms as you are of gourmet jelly beans," she confessed.

He grinned. "Pretty scary."

"I'd have been fine if the electricity hadn't gone out."

He reached over her shoulder and opened a cabinet. "Have you found any candles?"

"I just started looking."

Flashes of lightning aided their search. Shane moved down the counter, opening cupboards and drawers.

He stopped before the microwave and held up a shot glass. "Have you been drinking?"

Devin blinked. "I didn't know we had a liquor cabinet."

"We don't."

"I thought I smelled booze earlier."

Shane sniffed the shot glass. "Aged whiskey."

She wondered where he had hidden the bottle. The storm was building, and a stiff drink might calm her nerves. She scanned the counter. "Where's the bottle?"

He shrugged. "You tell me, I wasn't the one who needed a drink."

"I didn't need one until the storm broke."

They stared at each other, neither one blinking, until lightning flashed bright enough to blind a person. Thunder followed, the crash nearly deafening. Devin almost jumped out of her skin. She hugged herself, her shaking uncontrollable.

Shane touched her shoulder. "Go sit on the couch. I'll find the candles."

The hair on the back of her neck prickled as she sat in the dark, wrapped in her lilac comforter and her fear.

He joined her within minutes, a box of votives in one hand, and a book of matches in the other. She watched as he set the candles on the coffee table and struck a match. She held her breath as two of the votives refused to light, then breathed easier once the remaining four cast a soft glow on the room.

Shane sniffed. "Smells starchy, like a dry cleaner."

"White Linen." She recognized the scent.

He rested his arm along the back of the couch. Shifting slightly, he brushed her shoulder, then her cheek with his fingers. "Feeling better?"

"A little better." His touch was light, yet as jolting as

the lightning. Fear and pleasure tingled along her spine. The outer storm still crashed, but it was less threatening now with Shane in the room.

She looked at him in the flickering light. Shadows darkened his hair and his whiskered jaw. His eyes appeared more blue than gray. The thickness of his bare chest narrowed to a toned abdomen. She noted he wore only gray gym shorts as he crossed his ankle over his knee. His feet were bare.

She pulled the lilac comforter closer, over her shoulders and up to her neck. Shane McNamara was nearly naked, while she sat cocooned within her comforter.

"Were you sleeping when the storm hit?" he asked.

"Sleeping soundly. How about you?"

He raked his hand through his hair. "I was reading."

"The book must be a page-turner to keep you up this late."

His lips twitched. "Let's just say I was turning the pages."

"What were you reading?"

He hesitated a good long time. "*Scoundrel's Kiss*. I picked up a copy at The Bookie."

His admission took her by surprise. Knowledge that he found it boring set her teeth on edge.

He yawned. "I'm sure the plot improves—"

She punched him in his gut, a solid, straightforward hit. Her knuckles warmed from the heat of his flesh.

"Damn, woman." His breath came out in a whoosh. "Have you been working out?"

"Working with you is exercise enough." The calories she burned in anger would keep her slim and trim.

He rubbed his flat abdomen.

And Devin reveled in its tightness.

"You can't take a joke, can you?" he asked.

"It's hard to tell when you're kidding."

"The longer you're around me—"

"I've six weeks, no more." She lifted her gaze from the waistband on his gym shorts to his toned pecs. Such a nice body. And so off-limits. "That's not enough time to get into your skin."

Devin James was already under his skin, Shane hated to admit. Even sitting beside him now, wrapped like a tepee, she looked sexy as hell with her heightened color and defiantly tilted jaw. The woman had passion. He could see it in her eyes whenever her gaze lit on his body. She was interested, yet refused to get involved.

He recalled their lunch together at Sheckie's. If she could enjoy a man as much as she enjoyed food, she'd lick his platter clean.

Anticipation burned as brightly as the candles. "*Scoundrel's Kiss* isn't all that bad," he admitted.

"For a romance?"

"I like a harder ride when I read. Your plots are as soft and tender as Rose Coltraine's bosom."

"Your story lines are . . . are . . ."

"As stirring as my gunslinger's groin?"

She blushed, and he tugged the end of her braid. "We write for different audiences, Dev. Yet both our series sell."

Lightning flashed once again, and there was an instantaneous crack of thunder.

Devin snuggled deeper into her lilac comforter. While Shane wanted to crawl under there with her, he knew such a move would frighten her more than the storm did. Instead he could distract her, perhaps even chase away her fears with a little fun and games.

"Play with me, Dev," he said, repeating his earlier offer—an offer she'd rejected with a dirty look and a hike to her bedroom.

"Play *what* with you?" Devin and her comforter edged toward the far corner of the couch.

He rubbed his hands together. "Vic included a deck of cards. How about strip or stroke poker?"

She stiffened visibly. "My clothes stay on."

He jumped off the couch and went for the athletic bag near his desk. Shaking the contents onto the red carpet, he surveyed their options by candlelight. "Crossword puzzle? Checkers?"

Lightning spurred her to a quick decision. "A short crossword puzzle," she called over the thunder.

He grabbed the crossword book before she changed her mind and decided to color. He couldn't compete with a box of ninety-six Crayolas.

Settling back on the sofa, he flipped through the pages and finally found what he was looking for. He hid a smile behind the clearing of his throat. "Let's test your skills, Dev." He ran his finger over the blank boxes. "Three letters down: 'opposite of cold.' "

"Hot." She scrunched up her nose. "Is this the kiddie knockoff?"

He put on his best poker face. "Are you saying it's too easy?"

"I don't need my thinking cap."

"Trust me: these puzzles get tricky." He looked down at the page, then up at her. "Six letters across: 'protection.' "

"Pro-tec-tion." She sounded out each syllable, then licked her lips. "Guard?" She ticked off the number of letters on her fingers and thumb, then shook her head. "Shield!" She clapped, and the lilac comforter slipped off her shoulders.

Lightning flashed, thunder rumbled, and Devin shuddered. The comforter dropped below her breasts— beautiful breasts, barely concealed beneath a pale blue chemise. So silky, so soft, so easy on the eyes. The sweat

169

from his palm dampened the bottom corner of the page. "Protection? I was thinking more along the lines of . . . condom."

"Condom? Why would you think that?"

"It fits." He kept his gaze on the page, squinted. "Down again, Dev. We need a five letter word for 'penetrate.' "

Devin shifted on the sofa. She fanned her hand before her face. "It's getting warm in here."

It was getting downright hot. The lack of air-conditioning and the sight of her pale blue chemise had him nearly panting like the dog she thought him to be.

He lifted a brow and reminded her, "Penetrate?"

"Insert? Pierce? Thrust?"

Shane shook his head. "Too many letters. Let's try . . . probe."

She gnawed her lip. "Could be wedge."

He pried his gaze away from her mouth. "Or . . . enter."

She rolled onto her left hip, then ran her hands down the comforter that still covered her thighs. "Could be, I guess."

Shane cocked his head and scratched his jaw. "We've got 'hot,' 'condom,' 'probe.' Next word, six letters across: 'orgasm.' It starts with a C—"

"Culmination."

"Way too many letters, Dev."

"They will fit, trust me." She snatched a gray pencil with a silver-spur eraser off the coffee table and tossed it at his chest. "It might help to actually write in the letters."

Busted! He caught the pencil in midair, then twirled it between his fingers before jotting down the letters. "Snugs up tight, as long as two letters share a box." He looked up, smiled slowly, "I would have gone with 'climax.' "

"You'd have been wrong." She looked down her nose at him. "Puzzle porn. So very creative."

He'd thought it the perfect distraction, until the heavens flashed and shook, and Devin hugged herself once again.

Shane searched for another diversion. "Care to crown me?"

"With a shovel or a two-by-four?"

Her gaze glittered a little too brightly for his liking. "Checkers, Dev." He returned to the athletic bag and retrieved the game.

In less than a minute he'd set up the game board on the coffee table. He chose black, his lucky color, then allowed Devin to make the first move.

She surprised him with her competitive spirit. The crease in her brow, the hunch of her shoulders, and her study of the board caught and held his attention, so much so that he lost track of the game. One slender strap on her chemise now hung off her shoulder. So engrossed was she in winning, she neither noticed nor felt him straighten the strap.

"Captured number five!" She jumped another black checker.

Shane scanned the board. Damn if his men weren't dropping like flies.

"King me!" She'd stormed his back row; three of her red checkers were demanding to be crowned.

Most of Shane's men hadn't moved beyond two squares, and those that had advanced, had been captured.

Four more moves, and Devin threw herself back against the couch, her cheeks flushed, her eyes lit with victory. "Game's over!" A slow smile spread. "No contest, McNamara."

She'd beaten him with his own distraction.

Pushing herself forward, she began packing up the game.

"What, no rematch?" he asked.

She tilted her head, listening. "No more thunder."

The night had quieted. He tried the end-table lamp, and the bulb burned brightly. "Back to civilization."

She clutched the comforter to her chest. "Thanks, McNamara."

He lifted a brow. "For what? The puzzle porn? Letting you beat me at checkers?"

"For keeping the storm at bay."

"I make one hell of a lightning rod." He stood, took her hand, and pulled her off the sofa. He kissed her on the forehead. "Sweet dreams, Dev."

Awash in sunshine, Devin James stretched. Her eyelids felt heavy and her mind weary. Another day, another writing session. She wished she could sleep another hour.

Prior to midnight she'd slept with her bedroom door cracked, listening for any evidence of Shane and his late-night writing antics. She'd dozed sporadically, her sleep broken by suspicion. Then the storm had hit, so violent in its intensity that it had shaken the foundation of the cottage. In his very sexy way, Shane had distracted her with his bare chest, a crossword puzzle, and a game of checkers. He had been kind and considerate, a champion who'd chased away her fears. She liked that side of him.

Crawling out of bed, she headed for the shower, torturing herself with ice cold water. Goose bumps covered her body as she danced on one foot, then the other. She shivered, sneezed, and came wide awake. Wrapped in a velour towel, she then stood before her closet and considered what to wear.

"Dev, you up?" A hint of desperation scored Shane's voice as he thumped on the door. Devin realized too late that she hadn't closed the door completely after the storm. It swung wide now and bounced off the bedroom wall.

Shane entered, showered, but unshaven. Over his chest were stretched the words, *Mad Hatter Saloon, Paris, France* along with an image of a wild-looking gray hare with a black top hat tucked into a pair of torn-at-the-knee jeans.

Seeing him, Devin jumped, nearly losing her towel.

Seeing her, Shane stumbled over his own feet. "Nice towel. Egyptian Brown?"

She clutched the towel with one hand, and jabbed the other toward the door. "Unless the cottage is on fire—"

"No major fire, just a small spark."

"Then what's the problem?"

"Our secretarial temp has arrived," he informed her.

"Have you made her feel welcome?"

"She made herself welcome." He pinched the bridge of his nose between his thumb and forefinger. "How do you feel about sharing your workspace?"

"I'm not territorial."

He blew out a breath. "That's good."

She bit down on her bottom lip. "It sounds bad. . . ."

"Come look for yourself." He turned on his heel and left her.

Devin dressed hurriedly. The dark plum suit matched the circles under her eyes. She braided her hair, all thumbs and trepidation. She entered the main room with a smile on her face—a smile that soon faded.

"Good morning . . ." Or was it? She didn't recognize the room, the transformation was so startling.

Orange afghans had been thrown over the back of the sofa, and the enormous harem-style pillows now filled the space where the coffee table had once stood. A lime-green beanbag chair had replaced the Florida fan-back. A gold-and-scarlet silk scarf draped the pole lamp near the couch, casting the room in a fiery glow.

Devin willed herself to breathe. Her desk had been transformed into a shrine. Countless framed photographs of a young man with shaggy blond hair littered the desktop. Behind her desk sat a female with a heart-shaped face, shoulder-length brown curls, and wide blue eyes.

"Devin James, meet Joy Ford," Shane said, introducing the two of them.

Joy bounced up, waif-thin and full of energy. Devin saw a flash of red blouse and a black denim skirt as Joy grabbed her hand and primed it like a water pump. "I've read all your books and most of Shane's. It's an honor to be working with two such fine authors."

Strong for one so thin, Joy nearly dislocated Devin's shoulder. "Nice to meet you also," was all Devin could muster.

"Joy told me she wanted to create her own workspace," Shane said from his desk. He sat back in his chair, arms crossed over his chest, amusement in his eyes. "She pulled up in a Caravan and unloaded."

Joy nodded, her spiral curls bouncing. "Mrs. Farrell, my creative-writing teacher, stresses mood. An author needs the right ambience to create."

Devin looked around, uncertain as to what mood the

temp had created. The room was so . . . bright. Blindingly so.

"Joy is four weeks into her class, and maintaining a B average," Shane informed Devin. "We're her first secretarial job in three months."

"I get overlooked a lot at the temp company, but I think that Patton lady was desperate. I was the only temp with a five-week block of time available." Joy hugged herself. "Isn't that great?"

"Five whole weeks." Shane didn't look quite so amused. "Did Vic leave a forwarding number?"

"Not that I'm aware of." Devin was in desperate need of her wake-up cup. "Coffee, McNamara?"

"It's an island blend, Jamaican Me Crazy."

Devin bit back a smile as she entered the kitchen and poured herself the largest mug of coffee she could find.

"Coffee's bad for you, and caffeine's a known killer," Joy called from Devin's desk.

Too much sugar would rot her teeth, Devin wanted to say, but she held her tongue. Joy had discovered the cranberry-colored dish of gourmet jelly beans and was eating them by the handful.

"You should switch to herbal tea," Joy told her between bites. "My favorite's peppermint."

However bad coffee might be for her, Devin needed fortifying. One sip and the dark, rich caffeine kicked in. She poured the remainder of the coffee into a black plastic carafe and brought it with her back to the living room.

Settling on the couch, she set the carafe on the floor by her feet and cradled her mug between her palms. The scent of patchouli incense drifted from the afghans, strong enough to give her a headache. Thinking positively, she looked at Shane and asked, "Are we ready to write?"

"You betcha," he replied.

"What do you need me to do first?" Joy asked as she swiveled the chair in several fast circles, making Devin dizzy.

"Try sitting still," Shane said dryly.

The chair spun twice more before it came to a stop. "Do you do any warmup exercises to stimulate your mind? Any visualizations?" Joy asked.

"We simply breathe," Shane said.

"I focus on my muse." Joy picked up one of the photographs on the desk and kissed the glass. "Danny Stone, my boyfriend, my inspiration, my life."

My God, Devin thought. She caught herself staring, and forced a blink. She then caught Shane's rather pained expression.

She wasn't sure if she should laugh or cry.

Devin drank half a cup of coffee before she could trust herself to speak again. "Why don't you run two copies of the last scene on the disk," she suggested.

Joy fingered her curls. "Why two copies?"

Because I'm asking you so nicely. "One for me and one for Shane to review," Devin explained.

"Oh, okay. But wouldn't it be simpler for him to join you on the couch and read from just one copy?"

"Just as easy." Shane rose from behind his desk and strolled toward Devin. "One copy works just fine, Joy."

He dropped down next to Devin. "Is it noon yet?"

Twenty long minutes passed while Joy fooled with the paper feed. She tore enough paper to make a mountain of confetti. "Almost aligned," she said, only to sigh more deeply when the perforated edges of the paper went into the printer crooked once again. "I can do this. . . ."

"I think I can, I think I can," Shane quoted *The Little Engine That Could*. He then rose from the couch and crossed to her desk. "Let me help you." In less than thirty seconds he had loaded the paper.

"Nice job." Joy swatted him on his butt, then watched him walk back to the sofa.

Devin watched Joy watch Shane. The temp openly appreciated his backside, which Devin had also noticed on more than one occasion. Devin, however, hadn't drooled. Must Joy be so obvious? So interested? What about her highly photographed boyfriend, Danny Stone? Joy Ford was, indeed, fickle.

"The printout, please?" Devin said, hoping to nudge Joy back to work.

"Sure thing—give me a minute to familiarize myself with the computer."

Fifteen additional minutes swept by. Shane leaned forward on the couch and rested his elbows on his knees. "Is it on yet?"

"Almost on."

"What's the problem?" Devin fingered a button on her blazer.

"Can't find the switch," Joy confessed. "This computer's different from the one I work on in my computer class."

"My turn." Devin proceeded to help Joy set up for work. "Can you type?" She was afraid of the answer.

"I hunt and peck like a chicken," Joy readily admitted. "That's why I run a tape recorder, so if I miss anything important, I can catch it when I transcribe."

"A tape recorder," Shane repeated.

"Transcribe." Devin lifted a brow. "I think I need an aspirin."

She returned after taking two, exactly at the moment

Joy tore the printout from the printer. "Wow! This is hot."

"*Hot?*" Devin questioned the secretary's choice of words. "If I recall correctly, Rose Coltraine has just returned from the Triple C with the knowledge that Cutter is a thief."

"Your memory fails you, Devin. Must be age," Joy said.

Her age? Devin wouldn't turn thirty for another eight months!

Joy wrinkled the paper as she scanned the printout. "The last scene on this disk has Dare Calder walking in on Miss Rose's bath."

"Her bath?" Devin shot off the couch as if the cushions were on fire.

Shane was right behind her. He read over her shoulder as she whipped through the printed pages. Devin's heart slammed with the countless additions to their last writing session. When had this occurred? Before the storm? After the storm? Heaven help her. Working with Shane had become a nightmare.

"*When,* Devin, when?" Shane jammed his hands into the pockets of his jeans, his expression as mad as the Hatter on his T-shirt.

"When, *what,* McNamara?" Her hands shook as she folded the printed pages and set them back on the desk.

"When did you write this?" he pressed.

He was blaming her for the copper tub scene? "This isn't my work."

It wasn't his either. Shane knew. Devin lied like the rug he now paced. What the hell was happening here? Scenes continued to pop up on the computer that neither he nor Devin would admit to writing. It didn't make sense. While the scene accurately portrayed his gunslinger's character, it was not a joint effort, as stipulated in their contract.

He looked into Devin's face. She was so lovely, so innocent in her mask of deception. Refusing to argue before Joy, he grasped Devin by the elbow and tugged her toward the kitchen. He lowered his voice below the hum of the refrigerator. "Come clean, Dev. Prior to the storm, did you hit the wee hours with a bottle of whiskey and your naughty imagination?"

She stepped back, looking as stunned as if he'd slapped her. "I seldom drink, McNamara, and when I do it's something frothy, with fruit and an umbrella."

He pulled her closer. "What about the shot glass by the microwave? The scent of whiskey?"

"The shot glass was already on the counter when I entered the kitchen. That's all I can tell you."

Shane looked her dead in the eye. "I'm certain there's more."

"Was there liquor on her breath? Could she walk a straight line? What was her blood alcohol level?" Joy Ford had the hearing of a bat.

Shane glanced at the temp, and Joy shrugged. "Criminology 101. I take a lot of night classes."

Shane shook his head, and Joy tapped the computer screen. "You shouldn't be arguing; you should be applauding yourselves. This copper tub scene is fantastic. Your characters are so lifelike, they could step off the pages and walk right into this room." She cupped her ear. "I can almost hear them breathing."

An unexpected chill swept Shane's spine, as if he'd walked over someone's grave. The rash of goose bumps on Devin's arms told him she'd reacted in kind. Characters taking on lives of their own? It was too farfetched to imagine.

He released Devin, raked one hand through his hair,

and admitted, "The scene is good. I especially liked the bathing cloth clinging to Rose like a lover."

Devin poked him in the chest. "Calder remains a disreputable drifter, yet Rose has invited him to live at the Garter."

"Not in her bedroom."

"Miss Rose sleeps alone."

"Calder sleeps best with his head pillowed on soft breasts."

"Let's move beyond the gunslinger's comfort zone," Joy interrupted them once again. She pointed to the couch. "Whatever's holding you up, get over it. Have a seat and let's get to work."

"The temp has spoken," Devin said.

"Bossy little thing," Shane muttered.

"Give her a chance; she's just gotten here."

"She looks like she's here to stay. Forever."

"I'm waiting. . . ." Joy tapped her nail-bitten fingers on the desktop.

"We're ready to start," Devin said as she dropped down on the sofa next to Shane. "The next scene revolves around Calder's stakeout at the Garter."

Shane rubbed his hands together. "Calder might like to experience the nightlife before he holes up in the alley."

"He's restricted to poker, nothing more."

"That makes for a boring evening." Shane covered his mouth, yawning. "Now if you could convince Rose to slip into a thigh-high, low-cut gown—"

"In flesh tones?" Devin asked sweetly.

He nodded his approval. "Think she'd rouge her nipples?"

"When Calder vows celibacy."

Joy snorted. "Calder celibate? That will be the day."

Shane ignored her comment. "Although viewed in

bed and at her bath, Rose remains maidenly."

"*Old* maidenly." Joy snorted more loudly this time.

Beside him, Devin rubbed her temples. The same headache was working at Shane's brow. "Calder's living at the Garter, preparing for a night of poker. Where's Rose?" Shane asked.

"Adorned in a dawn-pink gown—"

"Any chance Rose could dress in a color other than pink?" Joy cut in.

"It's her signature color." Devin again fingered the button on her blazer. "A continuity factor within my Garter series."

Joy scrunched up her nose. "Heaven forbid we deviate from the obvious."

"Rose looks good in pink." Shane could not believe he'd just defended Devin's character.

Devin, apparently, could not believe it either. Her eyes wide, she looked at him as if hell had frozen over.

"How about jewels?" Joy asked.

"Garnets at her ears, neck, and wrists," Devin replied.

Shane nodded. "Tasteful."

"Somber," Joy said.

Devin worked the button a little faster. "I was going for elegant."

"Not quite successful, were you?" Joy smirked.

Shane heard Devin swallow her reply. He decided it was time to rein in the temp. "Work with us, Joy. Concentrate on getting down our outline for the next chapter."

"Gotcha." She went back to her hunt and peck.

Devin glanced his way. *Thank you,* she silently mouthed.

Shane rested his arm on the back of the sofa and

squeezed her shoulder. "Let's have Rose and Calder meet on the second-floor landing."

Devin agreed. "Once there, Miss Rose finances Calder's stake in the poker game."

"Calder's no charity case," Shane said.

"Rose hired him, and she will fund his hand," Devin insisted.

Joy looked up. "It's nice to see a woman supporting a man."

"Rose is not supporting Calder," Shane said to set Joy straight.

"How much money is she giving him?" Joy demanded.

"Enough to guarantee he'll win the poker game," Devin said.

"Does Calder get to keep his winnings?" Joy continued to work outside her job description. She talked more than she typed.

"He's not a greedy gunslinger," Shane said. "He'll repay Rose every cent."

"I'd demand an IOU."

"You're not Rose." Devin smiled tightly at Joy. "After a brief discussion on the second-floor landing, Rose descends the front staircase, and Calder takes the rear steps. Known to the players in the back room, Calder sits across from Wayne Cutter, with Marshal Dirk Morgan on his right."

"A lawman at his side would make Dare edgy," Shane said.

"The game will last for only a few hours," Devin reminded him.

He shook his head. "He can't relax with Tin Star at his elbow."

"Then move him!"

Devin had become as edgy as Calder. "Calder will sit

between banker Calvin Waite and the barber, Harry Wiggs."

Devin jabbed him in the ribs. "I've never had a barber in my books."

"It appears you do now." Joy chuckled as she continued her hunt and peck.

Devin's button held on by a thread. "In Rose's stead, barkeep Willis Eldridge—"

"Is that Willis with one L or two?" Joy questioned.

"Two," Devin answered. "The barkeep oversees the poker game. Seduced by the strongest whiskey, finest cigars, and deeply cushioned chairs, the gamblers throw caution to the wind."

"Where are the soiled doves?" Joy asked around a mouthful of jelly beans.

"They're regular characters in Shane's books, not mine," Devin said.

"You write great whores." Joy grinned at Shane. "I loved both Sally and Sue at Buffalo Annie's Saloon in *Texas Trails.*"

Shane recalled the characters. The women were big-boned, buxom, and bawdy. They outdrank wranglers and buffalo hunters, and drained men during sex. Calder had taken both women to bed simultaneously, and survived the night. "They almost stole the book," he said. "The sisters received a lot of fan mail."

Joy grew excited. "Maybe they could appear in *Calder's Rose.*"

"Maybe not." Devin's button popped off in her hand, and her blazer gapped a full inch.

Shane glimpsed a flash of skin and the curve of a satin demicup before Devin clasped the edges together. He blew out a breath. "Calder needs to concentrate on Cutter and the poker game. At present he's nursing one shot of whiskey, while Cutter's slugging down bottles."

"It's when Cutter wins an exceptionally large pot that he drunkenly mentions satin ribbons," Devin said. "Marshal Morgan is aware his wife, Penelope, loves hair ribbons. Just that morning while looking for a pair of socks, he discovered strips of blue satin beneath her dainties in the bottom drawer of their armoire."

"Ribbons he couldn't afford on his chicken-scratch salary," Shane said. "Quick to piece together the facts, the marshal realizes Penelope's daydreams center on Cutter and not on him. The more liquored-up Cutter becomes, the wilder the rancher's bidding."

Joy stopped typing. "Cutter sounds like such a loser."

"He can't compete with Calder's cunning and daring."

"I like that." Joy tapped the keys.

"Don't type everything Shane says," Devin said. "We have to agree before it's written in stone."

Joy gave an exaggerated sigh. "I'll delete it."

"Good idea," Shane said. "Cutter's losses soon mount, along with those of Marshal Morgan. When Dirk tosses in his hand, clean out of cash, Cutter slurringly suggests that he wages Penelope."

"The marshal's pledge to uphold the law forbids him from calling the rancher out," Devin continued. "A charged silence unfolds with the next hand. The back room is filled with tension felt by all but Cutter."

Joy swiveled her chair. "That's 'cause he's drunk as a skunk and feeling no pain."

Shane heard Devin's indrawn breath. The corner of her left eye now twitched and her mouth had pinched. He drew his hand to the back of her neck and began to massage away the tension. She leaned back into his hand and sighed. Shane continued with the story line.

"Having listened and learned and eventually caught the lust in Cutter's gaze whenever Penelope's name is mentioned, Dare Calder calls it a night. Pocketing his immense winnings, he tips his Stetson and slips from the room. Once in the alleyway, he loses himself in the shadows and awaits the thief."

"Outside the saloon, darkness hovers as thick and oppressive as Wayne Cutter's deception," Devin said. "A lone star casts pinpricks of light on the tin roof of the neighboring mercantile."

"Is that Parnham's Mercantile? Owned and operated by Delbert and Anna Parnham?" Joy asked.

"One and the same," Devin answered, still clutching the edges of her blazer.

"The mercantile sells family Bibles, patterned china, and sarsaparilla. Delbert refuses to peddle hard liquor, right?"

Devin nodded. "You know Cutter's Bend."

"I might have lived there in another lifetime," Joy said. "My great-grandma lived in the Wild West."

Shane wished he'd had a camera to capture Devin's look of disbelief. "Cutter's Bend is fictitious, Joy."

"How can you say that? Rose lives there, and Calder's settled in at the Garter."

Devin paled slightly. "You're discussing our characters as if they were human."

Joy sighed. "You write so true to life, they actually could be."

Devin's shiver extended to Shane. For the second time that morning, goose bumps rose on his flesh.

"Back to the book," he directed. "Dare Calder disappears into the shadows, all dark clothing and matching scowl. Hat tipped low, he rests a shoulder against the wood building. He flexes his right hand, itching for a fight."

"Calder sure can fight," Joy said in admiration. "In *Texas Surrender* he bested six men in a barroom brawl. His face and his knuckles were bloody and bruised. Lucky for him, a dance-hall girl named Abbie spent the night soothing his aches and pains."

"She sure did." Shane chuckled, until Devin elbowed him hard. He returned his attention to the book. "The creak of the side door alerts Calder to another presence. The man's Stetson looks more gray than white in the darkness, but he's still easy to track."

"Calder's got eyes like a hawk. He's been known to shoot a nut from a squirrel's mouth at eighty feet," Joy added in praise of the gunslinger.

"Poor squirrel if he ever missed," Devin muttered.

Shane nudged her knee with his own. "He never misses."

Devin blew out a breath. "Can we get back on track?"

He nodded. "Keep typing, Joy."

"I'm multitasking," she said, puffed with pride. "I can type and talk at the same time."

"Concentrate on the typing," Shane prodded as he continued to plot. "The moment the thief hits the bottom step, Calder pushes off the building and widens his stance. In a voice as lethal as his weapon, he orders the man to drop the money and turn around slowly."

"The thief has no intention of giving up peacefully," Devin said. "The man spins and fires on Calder. Calder feels a hot round of lead slash past him as he dives behind the stairs."

"He's not hurt, is he?" Joy asked.

"He'll be fine," Shane assured her with a smile. "Calder's draw proves smooth, liquid fast. He catches the butt, lifts the weapon, drags back the hammer, and when the muzzle slants up, he puts his first round through the robber's thigh. Man and money bag hit the ground with a grunt and the jingle of gold coins."

"Cautiously Calder approaches the downed man," Devin said. "Kicking the money bag and firearm aside, he stands, boots planted before the thief. Wanting to see the man's face, he tips back his Stetson with the barrel of his gun, then pulls up short."

Devin's sudden smile was pure satisfaction. "The man glaring back at him is not Wayne Cutter."

"Not Cutter?" The plot twist grabbed Shane's full attention. He felt an adrenaline rush. "Who is it then?"

"Figure it out later." Joy jumped up, pushed back her chair, and stretched. "I'm bored stiff. This story's dry as dust. Let's break for lunch."

Chapter Seven

"You want to break *now?*" Devin couldn't believe her ears. She'd been silently hatching a terrific plot twist, and the temp wanted to stop and eat. It was not yet noon.

"Give us another thirty minutes, and we'll do lunch," Shane said. "You can't stop when the writing's this good."

Joy was not to be swayed. "I'm hungry and you're out of jelly beans."

"There's a bag in my bottom desk drawer," Devin said. "Help yourself."

"Why not save some for later?" Shane suggested.

And Joy did. What she didn't pour into the fluted cranberry-colored dish, she stuffed into her backpack.

Devin watched her jelly beans disappear. "All gone."

"Thank God," Shane said.

Devin eased off the sofa, rolled her shoulders, then headed toward her bedroom.

"Where are you going?" Shane called to her back. "Don't leave me hanging on the story line."

"I need to change, or hadn't you noticed I'm gaping?"

"I noticed you'd been left holding the button."

She turned slightly. "I thought you'd peeked."

He smiled a slow, sexy smile that made her blush.

Devin walked a little faster. Once in her bedroom she slipped off her blazer and put on a mauve silk blouse. She returned in under five minutes.

"Quick-change artist," Shane admired. "I like a woman who gets in and out of her clothes quickly."

"I like a man who keeps his pants on," Devin returned.

Joy cleared her throat. "Child in the room. Flirt on your own time."

"We weren't flirting," Devin said as she sat down beside Shane.

Joy looked from Devin to Shane. Her grin was as knowing as it was needling. "You were getting it on. Words can be the hottest foreplay."

Foreplay? The temp was mistaken. Shane teased and taunted, but he hadn't been tempted since he'd seen Jamie Jensen at SunBake Boardwalk. That was just as well with Devin. An affair with Shane would . . . would . . . be wild and thrilling, and would scare the hell out of her. Her life was orderly and calm. She didn't need the zing of an affair to get her through the next five weeks.

"Let's get back to the book," Devin directed.

Shane deferred to her. "*Who* was the thief?"

"Calder tips back the downed man's Stetson . . ." Devin paused, heightening the suspense. "With an expletive, the thief glares up at him. Calder holsters his six-shooter. The man he's caught red-handed is none other than the most law-abiding citizen in Cutter's Bend: Marshal Dirk Morgan."

"The marshal?" Shane lifted a brow. "Run with it."

And Devin did. "Morgan clutches his leg as blood spreads and stains his baggy brown pants. Calder hunkers down beside him. Removing his black bandanna, he secures it over the wound—"

"Always the considerate gunslinger," Joy broke in. "Tending to others before himself."

"Calder's not hurt, Joy."

Joy looked at Shane as if he hadn't been following the story line. "Morgan shot at Calder."

"But he didn't hit him."

Joy shrugged. "Gunfire is gunfire."

Devin twisted one of the diamond-shaped buttons on her blouse. "Calder then asks the lawman how long he's been cracking safes. Morgan releases a tired sigh as he slumps back on the ground, where puffs of dust soil his beige shirt. He admits to breaking the law for the first time that night."

Shane snapped his fingers. "I know where you're headed. Morgan has turned criminal for his wife."

"A very pregnant wife." Devin smiled, pleased she and Shane were on the same page for once.

"Didn't they have condoms back then?" Joy asked.

"Protection was available," Devin informed her. "It wasn't, however, always practiced."

Joy sniffed. "Same as today. Unwanted pregnancies, unwanted babies, unwanted—"

"Type, Joy," Shane instructed.

And when Devin heard her hunt and peck, she went on. "Morgan's wife wants to travel back east to have her baby. His pay won't cover the train trip. He thought lifting a little cash might set his life to rights."

"Calder reminds the marshal that he's wronged Miss

Rose. Morgan is well versed in the law. He knows he could hang for his crime," Shane said.

"You can't hang the marshal!" Joy jumped off her chair and covered her ears. "He's a good character, strong and upstanding. Penelope's the bitch—get rid of her."

Shane motioned Joy back onto her chair. "The scene's not over until it's over."

Joy blew raspberries. "I hate suspense."

"Maybe it's time to break for lunch?" Shane suggested.

Devin rubbed her stomach. "I could go for a sandwich about now."

Joy curled her hand like a gun. "Get off that sofa and I'll take you down faster than Calder shot Morgan."

Devin lips twitched, and Shane smiled outright.

"Calder confides in the marshal that there could be a second thief," Shane said. "He cocks his head toward the corner of the building and asks the marshal if he cares to wait out the night."

"Morgan rises with a low groan," Devin said. "Favoring his wounded leg, he scoops up the money bag and hobbles to where Calder now stands in the shadows."

"Is it going to be a long night?" Joy asked. "I hate waiting. It's dark and the temperature has dropped." She rubbed her upper arms. "Morgan's still bleeding and Calder's as quiet as a corpse."

Devin nudged Shane with her elbow. "Joy's living our story line."

"Then she'd better duck or draw." He kept his voice as low as hers. "A second round of gunfire's about to explode."

"Should we warn her?"

"Naw. Readers like surprises."

"Just before daybreak, the side door swings wide and a shadowy figure takes the stairs two at a time," Devin continued. "The thief sports a white Stetson and there are two money bags slung over one shoulder."

Shane ran his hands down his blue-jeaned thighs, then back again. Devin tracked the movement, her gaze lingering on his zipper. She blew out a breath. Her fascination with a metal tab and tiny silver teeth made no sense whatsoever.

Her head jerked up as Shane drew her back to the story. "Gunslinger and marshal stand side by side, their guns drawn, the hammers cocked. Calder warns the thief that if he takes one more step, he'll be entering hell."

"The road to perdition," Joy said. "Get on with the showdown."

"The thief shifts his weight, ready to bolt," Shane said. "Calder fires two warning shots at the robber's boot heels."

"Make him dance!" Joy cheered.

"Calder hits the bronze spur on one boot heel and sends it spinning." Devin worked the button on her blouse.

"Careful, Dev, or you'll require needle and thread," Shane whispered in her ear.

The button was loose. She folded her hands in her lap. "Aware the next shot could take his life, the thief raises his hands high in surrender," she finished.

Joy clapped her hands. "Wayne Cutter turns to face his jury, right?"

Devin and Shane looked at each other and nodded as one.

"I'm such a good writer." Joy patted herself on the back.

"Write a little more, and we'll break for lunch," Devin said.

Wiggling her fingers over the keyboard, Joy agreed.

"While the marshal holds his gun on Cutter, Calder hefts the money bags from the rancher's shoulder. Fear shines in Cutter's gaze, and his thick lips twitch."

Devin glared at Shane. "Cutter doesn't have thick lips."

"The rancher's got lips like a puckered tuna," Joy butted in. "That's how I've always envisioned him."

"Me too," Shane said.

Devin pinched his thigh, and Shane grimaced. "I've never described Cutter in such a manner."

"Change it, Joy," Shane instructed as he rubbed his leg. He then turned to Devin. "I'd rather you punch than pinch."

Joy looked from Devin to Shane. "She sure touches you a lot."

Shane's smile slanted. "Not nearly enough, Joy."

The corners of Joy's eyes crinkled and she chuckled. "You look like a hands-on kind of guy."

Devin dipped her head and blushed. She must keep her hands to herself. "Calder next asks Cutter to explain his actions. Cutter hems, haws, and avoids the marshal's eyes as he blurts out his story. He's wooed Penelope into an illicit affair."

"Cutter would hump a snake in a woodpile," Joy muttered.

Shane coughed, almost choking, and Devin pursed her lips.

Joy's hunt and peck broke the ensuing silence.

"An affair! Marshal Morgan stiffens as straight as a barber pole," Shane continued. "He flushes crimson, then pales, breathing heavily through his mouth as Cutter confesses to giving Penelope sapphire ribbons, along with several other trinkets: a porcelain egg and a cranberry-colored vase. Also baby booties. Cutter admits Penelope now carries his child."

"Son of a . . . biscuit!" Joy exclaimed. "Poor marshal. Give me a gun—I'll shoot Cutter myself."

"Devin and I will take care of him," Shane assured her. "Morgan lunges at Cutter, and Calder steps between them. Calder asks the marshal to hear Cutter out."

"If looks could kill, the rancher would be buried on Boot Hill," Devin said. "He's given Penelope the baby Morgan has been longing for."

"Morgan is stunned. He's always wanted a son, yet Penelope hasn't let him touch her for six months," Shane said.

"The marshal needs to park his boots at Eve's Garden," Joy suggested. "A night with a whore will polish his tin star."

"Type, Joy," Shane said, more firmly this time.

Joy's hunt and peck picked up a little speed.

"The marshal swallows his pride and asks Cutter how long he's been sleeping with his wife," Shane said. "Hanging his head, Cutter states the affair began the night of Holcomb's barn dance. When the marshal was called away to break up a gunfight, Cutter gave Penelope a ride home in his buggy. Beneath a full moon and clear skies, they stopped near Sparrow Springs and had—"

"Buggy-creakin' sex?" Joy snorted indelicately. "Thank God for the invention of the automobile and the backseat."

"Amen to that," Shane echoed, and Devin swatted his knee.

He snagged her hand and clasped it tightly. "Mine now."

Devin tugged against his hold as he rested their hands on his thigh. She shivered when he slid his thumb along her forefinger, and across the heel of her palm, then rubbed a slow circle in its center.

The plot was lost to the sensation of his touch. Devin stared in Joy's direction, but didn't see her. She felt nothing but Shane as he cradled her hand. Denim brushed her knuckles as he turned her palm slightly, then stroked the sensitive flesh at her wrist. Her heartbeat quickened, and her breathing deepened.

"I'm all caught up with the story." Joy stopped typing.

Devin was caught up in Shane—so much so that she could barely concentrate on the scene. "Umm, the buggy . . ."

Shane saved her with a knowing smile. "Cutter further confesses that Penelope is blackmailing him, and he's been stealing from Rose Coltraine, the most respected woman in town."

Respected? This from Shane, whose gunslinger stalked Rose with his sexuality. A gunslinger who was as wild as the West, and who lived to bed women. Devin wondered what Shane was after.

Steeling herself against the heated stroke of his thumb, she said, "The rancher's confession causes the marshal to reevaluate his life. Morgan's nostrils flare, and white lines bracket his mouth. Tension holds him proud, when his wounded leg would bring a lesser man to his knees. No man deserves an unfaithful wife."

"Calder has heard his fill," Shane said.

"I'm also done listening," Joy couldn't stay out of the conversation long. "Send Penelope packing."

Devin sighed heavily. "We're getting there, Joy."

"Just as fast as we can," Shane added. "Both Cutter and Morgan have been swindled by the swish of Penelope's petticoats. Calder suggests a one-way ticket on the next stage. The high-noon stage heads east. Penelope will have a reserved seat."

Joy drummed her hands on the desktop. "Go, gunslinger!"

Shane linked his fingers more tightly with Devin's. His hand was large, strong, and comforting. His arm brushed hers as he leaned a little closer. His heat, his scent, his masculinity played with her senses. Her common sense insisted they separate, but the woman in Devin liked Shane near. Settling deeper on the sofa, she crossed her legs, her right hip rolling and resting against his.

He squeezed her fingers. "Cutter and Morgan eye each other, then turn their gazes on Calder. Calder then demands they repay Rose Coltraine. The men agree Calder should take the money. The two men assume they are under arrest and will soon be sharing the same cell."

"Better a cell than sharing the same woman," Joy said.

"Both men nod and surrender to their fate," Devin said. "Dare hefts the money bags, turns on his heel, and heads toward the stairs. Over his shoulder he tells the men he's known the night to hold many secrets. The mistress of their misery is about to part town."

"Fresh starts. Forgotten betrayals. Gunslinger justice." Shane raked a hand through his hair. "Understanding penetrates the morning air and the men breathe a whole lot easier, until Calder draws one promise from each man. Morgan is willing to oblige his request, whereas Cutter scuffs his boot in the dirt, reluctant to comply. The marshal jingles the keys to the jail, and Cutter nods his agreement."

"What were Calder's requests?" Joy swiveled in her chair.

"The requests will unfold in later chapters," Shane said.

"Dare Calder then enters the side door of the Scarlet Garter." Devin was ready to wrap up the scene. "Rose Coltraine deserves the return of her money. And perhaps a little courting after all."

Shane groaned. "Courting?"

"Poor Calder," Joy groaned as well. "Rose is so prudish. He's going to have to work his butt off to get into her drawers."

Devin gaped, and Shane grinned. "My work's cut out for me."

Joy blinked. "Your work? Calder would do just fine on his own."

"They are characters, Joy. Characters we've created," Devin reminded her for the second time. "Calder and Rose need our direction."

"Not all the time," Joy said flatly. "I'm certain they could manage without you."

Joy's words made Devin shiver. She squeezed Shane's hand, seeking reassurance that she wasn't the only one freaked out by the temp's unsettling point of view.

He patted her hand as he rose and pulled her up beside him. "Let's break for lunch," he suggested.

Joy beat them to the kitchen.

Her opening and closing of cabinets covered Shane's whisper. "Five hours seemed more like five weeks."

Devin shook her head. "I'm not certain I can work with her day after day."

"I know I can't," Shane said near her ear.

"What's our option?"

Shane's gaze was hot with intent. "As I suggested earlier, we sleep together, for the sake of the book."

Sleep together . . . to keep the story line on the straight and narrow.

Devin looked at Joy, who had pulled so much food from the refrigerator, it filled the entire counter. She was taking bites out of each item, then moving on. No plates, no silverware, no manners.

Joy or Shane? She weighed the alternatives carefully. Her shoulders sagged as the scales tipped in his favor.

"There will be rules written, posted, and strictly followed," she informed him. "No bedrooms. We pull out the sofa bed and sleep out in the living room. We stay fully clothed. You'll sleep under the sheet and I'll sleep under the comforter. You stay on your side of the bed. There will be no touching, no kissing, no . . . no . . ."

"Hot, sweaty, pulse-pounding sex?"

His words slipped past her guard and she swallowed hard. "I'll . . . I'll be sleeping with a steak knife."

"Smooth or serrated?"

She looked directly at his groin. "Serrated. Two-sided and sharp."

He stepped back and allowed her to pass. "You're scaring me, Dev."

Devin walked around him, only to come to an abrupt halt at the corner of the counter. Shane walked into her back. They both stared as Joy made her way down the counter like a buffet.

"You've got enough food to feed an army," Joy said around a cold chicken drumstick.

A one woman army, Devin noted. For one so thin, Joy could put it away. Devin pulled open the refrigerator door and stared at the remaining contents. "Ham and Swiss, or I can cook you a hamburger?"

Joy hadn't yet gone for the raw meat.

Shane positioned himself on a barstool. "A sandwich is fine. I can fix it myself—"

"I don't mind." His look of disbelief prompted her to add, "It's one sandwich, Shane."

He watched her gnaw her lower lip as she spread margarine on the bread and added a little mustard. She then licked her upper lip as she layered the ham and Swiss. Devin James had a beautiful mouth. A most kissable mouth, one he wouldn't mind tasting again soon.

Her agreement to prepare him a sandwich had surprised him. She'd always thought him dog-dish low. But after watching Joy devour a week's worth of food with her fingers, he'd gained several brownie points. The temp made him look good.

Maybe Joy should stay an extra day? He watched her inhale a container of macaroni salad. He was certain some of the pasta had gone up her nose. She would be on her way within the hour.

He waited until Devin had served his sandwich before he questioned Joy. "What are your plans for the future?"

Joy looked at him with mayonnaise at both corners of her mouth. "I'd planned a vacation after this temp job."

He handed her a napkin. "Vacation?"

Joy wiped her mouth, looking wistful. "Danny and I wanted to work our way cross-country. See the sights, camp at state parks, make love under the stars." She looked from Devin to Shane. "Danny and I are a lot like the two of you."

Devin choked on her sandwich. Shane stood and patted her on the back. "Explain this likeness," he said to Joy.

"We're like magnets, and opposites attract."

Devin set her sandwich down after the second bite. "You're mistaken, Joy."

"If I'm mistaken, then you're blind." Joy crunched on a carrot stick.

"We both walked into this writing relationship with our eyes wide open," Shane said.

"Wide open, but sneaking peeks." Joy jabbed a radish at Shane. "You're constantly staring at Devin's mouth, and she"—Joy nodded toward Devin—"seems fixated on your zipper."

"My mouth?" Devin covered her lips with two fingers.

"My zipper?" Shane felt himself stir.

"Whether you recognize it or not, your togetherness is a turn-on." Joy reached for her third dill pickle. "If you'd let your characters write the book, you'd have more time for each other."

"Our characters write . . ." Shane thumped his head with his palm. Joy Ford was a Looney Tune.

"We don't need time for each other," Devin said softly. "We need to complete *Calder's Rose* and get on with our lives."

Get on with their lives? An unidentifiable heaviness settled on Shane's chest, and he found it difficult to breathe. He pushed his sandwich aside at the exact moment Devin did the same. The edges of their plates clinked.

Joy popped three Doritos into her mouth. "You even finished eating at the same time," she said around the crunch.

It was time to terminate Joy Ford's employment. Shane stood and pulled his wallet from the back pocket of his jeans. He removed a blank check. "How would you feel about starting your vacation earlier than planned?" he asked.

Joy's expression looked as crushed as the crust on

her bread. "But . . . but . . . I've only worked half a day."

"And you've done . . . quite a job," Shane assured her.

"A good job?" Joy pressed.

"You did your best." Devin ran her fingers along the countertop. "Perhaps temp work isn't your calling."

"You think?" Joy tilted her head, suddenly thoughtful.

"Perhaps you need to explore your options," Shane suggested.

"I'd love to go exploring," Joy said. "But that takes money. My talents as a writer and computer programmer only get me so far."

Not far enough. Shane stood and crossed to his desk for a pen. He then wrote out the check, adding enough zeros to get Joy and her boyfriend all the way to California. But not back.

Returning to the kitchen, he handed Joy the check. "A bonus for all your hard work."

Joy was momentarily speechless. "What do I tell the agency?"

"The truth," Devin said. "You want to explore your career options."

"Can I use you as a reference?" Joy asked.

"Have your next employer call us," was as far as Shane would commit.

Joy set all the food aside and smiled as she first hugged Devin, then embraced Shane. For one so thin, she sure could squeeze, he mused. She didn't release him for a good long time. "Thanks in advance for dedicating the book to me."

Shane's jaw hit the top of Joy's head. Her assumption was way off. "As long as our plot remains confidential, we'll mention you in the acknowledgments."

Joy patted him on the bottom, then cupped his left buttock. "This crow don't caw."

Shane shifted his stance, moving beyond her reach, and bumped into Devin in the process. The brush of their bodies felt good. She was soft and warm and could make him hard in a heartbeat. He liked that last quality in a woman.

"Shane?" Devin's light touch on his arm burned like fire.

Down, boy! He mentally shook himself. "What's up?" Besides his erection.

"Joy was preparing to leave," Devin informed him.

They joined Joy by Devin's desk. "Would you mind leaving the tape of our writing session?" he asked, just in case her hunt and peck left more gaps than he and Devin could fill in.

Joy bit down on her lower lip. "No can do. The batteries died in the recorder at the start of the poker game. I'd planned to transcribe from memory."

"I hope my memory is as good as yours." Shane looked at the computer screen and prayed for total recall. Throughout the morning Joy had typed key words, but not a single sentence. *Poker, satin ribbons, determined Calder and drunken Cuter*—Cutter spelled with only one T—were the only clues to their five-hour session. He and Devin had a lot of blanks to fill in.

Thoughts of strangling Joy grew a little too vivid.

"It's time to pack up," Joy said.

Shane blinked away the image of his hands around her neck. He gathered up her photo collection. "I'll help you load your van."

Devin moved to the couch and the orange afghans. "So will I. With the three of us working, we'll have you on the road in no time at all."

No time at all took one solid hour. Joy rearranged

the contents of the van three times before she was satisfied with her home on wheels. Devin and Shane
stood at the front window as she drove away.

"That was the longest morning of my life," Shane
said as he followed Devin to the kitchen to clean up
Joy's leftovers. "We don't need a third party to drive
each other crazy."

Devin stuffed a head of lettuce along with several
carrot and celery sticks into a plastic container. She
snapped down the lid with a great deal of force. "She
ate all my jelly beans."

"The loss being?" Shane poured the remainder of
Joy's orange soda and cherry cola down the drain.

Devin swung open the refrigerator door. "I liked
them."

He made a face. "I didn't."

"One of our many differences."

"Joy thought us magnets." He put the loaf of wheat
bread in the bread box, then leaned against the
counter, arms crossed over his chest.

"You believed her?" Devin collected the pickles, mayonnaise, mustard, and the tub of margarine. "The
same Joy who thought our characters were real?"

"They are pretty lifelike."

"We breathe life into their creation." She closed the
refrigerator door, grabbed a sponge from the sink, and
began wiping down the counter.

"A minor technicality." He smiled to himself as Devin worked around him, leaning in close, brushing her
arm against his ribs, her hip against his thigh.

Once finished, she rinsed out the sponge and turned
to him. "What's next, McNamara?"

He nodded toward the sofa and feigned a yawn. "I
believe it's time for bed."

She shook her head, blushing. "Not a chance, Sandman."

He pushed away from the counter, restless and needing to move. "I think I'll pound the pavement." While sex would prove more satisfying, a good run would tire him out. For the short term. He turned on his heel and strolled toward his bedroom to change clothes. "I'm gone."

Devin was glad Shane had left. His restless energy made her nervous. She followed his progress from the front window as he jogged down the driveway and the dirt road until he hit the main paved street that led north into Naples. He was wearing a sleeveless gray T-shirt cropped at his abdomen that shifted over the hard play of muscles across his shoulders, and charcoal gym shorts layered over more snugly-fitting bike shorts.

His tight butt, sinewed thighs, and strong calves proved exercise agreed with him. She liked watching him run.

With Shane out of sight, Devin opted for a swim. She slipped off her mauve blouse and plum slacks and pulled on a Caribbean green bandeau swimsuit. She pulled her hair free from its braid. Only a beach towel trailed her to the shore.

It was high tide, and, the waves were perfect for body surfing. Devin rode each one before floating on her back in the shallower water. Cradled by the gulf, she grew drowsy. The promise of a catnap on her towel drew her toward the sugary sand.

Blinded by the sun's brilliance, she didn't see Shane right away. He stood two feet from her towel, slick with sweat, sin in his smile. "Care if I cool off?"

Her heartbeat pounded like the surf. "Take a cold shower."

"The gulf looks enticing."

So did Shane, as he slowly stripped off his T-shirt and gym shorts, leaving only the tight-fitting bike shorts. The dark hair on his chest narrowed to the washboard ripples of his abdomen. He looked firm, fit, and too fine for his own good as he crossed the sand, sensual intent darkening his gaze to shark gray.

Devin shrieked, and charged into the water.

Shane was on her before she reached the sandbar. He swam like a competitive swimmer, his strokes powerful and sure. Diving beneath the surface, he caught her left ankle. He slid his hands up her leg, drawing her under. She swallowed a mouthful of salt water as she squirmed and slapped at him, the water slowing the force of her swing.

They surfaced, gasping and sputtering and shaking water from their hair and eyes. He tickled her until she nearly drowned from laughing. She collapsed against him to catch her breath. His eyelashes were spiked, and his expression was both watchful and dangerous—a little too dangerous.

Sex was there; she sensed it and knew he sensed it too. His hands on her waist, he lifted her high and pressed her close. The warmth of his breath fanned her belly through the thin bandeau, drawing her stomach tight.

Time stopped except for the shifting tide as he kissed the indentation of her navel, then between her breasts. The feel of his mouth remained as he eased her down his body of deep cut muscle, prominent sinew, and rigid sex. He guided her legs around his hips and pressed into her.

She'd been attracted to Shane, but hadn't realized the strength of that attraction until she rocked forward on his hardness. Her body was liquid lust as she dissolved into him.

Shane shuddered. His eyes narrowed and his jaw clenched as he ran his hands over her lower back and buttocks and along the backs of her thighs. Surrounded by sun-speckled ocean, they felt anticipation mount with every heartbeat. He took her mouth slowly, a light brush of lips, corner to corner, expectancy riding as high as the waves.

Heat expanded in her belly as his hands and mouth stroked, felt, and searched more deeply. She clutched his shoulders, his nape, raked her fingers through his hair. She returned his kiss with the same demands he made of her. Her breathing grew as ragged as his as their bodies rocked with the waves.

She tightened her legs about his hips, feeling his hardness and length, and all he could give her.

His legs were braced, his stance wide, solid, firm, her thighs wrapped about him . . . in the exact position he'd held Jamie Jensen on SunBake Boardwalk. The image drove the desire from her body as if she'd been punched.

Shane and Jamie were meant to be together.

She stopped kissing him. Stopped rubbing and rocking against him. She feared her heart would stop beating when he also stopped thrusting; the waves were now creating the only motion between them.

Still cupping her bottom, he released a strangled breath and leaned back slightly. "Talk to me, Dev."

She had no ready explanation. Looking at him, she felt his discomfort. His eyes were closed, and his jaw worked. He ached for a release she could not give him. A release she had denied herself.

Her withdrawal was clearly testing Shane's control. With a long-suffering sigh, the last of the tension left his body. His breathing was nearly back to normal. Resting his forehead against hers, he looked her in the eye. "Why did you stop what we started?"

She licked her lips, tasting salt and Shane. "I-I was afraid—"

"Of getting naked?"

He was so blunt, he made her blink, then blush. "That, and of making a mistake."

"A mistake?" He ran his tongue along the inside of his cheek. "You're calling us a mistake?"

"A major mistake if . . . if . . ."

"We'd ridden the final wave?"

Silence stretched between them until Shane threw back his head and blew out a breath. "A mistake."

The wind had shifted and the waves built, now slapping his back and splashing over his shoulders and into her face. Shane carried her toward shore, releasing her in shallower water.

Devin took a long time straightening her bandeau.

He took a long time watching her do so.

She looked up slowly. He stood so tall, tan, and handsome. The sun had dried his hair and chest. His bike shorts hugged his groin, his arousal still evident. The pain of knowing Jamie Jensen claimed his future squeezed the breath from her lungs. In the depth of the gulf, she'd embraced Shane with her body and soul. She'd responded to him with trust and abandon and love in her heart. A love he would never return.

Distancing herself would not be easy. But once their writing session ended, Shane would pack his bag, close the door on the cottage, and never look back.

Shane looked over his shoulder to be sure Devin was not far behind. With the sudden shift in wind, the currents tugged strongly. He didn't want to lose her to the undertow.

She approached him slowly, with her head down and dragging her feet. Her withdrawal scared the hell out of him. They'd ridden the waves and each other's bodies until he'd been afraid they'd drown from the pleasure. He'd felt her desire build and throb and mirror his own pulse-pounding need . . . until she'd pulled back. Way the hell back. So far back he could no longer reach her.

He kicked a mound of sand, as much at odds with himself as he was with her. Their water play had aroused more than his desire. He liked that side of her, loose, playful, fun to be around.

He had loosened her up, only to get lost in her.

But Devin didn't seem to feel the same bond. She'd grown silent and distant, now staring over his shoulder at a palm tree in preference to looking at him.

He slapped his palms against his thighs, then clenched his fists. What he'd considered monumental, she'd called a mistake.

It was downright disconcerting.

He scooped up his T-shirt and gym shorts, then tossed Devin her towel as she crossed the sand toward him.

"I bought you a present," he said, hoping to clear the air between them.

"You did?" Her lips parted. "When have you had time to shop?"

"I took a detour while I was out jogging."

"And you thought of me?"

With every pound of the pavement. "When I returned and you weren't at the cottage, I left the gift on your desk."

One corner of her mouth curved. "Is it bigger than a bread box?"

"Smaller," he replied, playing along.

"Bigger than a can opener?"

"Close to the same size."

"A gift is good. Let's check it out." Sunburned, her hair tangled from the waves and his hands, she wrapped the towel about her waist and started toward the cottage.

Shane fell into step beside her. They walked in silence, keeping a full body width between them.

At the cottage he pushed open the sliding glass doors and let Devin pass ahead of him. She walked straight through the lanai and kitchen and directly to her desk. She stood at its corner and stared at the clear plastic bag. Shane caught her blinking, her eyes overly bright. She bit her lower lip, and her expression softened.

He nudged her shoulder. "You like?"

He heard her swallow. "Very much."

"They're not your fancy-schmancy brand."

"They're still jelly beans." She touched his elbow. "Thank you."

"You're most welcome." He watched as she untied the decorative straw ribbon on the bag and tasted several of the jelly beans. With each sampling she took the time to savor the flavor.

"Mmm, these are good. Care for one?" she asked.

He wanted to taste the flavor on her tongue. "Maybe just one." He selected orange. To his surprise the jelly bean tasted as juicy as fresh fruit. "Stick with this brand, Dev."

"Where did you find them?"

"Down the road at Sugar's, in the Barefoot William Plaza. There are lots of shops and also a restaurant,

Saltwater Cowboys; I thought we'd try it for dinner."

"Dinner?" Her fingers shook as she resealed the bag.

Shane didn't like the panic in her voice. "It's not a date, Dev; we'd merely share a meal."

He didn't like her mental debate. "Guess I have to eat sometime," she allowed.

That *sometime* would include him. Shane absently scratched his abdomen. The salt from the gulf had dried on his skin, and now itched. He needed a shower.

From the corner of his eye he caught Devin watching his fingers on his bare belly. He liked her eyes on him. Liked how her gaze narrowed and her pupils dilated just enough to show her interest.

He shifted slightly, afraid his body would show her exactly how much he liked her looking at him.

"Time to shower, answer my e-mail, and shoot off a few letters," he informed her.

She blinked. "What about the book?"

He glanced at the Art Deco clock. "It's after three. Let's hang loose until five, then have an early dinner. Afterward we'll work on *Calder's Rose*." And work they would. After Joy Ford's hunt and peck, they faced a writing marathon.

Devin nodded and, without further word, headed toward her bedroom. The urge to follow her was strong. But the timing wasn't right. He'd join her only when she wanted him as badly as he now wanted her.

Shane returned to the main room in under thirty minutes. Devin was indeed a quick-change artist. She was perfectly turned out in a dark green pantsuit, saddle shoes, and her tight-ass braid. He wished she'd dress down on occasion, as he was in his *Rum Raven, San Juan* T-shirt and patched black jeans. The raven on his shirt held a bottle of Bacardi in its claw, and a shot glass in its beak.

Reclining against two throw pillows, Devin glanced up from the book she was reading. She studied his shirt. "That bird looks looped."

He'd been looped as well the night he bought the shirt. He recalled the bar, the steel-drum music, the moonlight and—

He looked at Devin, and the woman he'd been with in Puerto Rico faded from memory. Damn, he must be whipped.

Devin stretched, and Shane caught the title of her book: *Tame the Corral* by Jackson Blackmore. What the hell?

"Why are you reading Blackmore?" he asked, disillusioned by her choice in authors.

She looked up, blinked. "His titles draw me in."

"His titles don't make a lick of sense."

"I've always found them right on the mark."

Surely she wasn't serious. He dropped down next to her. "Have you ever met Blackmore?"

"Once, years ago." She flipped to the inside back cover and studied Blackmore's photograph. "He's a nice-looking man."

Shane shrugged. "If you like buzz cuts and weak chins."

"He looks considerate and kind."

"All that from a headshot?"

"Read his author bio."

Jackson Blackmore was an animal activist and philanthropist. When he wasn't writing, he did volunteer work at a list of organizations that stretched two paragraphs. It read more like an obituary than a bio.

"The man's a saint."

"Cut the sarcasm, McNamara." She shooed him

away. "Find something to do. I want to finish this book."

He had no reason to be jealous of her reading material, but for some unidentifiable reason, he was. "Why aren't you reading one of my Westerns?"

"I've read all the Texas trash I could stomach."

She'd struck deep. He covered his heart. "You wound me, Dev."

"I'll wound you even deeper if you don't leave me alone."

Leaving her alone was not an option. He was still keyed up from their swim and the newfound feelings that plagued him. He wasn't handling rejection well. He knew it, but couldn't control his need to get on Devin's nerves.

"I started Blackmore's book, and read all of ten pages. I knew the cattle rustler was—"

Devin glared at him. "Don't you dare tell me the ending!"

He crossed his arms over his chest. "It's on the tip of my tongue."

"Bite down, Shane."

The urge to tell was too strong. He opened his mouth . . .

And Devin covered her ears. "I can't hear you."

He waited until she could. "Wallace Waite."

Devin reared back, as mad as he'd ever seen her. "You jerk!"

If looks could kill, Shane would be dead. When Devin threw the book at his head, he ducked. When she punched him he suffered the blow. When she leaped over the cushions with murder in her eyes, he grabbed her wrists and pulled her across his lap.

She struggled for a solid minute, then ground her teeth and demanded, "Why did you spoil the ending?"

He'd wanted her attention on him and not on the book, so his inner child had turned bratty. *Grow up, McNamara.*

"I, uh, thought your time would be better spent . . ."

"Doing what, Shane?"

He looked around. "Coloring. You've yet to crack the Disney Classics."

"You are unbelievable." She jerked free of his hold.

"I thought coloring relaxed you." He looked at her closely. "You could use a little relaxation."

"I was relaxed, you imbecile, settled in for the afternoon with a good book."

Good book, his ass. With a Jackson Blackmore Western, you really could judge the book by its cover.

Devin rose from the sofa. She claimed her coloring book and crayons from her desk, then settled two cushions to his left. She cracked the book and began to color slowly, methodically, neatly, staying inside the lines.

Shane edged a little closer. A part of him wanted to put his arm around her and whisper in her ear. Ten seconds of sweet nothings and Devin of the dark suits and tight-ass braid would jab him in the gut. He wouldn't push his luck. Not this time. She deserved his respect and what few manners he took to heart.

He studied the picture she was coloring and grew concerned. Maybe Devin was color-blind. "Snow White doesn't have red hair."

"She does when she's angry."

Point taken. He rose, stretched, and left Devin to her dwarfs, who were rapidly joining snow white as redheads. Crossing to his desk, he settled in with the Internet.

Time ticked by, one hour, then two. Shane glanced at Devin, checking her mood. She was still coloring, and looked more relaxed. She hadn't glanced up once. He knew that for a fact, since he'd sneaked frequent peeks in her direction.

She entertained herself quite nicely. A first for Shane. He'd never been in the same room with a woman for longer than ten minutes before she'd demanded his full attention. Most of his companions wanted more than conversation—cuddling, kissing, sex. Devin went against the norm, allowing him more freedom than he sought in her presence.

He craned his neck. From what he could see, Devin was working on a page with Cinderella at the ball. To his immense relief, Cindy had blond hair. Apparently Devin was no longer mad at him.

"Ready to eat?" he asked.

She nodded. "Whenever you are." She closed her coloring book and returned the crayons to their box.

He closed down his computer, then stood. He patted his stomach. "I'm thinking buffalo wings. Fire-breathers, Dev."

"They sound hot."

"Hot as hell. It's time to tame the dragon."

Dare Calder stumbled against the sofa Devin James had recently vacated. He dropped down hard. He'd never felt so puny. "Darn tuckered out," he mumbled.

"Breathing has become quite difficult," Rose Coltraine said, panting. "My heartbeat has slowed."

Calder looked at Rose. The saloon proprietress had grown pale, a mere shadow of herself. And he knew he'd shrunk, standing under six feet.

Sadly, the vivid colors of life had begun to blur. His black denims were closer to gray, and the polish on his six-shooter was dim.

The bloom was off the rose. The pink hues Miss Coltraine favored were now a dull snuff shade. Tobacco was not her color.

Dare Calder knew the reason behind their failing energy. Attraction now stirred in their creators' souls. Devin and Shane had kissed and touched, and now held an emotional truce. He prayed it would be short-lived. They were about to break bread; perhaps even enjoy their shared meal. Their truce put a hitch in Calder's giddyap. It diffused his presence, spreading him thin as air. He couldn't live on their happiness. He needed them riled.

Only Devin's uncertainty secured his life force. She'd called Shane a mistake. That mistake kept Calder breathing.

He wasn't about to give up the ghost. Not without a damn good fight. Joy Ford had felt their surging life-blood, she'd sensed he and Rose were more than characters.

"It's time to lay a false scent," he declared. "I'm about to put a twist in this tale."

"I'm here to help you, sir," Rose rasped, her voice no more than a whisper.

"Save your strength, darlin'." It took great effort for him to wink. "I want your heart strong, pumpin' as wildly as my hips, when I take you to my bed."

Rose Coltraine lost all color.

Chapter Eight

Scarlet Garter

"Got a hankerin' for Miss Rose, don't ya?" Doc Wabash curved his eighty-six-year-old spine against the back of the wooden rocker set out just for him on the boardwalk in front of Cormet's General Store. He hooked his thumbs in his prize red suspenders and rocked back. "Goin' courtin', son?"

Dare Calder leaned against the door frame, and rolled a cigarette. He listened, but didn't reply. He'd never been one for idle chitchat. Positioned to keep an eye on the comings and goings at the Scarlet Garter, he watched the town heat up on a Friday night.

All about him, women in long dresses, shawls, and bonnets, along with their menfolk dressed in black suits, string ties, and bowler hats, strolled the rustic planks. Wagons rattled up and down the street. Eager cowhands rode into town, young, brash, and letting off steam occasionally with a whoop and a holler.

Amid it all, Doc Wabash produced a toothpick from the front pocket of his worn shirt and shoved it between his false teeth. "Strange new faces every day," he commented on those passing by. "Town mushroomed from fifteen hundred to five thousand in under two years. Was a time when everyone knew everyone else. Nice and homey-like. Now not even I can keep track of who's headin' in, who's lightin' out."

"I'll be goin'," the gunslinger said flatly.

"Goin' courtin'," Doc chuckled, a deep rattle of bones and age. "My advice to you, boy: taste all the words before you spit 'em out. A man'll say most anythin' to peek under a petticoat. One peek ain't worth exchangin' vows."

Calder slapped the old geezer on the shoulder before stepping off the boardwalk and out from under the overhanging second-story porches that covered the wooden planks in front of most stores the length of Bonanza Street. Grinding his cigarette out in the dust with his boot heel, he crossed the street. His spurs jingled a little, and tiny puffs of dust rose from his boots as he walked. There was a grim set to his jaw and a determined hardness to his gaze. There was no quit in him today.

That very morning, as the sun edged over the horizon, he'd met with Miss Rose in a separate sitting room just off her bedroom and related the details of the robbery. He'd returned the stolen bags of money and relinquished his winnings from the poker game.

Point-blank, he'd informed Rose that the two men she respected and admired the most had stolen from her. One was now proved an adulterer; both were thieves.

Her spine straight, her chin held high, Rose accepted the gunslinger's justice between sips of hot chocolate and small bites of a buttermilk biscuit. Though she'd wished to interrogate Wayne Cutter herself, she understood Calder's determination to protect her from the man.

"Retribution comes in many forms," Calder had told her. "Penelope Morgan's memory will haunt both men like a living ghost for the rest of their lives."

Rose had thanked Calder with a handshake and a smile of gratitude. He had wanted to kiss her, had wanted to collect on their agreement of two kisses for Wayne Cutter's downfall. He'd hoped to kiss her into forgetting that good men like Cutter and Morgan faced temptation and lost, and that even the worst men like himself found redemption with the right woman in their arms.

Someday soon he would collect on those kisses.

Now, as dusk turned to darkness, he entered the Scarlet Garter and took the stairs two at a time.

The hour had come for courtin' Miss Rose Coltraine.

He found the hallway empty, the door to her room ajar. He knocked, then kicked the door open before he received an answer.

Miss Rose sat at a rolltop desk, plumed pen in hand, working over a ledger. She tilted her head in question. "Mr. Calder?"

His intrusions no longer startled her, Dare realized. She had adjusted to his untimely visits. "Evenin', Rose."

She brushed the white feather along her delicate jaw. His gaze had not left hers, and now color was coming into her cheeks, as delicately pink as her gown. "Something on your mind, sir?"

"A woman."

"Which woman, Mr. Calder?" Rose asked, obviously

baffled. "Each time I pass you on the street, I can't help noticing how the townswomen never fail to look at you twice. And when their eyes meet yours I can almost hear their hearts pound. A reaction that you enjoy and encourage, usually with a bold wink."

"Nice to know you've been watchin' me, Rose, 'cause I've been watchin' you too."

He walked toward her, straight, tall, purposeful, stopping before her desk. Their eyes met—and held. Her gaze was wide, uncertain. She set down the plumed pen and folded her hands in her lap.

Determination prodded him. "I'd like to start seein' you."

She blinked. "Seeing me? Out paths cross daily, sir. You're a hard man to miss."

As he looked at her, something fierce and foreign fought to replace his harsh outlook on life. A tightness twisted in his chest that even a deep breath could not unwind. "I'm talkin' courtin', Rose."

"Oh . . . my."

"I'll not be hobbled," he warned in advance. "No city suit, no slicked-back hair, no bouquet of pansies in my hand."

She ran her palms down the wide pleats on the skirt of her pink gown. "My only request is that you shave, Mr. Calder."

He scrubbed his knuckles along his jaw. "I was born with whiskers. My face will never be clean-shaven."

"I see. . . ."

"There'll be no heartfelt poems or declarations of love." He wanted his intentions laid as wide-open as the land he'd soon roam again. "I'm a drifter, Rose, not a family man."

A fleeting expression crossed her features. Something akin to pity darkened her gaze. "You have no wish for a son to carry on your name?"

"I'd rather take a bullet to the groin."

His bluntness startled her. She blinked, and he cut to the chase. "Henry Sweet's Café. One hour."

She studied the starched folds of her skirt, a beautiful woman, pensive and perceptive . . . and unresponsive.

Rose Coltraine needed more from him, and he had so little to give. "Perhaps a twilight buggy ride, sharing the moon and the stars." His throat nearly closed on the invitation.

"Such sweet words, Mr. Calder."

He swallowed hard. "They don't come easy, Rose. A man who lives by the gun will forever be alone. But there are times even he seeks the warmth of a woman."

"Until recently you've slept at Eve's Garden."

She wasn't making this easy for him. "I'm presently standin' before you at the Scarlet Garter. Care to dine with me?"

Her silence held far longer than he liked. A deep restlessness settled in his bones. He paced from her rolltop desk to the door and back again. Her silence spoke louder than words. He waved his hand in dismissal. "Forget I ever—"

"I'd like to have dinner with you," she slowly accepted. "I'll meet you at Sweet's Café at five o'clock."

Rose Coltraine would meet him at Sweet's. She would not allow him to escort her down the boardwalk in broad daylight. He was not a suitable suitor. She had refused a public courting.

Disappointment curled in his belly.

His chest tight, Calder tipped his Stetson, turned on his heel, and hit the door in two long strides.

* * *

Ninety minutes passed before Dare Calder joined Rose Coltraine at Sweet's Café. It wasn't his fault he'd run late. He'd never turned his back on a fight, and tonight was no exception.

After he'd left Rose, he'd returned to the bar for two fingers of whiskey, and to study the crowd. Bounty hunter Art Noble had yet to track him to Cutter's Bend. But that didn't stop Dare from noting each new arrival through the bat-wing doors.

Two young mustangers had caught his eye. The men drank heavily and were hunting trouble. The barkeep had been too busy serving customers to notice their polished six-shooters. Until Rose hired new gunmen, it was Calder's job to keep peace at the Garter. He watched as the two men pushed through the crowd, eyes shifting, seeking a mark.

The mark became Ty Billingsly, a middle-aged, square-faced man bent more on drinking than playing cards. He was down to his last silver dollar.

The young guns circled the table and moved to his back. Dare Calder moved right along with them.

"Get up, old man. You're in my seat." The taller of the two men shoved the back of Billingsly's chair, gaining the older man's attention.

"Why'd you take Logan's seat?" the shorter trouble-maker pressed.

"Make him get up, Del," the one known as Logan commanded.

Del hefted Billingsly from the chair.

Billingsly resisted. His wild swing missed Del by a country mile.

"Wanna play rough?" Del spat in the older man's face.

"Not as rough as I do." Dare Calder stepped forward. His left hand brushed back over metal as his palm cocked the hammer. "I'm no judge of a thousandth of a second anymore. That could be the difference between your livin' or dyin'."

All conversation ceased. An air of menace surrounded Calder. Primed for bloodshed, he waited for the wild youngsters to make their move.

Del came to his senses first. He shoved Ty Billingsly back onto his chair. "There's a seat yonder that'll do me fine."

His partner, filled with liquor and excess energy, itched for a showdown. "Think you can kill us both?"

"I could drop this entire room." Calder showed Logan how fast he would go down. In the blink of an eye his gun cleared leather, the barrel pointed at the rowdy's heart. "You've no business in this establishment. Care to continue breathin', or shall the undertaker measure you for a box?"

"Just passin' through. We'll stay the night and be gone by sunup." Logan curled his lip and took his last verbal shot. "But we'll meet again. Be assured, gunslinger."

Calder holstered his gun. He'd saved the Garter from a costly fight. Broken shot glasses and bottles of whiskey, overturned tables and chairs, shattered mirrors, perhaps bloodstains on the hardwood floor—the damage would have shut down business for a long, long time.

In his mind Rose Coltraine owed him a sweet kiss of gratitude.

Now he strode with purpose down the boardwalk, toward Sweet's Café. Soft kerosene light spread from the café front window, casting a glow onto the long wooden planks. Through the window, Calder spotted Rose sitting at a table for two.

Two. Her dinner companion was rancher Wayne Cutter.

"Table for two, McNamara," Shane said to the hostess as he and Devin entered Saltwater Cowboys. He immediately liked the eclectic feel of the place.

An enormous seahorse sporting a red Stetson dominated the entry to the popular beachside bar and grill. The waiting line stretched into the parking lot. He decided sitting in the bar with a cold beer was preferable to standing on the hot asphalt.

Inside, the scents of fried fish and hush puppies mixed with the tang of barbecue. The restaurant was a unique combination of Old West and southern seashore. High against the rafters, fishermen's nets clutched both starfish and tumbleweeds, while wagon wheels hung from sand-cast walls and giant coral whitened the sawdust floors. Deeply inset tables decorated with shells and horseshoes were topped with thick aqua glass.

Waitresses bumped hips with customers as they took orders and served food. The place was loud and friendly.

"Left, Devin." He motioned toward the low-slung western bar door. "I could go for—"

Jamie Jensen. The door parted with the force of the singer's personality. Ross Hunter strolled in her wake, followed by several members of her band, Southern Comfort.

"Shane!" Jamie's shriek turned heads.

He felt Devin draw back slightly, and made a grab for her elbow. He pulled her to his side. She was too polite to make a scene and resist his hold in public.

In the space of a heartbeat Jamie parted the crowd and came to Shane. Skintight white leather riveted with silver studs skimmed her curves. The zipper on her jacket rested at her cleavage. Body glitter shimmered on her breasts, adding to her glow.

"We meet again." Jamie's voice rang with satisfaction.

Jamie came at him full force. He lost hold of Devin's elbow as she took a step back. His attempt to dodge J.J.'s hands and hips turned into an outright struggle. The singer raked her weapon-length nails down his black polo, then snugged her hips against his black jeans. A very warm welcome from a hot country star. Shane's only heat came from embarrassment.

"I'm so glad to see you," J.J. breathed against his mouth.

Shane backed away, and squarely into Devin. The heel of his leather loafer crushed the toe of her saddle shoes.

"I need that foot." She hopped back, pinching his arm hard enough to bruise.

"Sorry," he mumbled as Jamie nibbled at his lips.

Shane's breath exploded in a frustrated sigh. He sought Ross Hunter over Jamie's red head. "Evening, Ross." Shane extended his hand.

"Good to see you, pard," Ross replied.

Once he'd shaken Ross's hand, Jamie interlaced her fingers with his. "You're mine for the night."

Oh, no, he wasn't. Shane set her aside with both force and finesse. "I'm not on the menu, J.J."

J.J. sniffed. "Still resisting?"

"I'm still convinced we're better apart." A hemisphere apart.

"I have faith in fate."

Dipping two fingers into her cleavage, she pulled out a picture. "I still hold you close to my heart."

Jostled by the crowd moving around inside the grill

and bar, Shane glanced at the tiny photograph taken eight months and eight hundred fights, misunderstandings, and disagreements ago. The photo showed them sitting on a cream satin love seat in a hotel room during one of her tours. Atlanta, he recalled. They looked as sewn together as the fabric covering the settee for two.

He hadn't been smiling then, and he sure as hell wasn't smiling now. "Not a Kodak moment."

"I've albums filled with us." She tucked the picture back between her breasts.

Shane hadn't a single picture of their time together. The flash of her camera would never again go off in his face. "No more snapshots."

She licked lips glossed to the shade of Southern peaches. "Just one more close-up?"

He held her hands at her sides when she would have wrapped them around his neck. He needed air. He stepped back.

Where was Devin? He instinctively knew she no longer stood behind him. Turning to his left he caught the swing of her wheaten braid as she wound through the crowd, now headed toward the door.

His heart kicked in panic. She couldn't leave. He wouldn't let her.

"Excuse me," he said to Jamie, who gaped at his departure.

Dodging waitresses and customers, he made his way toward Devin. He caught her with one foot out the door.

"Leaving so soon?" He kept his voice light.

She looked at him for a long moment. "I'm surprised you noticed."

He'd noticed all right. "Where were you going?"

"To get a little fresh air," she informed him. "The

crush of the crowd was a bit overwhelming."

"Would you rather eat elsewhere?"

She looked up and stared across the room. "No, you'd be happier here."

Not necessarily. "I'd be grateful if you stayed."

Her brows furrowed and she appeared confused.

"I'd be even more grateful if you would join us for dinner," Ross Hunter put in as he came to stand beside Shane. "One meal, a personal favor, pard."

"Joining your party isn't an option," Shane said firmly. "Devin and I—"

"Devin?" Ross acknowledged her for the first time.

"Devin James, coauthor of the book we're working on. Devin, meet Ross Hunter, Jamie Jensen's band manager," Shane said.

Shane watched as Ross took her in. Although Ross never looked beyond her face, he studied her closely. Ross's expression shifted from one of politeness to one of interest. Shane had the strangest sensation that Ross saw something in Devin that Shane had yet to see.

"Nice to meet you." Ross held out his hand.

Devin shook it. "My pleasure."

Ross then jammed his hands into the pockets of his gray chinos and shuffled his feet. "Jamie will have my head—"

"If you don't bring Shane back on a platter," Devin supplied.

Ross shrugged. "I merely do her bidding."

Shane shook his head. "Her whining can bring grown men to their knees."

"Stand tall, Ross." Devin patted his shoulder. "We'll join you for dinner."

"It'll be eat and run," Shane added.

Shane kept his eye on Devin as they made their way back toward Jamie and her band.

Shane made quick work of the introductions. "Devin James, my writing partner, meet Jamie Jensen, country's finest."

Devin smiled, and the singer dismissed her with a cool nod.

"This is Lake Crawford, lead guitar, and Bowie Sawyer, keyboard," Shane continued. "Montgomery Austin and Davie Crowe are still in the bar."

Shane didn't like the way Lake Crawford stepped forward and took Devin's hand. He clasped it overly long, and his smile held too much interest for Shane's liking.

"Your table is ready, Miss Jensen." The hostess approached, menus in hand, as she directed the group to a rectangular table in the far corner of the room.

"I love my privacy." Jamie Jensen hitched her chair so close to Shane's that the edges overlapped, pinching his thigh.

He pressed the back of his chair against the sandstone wall, creating a hairbreadth of space. Dinner for two had turned into a disaster for six.

He looked around Jamie to where Devin now sat, between the singer and Lake Crawford. He didn't like the way Crawford had cozied up to Devin. It irked him royally. He knew men like Crawford with their lazy but lucky let's-get-naked smiles. Hell, Shane had practiced that smile from his crib. Perversely, he didn't want that smile used on Devin. Not by Lake Crawford, anyway.

Poor, besotted Ross Hunter sat beside Lake. Although he exchanged conversation with the band members, his gaze singled out Jamie with long, lingering looks.

Jamie ignored Ross, which was her style. She was focusing all her energy on winning Shane back. Shane was not a trophy for her shelf. Never had been, never would be.

He fisted his hands in frustration. The manager wanted Jamie. Better than anyone, Ross knew J.J.'s faults. He'd managed Southern Comfort from the start of her career. If he could live with spoiled and self-centered, more power to him. Perhaps Ross had glimpsed a side of Jamie that Shane had never seen.

"I love you, Shane." Jamie took his hands and smiled expectantly, waiting for him to reciprocate.

J.J. had tunnel vision. If he was the least bit encouraging, she'd take it as a sign they were getting back together. She clung to a past that had no future. His tomorrows no longer centered around her. "You're a good friend, J.J."

"Friend?" Her lovely mouth pinched in a not-so-pretty line.

"A good friend—"

"But an amazing lover. Let me convince you." She kissed him full on the lips.

"Care to order?" Their waitress cast a congenial smile over the table at large.

"More than ready," Shane said, pulling back from Jamie.

"What looks good, sir?" the waitress asked.

"The exit," Shane muttered to himself, then ordered. "A large basket of fire-breathers, extra celery and bleu cheese dressing."

Jamie turned on him, pouting. "I wanted fish."

"Then order fish," Shane said simply. "Devin and I decided on buffalo wings before we hitched up with you."

The singer had enough fire in her eyes to barbecue baskets of wings. "I'll have grouper fingers, crispy, and a side of curly fries."

"Split a vegetable platter with me?" Lake Crawford asked Devin when it came his turn to order.

Devin nodded. "Sounds good."

It didn't sound good to Shane. When the food arrived and the good-time cowboy dipped a baby carrot in ranch dressing and fed it to Devin, Shane had the urge to upend the platter in Crawford's lap. He shot Devin a disapproving look. Wide-eyed, she lifted her shoulder and had the nerve to shrug off his concern.

"Feed me, baby."

J.J.'s request irked Shane. He didn't need to feed her. The woman had two perfectly good hands, ten functioning fingers.

"I'm hungry, Shane," she said insistently.

Shane glanced at Devin. She was helping herself to the buffalo wings. Nibbling on one, she swallowed slowly, her obvious pleasure in the food seductive. Bowie Sawyer couldn't take his eyes off her, and Crawford edged closer in anticipation of her next bite.

When a drop of barbeque sauce stained the lapel of Devin's green blazer, Crawford dove for the water glass. Wetting a napkin, he scrubbed at the spot. Devin's heightened color told Shane the man's hand had brushed more than linen.

If Crawford touched her again . . .

Shane rubbed the back of his neck in an attempt to relax. Relaxation evaded him. This was not the meal he'd envisioned when he'd invited Devin to dinner.

Jamie stirred at his side. She flattened her palm on his knee and scratched her lethal nails toward his groin. Nails that could end his ability to father children. "A woman could starve to death waiting for her man to feed her."

He was not her man, and he had no intention of feeding her.

Memories of a vanilla milk shake dumped in his lap, and a chili burger ground into his favorite Levi's jacket, reminded Shane how Jamie retaliated when denied her way. During their months together, he'd taken enough clothing to the dry cleaners to open his own franchise.

Still, he refused. "Help yourself, J.J.; food's getting cold."

She glared her displeasure as he grabbed a buffalo wing and stripped the meat with his teeth.

Hot, hot, hot! He'd wolfed down the wing, and was now breathing fire. The barbecue sauce burned his gums and tongue and caused his eyes to water. He gasped, coughed, swore the sauce was burning a hole in his esophagus.

Devin's braid swung into his vision as she leaned across Jamie and said, "Careful, McNamara. Lake said the wings should be savored." Her pink tongue flicked barbecue sauce from the tips of her fingers. "A little celery between bites cuts the burn."

Lake said! Hell, he knew how to eat buffalo wings. He'd lived on fire-breathers half his life. He grew angry over the fact that Crawford had introduced Devin to her first hot bite when it should have been he.

Devin wished she were sitting closer to Shane. She further wished she could escape Lake Crawford. The man came on too strong. She'd rather eat alone, bellied up to the bar, than have Lake feed her one more vegetable.

She tried to catch Shane's eye, but the back of Jamie's head blocked her attempts. She hadn't seen the singer's face since they had sat down. Engaged in intimate conversation, Shane and Jamie looked as if they lived only for each other.

Envy touched Devin's heart. If she'd been coloring a picture of herself, she would have colored her eyes green.

Devin sighed, and somehow Lake took her sigh as meant for him. He made his move. Sliding his arm along the back of her chair, he leaned close and stroked her neck. "You, me, my hotel room."

Devin blushed. She prayed the entire table hadn't overheard.

Of all the people to hear, Shane had caught Lake's invitation. "Crawford." His voice was low and tight as he nodded toward the door. "You, me *outside*."

"Now?" Crawford straightened, visibly confused.

"Right now."

Shane stood so quickly he banged his knee against the table leg, jarring both food and beverages. Several beers slapped the rims of their mugs, and a dozen cherry tomatoes rolled off the veggie platter. One overly ripe tomato splattered against Jamie Jensen's silverware, spitting seeds onto her knife.

"What's going on?" Jamie demanded.

Ross hunter rocked his chair back on two legs. "Let it go, J.J."

Jamie grabbed Shane's arm as he rounded her chair. "You will come back, won't you?"

"It all depends on Crawford," he said, more tense than Devin had ever seen him.

"Whatever's going on, fix it, Lake," Jamie called to the two men as they left the table.

Lake shrugged, looking puzzled. "I wasn't aware there was a problem."

"Definitely a problem," Devin heard Ross mumble as he returned his chair to the floor with a thud.

Devin hadn't a clue as to the cause of Shane's irritation. But mad he'd been. And for whatever reason, his anger was directed at Lake Crawford.

Maybe she should follow them. . . .

Jamie laid her hand on Devin's arm. Her smile was anything but friendly. "So you're the workhorse."

"Workhorse?" Devin wasn't sure what Jamie meant.

"The sidekick who's pushing Shane to work when he'd rather spend time with me."

Shane, the man of a million breaks, couldn't find time for Jamie? It didn't make sense. "We have a book to complete."

Jamie picked at her grouper fingers. "Tell me about this book."

Devin was hesitant to talk about *Calder's Rose*. Until a novel reached completion, she kept the story line under wraps. "It's progressing nicely."

"Is this the first time you've written with a partner?"

Devin traced the edge of her napkin. "I believe it's the first time either of us has written with a partner."

"Tell me about your relationship," Jamie pried.

"It's strictly business. Silver Star Publishing has given us six weeks to produce a romantic adventure novel. We're on a tight deadline."

Jamie flicked the base of her water glass with one long nail. "Maybe with this book he'll pitch more than manure."

Devin blinked. "You're saying his books are . . . are . . ."

"Crap. The man's knee-deep in a dead-end career."

"He's very successful—"

Jamie waved her off. "Don't defend his maverick mentality. The man's a throwback to the Wild West."

Devin liked that side of Shane, his quick-triggered wit, killer smile, and easy swagger. His unruliness. "He's definitely his own man."

"A man I want, maverick or not." Possessiveness flickered in the singer's amber gaze. "He's promised that once the book is completed, he'll join me on my tour."

Devin's chest grew so tight she could hardly breathe. She resisted the urge to massage her heart. "I know he's looking forward to your concert tomorrow night."

Jamie tossed her red hair over her shoulder. "Of course he is, and don't you forget it."

Nothing about this conversation would ever be forgotten. Devin had never felt more down. On the upside, however, Shane would now buckle down and write like a madman. His anticipation of joining Jamie on tour should motivate him to bring the book in on deadline.

"Shane, you're back!" Jamie jumped off her chair and grabbed his arm.

"Only to get Devin. We're leaving," he informed the singer.

Devin looked from Shane to Lake Crawford, who had dropped back into the chair next to her. Lake shoved his thumbs in his belt loops and sat still as stone.

"You can't leave," Jamie said sharply.

Shane pulled out Devin's chair, nearly unseating her. "Devin and I have a book to write. We'd planned to grab a quick bite and return to the cottage, not spend the evening socializing."

Jamie eyed the two of them suspiciously.

"That's the truth," Devin said as she stood.

Jamie pulled on Shane's arm. "I want you to stay."

Shane removed Jamie's fingers from his arm, one by one. "This isn't negotiable." He saluted the table. "Night, everyone."

"See you—" Devin was never allowed to finish.

Shane's grip on her elbow was almost painful as he turned her toward the door.

"I can find my own way." Pulling free, she bumped into a waitress serving a table of eight. "Sorry."

"I can find it faster." He snagged her hand this time and pulled her in his wake, parting the crowd with his haste and dark expression.

Comprehension failed her. Shane McNamara was deserting a famous country star and a night of enviable sex to quibble with his writing partner over his hero bedding her heroine.

She shook her head. The man was one bullet shy of a loaded cartridge.

"Dinner proved interesting," Devin said as she slid into the Porsche and fastened her seat belt.

Shane remained silent as he started the engine. The engine vibrated with power as he hit reverse, then slammed into first and peeled from the parking lot at race-car speed.

Sexual frustration? Devin wondered. Some men found speed a form of release. Whatever the reason, Shane was driving like a bat out of hell.

Covering his hand, she refused to let him shift into fourth. She jabbed her finger toward the nearest side street. "Pull over, McNamara. I want to live to finish our book."

Shane hit the brake and slowed so quickly she braced both hands against the dashboard. Only the restless rumble of the sports car split the night as he parked on the shoulder of a dead-end street and let it idle.

"Care to share the madness?" she asked.

He thumped the steering wheel with his palm. His gaze was as metallic as an overcast sky. "I'm hungry."

Hungry for food or Jamie Jensen? "I thought you filled up on buffalo wings."

"I didn't have a veggie platter to round off my meal."

His sarcasm was unwarranted. "Lake and I would have shared; you need only have asked. There were plenty of vegetables to go around."

Lake and Devin. Shane felt the full confinement of his seat belt when he wanted to leap from the Porsche and pace the roadway. "I didn't want to interrupt your intimate hand-to-mouth."

Her chin lifted a notch. "Lake fed me three carrots."

He had counted four carrots, six celery sticks, and eight slices of yellow squash, even with Jamie's distractions.

"Didn't you enjoy your meal?" she asked.

"The little I ate." He'd been too busy watching Crawford to finish off the wings.

He had nearly leaped over the table when Lake stroked Devin's neck. The unwanted image plucked a jealous chord. Jealousy was as foreign to him as an out-of-body experience.

"Care to share your chat with Crawford?" Devin asked.

He stared out his window, avoiding her gaze. "We discussed you."

"Why me?" He heard the genuine surprise in her voice.

He ran his hand through his hair, feeling uncomfortable as hell. "I told Lake to stay away from you until we've completed the book."

"Why would you say such a thing?"

Jealousy made a man say things he might not say when sane. "You need to pull your own weight."

Her voice hitched. "I haven't thus far?"

"So far so good," he relented. "But—"

"But *what?*"

"Visiting Crawford's hotel room would have been a mistake."

"A mistake?"

"A mistake worse than us." He finally met her gaze. "Crawford's a one-night stand. And sex zaps the creative flow."

"Sex zaps? How have you ever finished a book?" She sat and stared at him for so long, he waved his hand before her eyes to make her blink. "What made you think I would leave with Lake?"

He wasn't sure she would have, but he'd been scared as hell she might. "I didn't know, actually. Our conversation was purely precautionary."

"Big-brother precautionary?"

He'd never looked at her as a little sister. "Exactly."

"The book comes first, Shane." She fingered the strap on her seat belt. "I thought you knew that."

Where Devin was concerned, he no longer knew his own name. She confused him to the point that he didn't know what was up or down. He felt as if he were moving more backward that forward with her.

Vulnerability sucked. It was time to head home before he threw himself a pity party.

He jammed in the clutch, shifted, and spun the wheel sharply. It was time to retreat to *Calder's Rose.* He might not have much of a say in Devin James's life, but he could dictate the actions of his gunslinger. Dare Calder was the only constant in his life.

Back at the cottage, he and Devin exited the vehicle and walked toward the front door. A cold chill burst from the interior of the cottage as Shane unlocked the front door. He pushed her protectively behind him as he entered ahead of her. His shoulder blades twitched, and then he stiffened, dead certain someone was watching him.

"It's cold as a morgue in here." Devin stood so close behind him, her breasts pressed into his back. He felt her shiver.

"The cottage feels haunted." She flipped on the pole lamp near the sofa, and Shane searched the shadows.

No one. He returned to Devin, whose color had fled. He didn't want her scared. "I've no time for ghosts or horror stories, but things that go bump and grind in the night really turn me on."

She blushed, then noted. "The room has grown warmer."

"I'm a hot-blooded male."

She looked as him with apparent appreciation. Maybe she wasn't as immune to him as she'd have him believe. He had no time to test his theory. Over Devin's shoulder, he caught the flash of her screen saver, a continuous parade of her book covers.

He walked toward her desk. "I thought you'd turned off your computer."

"I did, when Joy left."

He scratched his head. "It's on now."

"How can that be possible?"

"I haven't a clue, Dev."

She touched his arm. "Was someone here?"

"That's what I'm trying to figure out."

He took her hand and drew her to her chair. She sat down slowly. He dragged the fan-back next to her leather swivel. "Pull up *Calder's Rose*."

He was apprehensive about what they would find. He had the uneasy feeling there would be changes to the manuscript. Changes he could neither define nor explain.

He soon discovered more changes than he could count.

The alterations didn't bother Devin as much as the fact they'd been made without her knowledge. When had Shane managed to fill in the blanks that Joy had left with her hunt and peck? When had he found time to have Calder court Rose Coltraine?

She was suddenly afraid to ask him. Afraid he wouldn't have the answers she needed to hear. They sat in a nerve-racking silence that was almost frightening.

Devin swallowed. "Except for the hour you went jogging and I took a swim, we haven't left each other's sight."

"What's been written would have taken even a fast writer longer than sixty minutes to produce," Shane said.

"It's good writing," Devin admitted.

"Lifted straight from our imaginations."

"It's almost as if someone were reading our minds."

He leaned back and crossed his ankle over his knee. "Who would be capable of doing that?"

"No one . . . living?"

They looked at each other then, uneasy with the thought they were both considering.

Shane shook his head. "There has to be another explanation."

"I'm not fond of the paranormal." She ran her fingers along the edge of her desk. "Evidence to the contrary would suit me just fine."

"Let's think this through." He stood and started to pace.

Devin turned off her computer. Seeing the words there made her edgy. She moved to the sofa. "I've got all night."

"Things that go bump and grind..." His words faded to a slow smile as he strolled to the corner of the couch. "Ready to pull out our bed?"

Devin clutched a throw pillow to her chest. She feared Shane McNamara more that the paranormal.

"Nice bosom, Miss Coltraine." The power of Dare Calder's gaze touched her physically.

Rose studied him closely. Tan and fit, he once again rippled with strength. "Keep your voice down, Mr. Calder"—she nodded toward the sofa bed where Devin slept and Shane dozed off and on—"or you'll disturb their slumber."

"I like feelin' alive," Calder admitted, his voice loud enough to wake the dead.

Rose lowered her voice to a whisper. "We're living on borrowed time," she reminded him. "Shane and Devin's attraction is inevitable."

"Their fallin' in love would kill us, but that ain't goin' to happen. Fear in their hearts will keep our hearts beatin'."

"Fear is a powerful emotion," she agreed.

"McNamara ain't lily-livered," Calder begrudgingly defended Shane. "He has, however, grown apprehensive and cautious, and protective of Devin."

"As well as he should," Rose approved.

Calder tipped back his Stetson and rubbed his whiskered jaw. An unholy light filled his gaze. "Then there's that Jensen woman. Pretty little filly. Shane may choose her over Devin."

Something snapped inside Rose. "Shane wouldn't know a pearl from an ox turd."

Calder's jaw hit the floor.

Mortified, Rose covered her mouth with both hands.

She'd sinned! Her sterling reputation would be tarnished by her reprehensible outburst.

"Hoo-boy!" Dare recovered first. His lips twitched, his gaze alive with laughter. "The prude's got spit in her after all."

She clutched her hands together as if in prayer. "I beg your pardon, Mr. Calder. Bitterness overtook me."

"Apology accepted, Miss Coltraine."

Rose sighed. "In truth, I prefer their anger to their jealousy."

Calder shrugged. "I'll breathe whichever emotion keeps me alive."

The man was selfish and tough as saddle leather. "While we live, let's continue with our story."

He moved disturbingly close. "Courtin' time, Rose."

No words could express her sudden fear of him. He would trample her heart.

"You got lockjaw, woman?" He swore against her silence. "Look, lady, the quicker we get to courtin', the quicker I cut trail."

She meant no more to him than trail dust.

Near the center of the room Shane McNamara stirred. The comforter and sheets rustled as he turned toward Devin James.

Rose and Dare stepped back into the shadows.

"Damn, Shane has wakened," Calder noted.

Rose sighed softly. "He's watching Devin sleep once again."

"That has to be borin'."

She craned her neck. "He doesn't seem bored. His face is relaxed, and he's . . . and he's smiling, sir."

"The man's gone simple."

"I'd say he looks content."

"That's not what I'm wantin' to hear, Rose."

With those words, Dare Calder walked into the darkness.

Chapter Nine

Devin James awakened slowly. She felt warm, safe, and aroused. She opened her eyes and died a slow death. Sometime during the night the sheet, the comforter, and pillows arranged between her and Shane had given way beneath the force of their attraction. The two of them were now pressed together like magnets. Only a breath separated them. Her face was buried against his shoulder, and her body embraced his.

"Good morning," Shane said against her ear.

Devin eased back and tugged down her sweatshirt, which was close to revealing her breasts. She met his amused gaze. "How long have we—"

"Been wrapped like ivy?" He chuckled as he hiked up his sweatpants from where they dipped below his navel. "Since midnight."

Seven hours had since elapsed. Seven hours of being held in Shane's arms. Seven hours during which she'd slept, when she could have enjoyed every solid inch of him. A good number of those inches were pressing her abdomen.

She wanted to rub against him. Her desire was strong, but so was the image of Jamie Jensen at Saltwater Cowboys. The singer's claim that Shane would join her tour once the book was completed prodded Devin to rise.

She rolled off the sofa bed and stood by the armrest. She looked around the room. "Was it quiet last night?"

"No computer action," he informed her as he also slid from the bed. He stretched then, lean and tall in his navy sweat suit.

She pulled at the sleeve of her red sweatshirt. "That's a relief."

He turned toward his bedroom. "I'm going to catch a shower."

"I'll start the coffee."

"Make it Hazel Nutcracker. We've lots of work ahead."

The smell of coffee welcomed her back to the living room. Shane was already there in his *Night Wolf Tavern, Wolfsburg, Germany* T-shirt and worn jeans. He'd already stripped the sheets and comforter from the sofa bed, and folded them on a chair. All evidence of their night together disappeared as he shoved the bed back into the sofa. Devin replaced the cushions and decorative throw pillows.

"Coffee's on your desk," Shane said.

She went to turn on her computer.

The telephone rang just as he approached her desk. He grabbed the receiver. "Writer's cottage."

A man on the other end of the line asked for Devin James.

Shane turned his back on Devin. The line was clear

as a bell, yet for reasons unknown he pretended a poor connection. "Devin who?"

The man cleared his throat and repeated Devin's name with the clarity of a professor addressing a class.

He felt instant dislike for the man with the scholastic tone. "Who's calling?"

"Skip Huddleston."

Devin tapped his shoulder, causing him to jump. "For you or for me?"

He held the phone just beyond her reach and whispered, "Yippee Skippy. Are you here for him?"

She lifted a brow. "Any reason I shouldn't be?"

"I thought we were going to write."

"Give me five minutes."

He looked at his watch as he handed her the phone. She had exactly five minutes.

Devin dropped onto her chair and swiveled it sharply, giving him her back and her tight-ass braid. "Hello, Skip, what a pleasant surprise."

Not at all pleasant, in Shane's opinion.

"Yes, I'm fine. Eating properly and taking my vitamins."

The man was checking her nutrition and health? Shane rested his hip on the corner of her desk, and "accidentally" hit the button for the speakerphone. He liked three-way conversations.

Skip's voice entered the room, sounding remote and reserved. "It's quite cold here, close to zero. How's the weather in Naples?"

"Buck-naked hot," Shane answered for Devin.

"Buck what?" A mild inflection broke Skip's monotone.

"Warm, very warm." Devin turned, hit the off button on the speakerphone, and glared Shane away from her

243

desk. She covered the mouthpiece on the receiver. "Find something to do."

Something to do . . . He circled the coffee table, then caught sight of the bouquet of carnations. He stroked one stem until it snapped in two. Catching Devin's frown, he held up his hands. "Purely accidental."

He could tell she didn't believe him. Snatching a second carnation, he inched back toward her desk. "He loves me, he loves me not, he loves me." Shane picked off the petals until "he loves me not" landed on the heap.

Her lips pinched, Devin scooped up the discarded petals and dropped them into the trash can. She once again turned her back to him.

Shane's bratty inner child goaded him forward. He sneaked up behind her, filled with sinful thoughts.

"The book is going well," Devin continued. "Shane McNamara?" A significant pause, followed by, "Tall, dark-haired. Average-looking, no distinguishing features."

Average-looking? Vanity prodded him to glance in the decorative mirror near the Art Deco clock. Hell, he had strong, even features. A little rough around the edges, but no woman had run from him screaming.

"Shane helpful? At times. Our techniques differ greatly."

Technique? Shane had had years to perfect his technique. Especially when it came to loving. He bent near her ear and blew softly.

Devin swatted at him as if he were a pesky fly.

A pesky fly that flicked its tongue against her lobe with just enough moist heat to make her shiver. Her swat became an all-out slug.

He faded left and nuzzled the soft spot right beneath her ear.

She stilled, and Shane rubbed the shadow of his beard against the heightened flush of her cheek. The corner of his mouth brushed hers before he dipped lower and nipped the delicate tilt of her chin.

"Please repeat that, Skip."

Shane smiled. She'd lost her train of thought.

He wanted her to lose all presence of mind. Nuzzle. Nip. Lick. A kiss just beyond her lips. His wicked ministrations made her stutter. "Y-your thesis is taking you where?"

"Where's he going?" Shane asked.

"Berlin," she answered him, then returned to Skip. Another minute passed, and her face suddenly fell. "Your research should come first." A further pause. "We would be miles apart."

"Love the one you're with." Shane kissed her full on the lips.

For a split second she allowed the kiss, her mouth soft and pliant against his before she swiveled sharply, the chair arm missing his groin by no more than half an inch.

I'll kill you in your sleep, she mouthed angrily.

"Relax, Dev." Pressing his thumbs to the sides of her forehead, he began a slow downward massage, working the outer shell of her ears, the natural hollows of her cheeks, the pulse at the base of her throat. With all five fingers splayed over her collarbone, he circled the top of each breast. Her nipples peaked with arousal beneath the white linen blouse.

Devin jerked the lapels of her cinnamon blazer together. "Skip, one minute, please," she said into the phone.

Shane thought he had her. Thought he had her good when Devin slid her hand over his, interlaced

KATE ANGELL

their fingers, then drew his hand over her lips. He awaited her kiss. . . .

She bit his palm. Her teeth marks marred his flesh, crossing his heart line and lifeline. He jerked back, nearly falling over the arm of her chair. She elbowed him then, so sharply he swore he'd have a bruise. A final push sent him the extra distance to the floor. He landed hard. His oath took the Lord's name in vain.

She ignored the evil eye he cast upon her.

He, however, caught her fallen expression when she hung up the phone. He kicked himself for such childish behavior. He must take control of his inner child, a brat he never knew existed until Devin James hit an emotional nerve and turned him inside out.

Jealousy would be the death of him.

He gripped the edge of the desk and pulled himself to his feet. He rubbed his tailbone. "Slipped disk, I swear."

She rubbed the bridge of her nose. "Does it hurt as much as a breakup?"

His heart slowed, and he held his breath. "Breakup? You and Skip?"

"We agreed a long-distance relationship wasn't workable."

"You could pack up your laptop and join Skip in three weeks," he felt compelled to say. "Writers can work anywhere."

"I'd rather work stateside." She sighed heavily. "I don't know how you've maintained your relationship with Jamie Jensen. She travels all over the world. At least when we've completed *Calder's Rose*, you can join her tour."

Maintained a relationship? Join her tour? Where had Devin gotten such crazy notions? Surely not from him. Actions, however, spoke louder than words. Thinking back, Shane was certain she'd seen Jamie kissing him on SunBake Boardwalk, then again at Saltwater Cowboys.

Devin believed he still loved Jamie. Her reasons for pushing him away now became quite clear. She wasn't into sex for the fun of it. She would never have gotten involved with a man who loved another woman.

It would have been a mistake.

Devin had misread his intentions toward Jamie. Tonight, after the concert, he'd set Devin straight. With Skip headed for Berlin, and Jamie on to her next concert, he and Devin could explore their feelings, along with each other.

He'd prove to her they were not a mistake.

His heart felt suddenly light.

"Do you feel like writing for a while?" he asked. "Or would you rather mend your broken heart?"

She attempted a smile. "I'd rather write; work will help me heal."

Shane dropped down on the fan-back chair next to her leather swivel. "Let's see . . . Rose Coltraine has stood Dare Calder up for dinner. Pride keeps him from storming Sweet's Café. He's committed to a meal, yet Miss Rose has not granted him the same courtesy. Wayne Cutter has cozied up to her in his absence. Rose is toying with the idea of confronting the rancher about his theft. Let's outline from there."

Devin's typing was smooth and methodical. "Dressed in his Sunday finest, Cutter sits across from Rose."

"His wide girth once again bends the legs on the chair. The rungs squeak like a stuck pig. He'll soon be sitting on a pile of splinters."

Devin glared at him. "I won't make him the butt of your joke." She paused. "Rose, on the other hand, glows in a dignified pink gown with red rosettes."

"A second man hovers near the dining couple," Shane went on. "Calder recognizes him from the poker game. Tough, young, and brash, with dangling arms and itchy fingers, Smitty Sloan protects Cutter's back. Cutter claims rheumatism in his right hand. Sloan shoots with his left."

Devin tapped her fingers on the desktop. "Cutter is not rheumatic."

"Doc Wabash says he is."

"Wabash no longer practices medicine." She blew out a breath and continued, "Cutter lifts a bottle of white wine and refills Rose Coltraine's glass. She dips her head and smiles."

"Calder's scowl darkens," Shane said. "Quick as thought, he acts. There are ways to wound without gunfire. The back door offers him such an opportunity. He hightails it around the side of the building and cuts through the pantry to the kitchen. There he finds Henry Sweet slicing generous portions of rare roast beef onto a platter. A creamy horseradish sauce simmers on the stove."

"Calder tips his Stetson," Devin said. "The owner of the café continues to carve the roast."

"Calder reaches into the pocket of his dark trousers and extracts a gold piece," Shane said. "He then slips the gold piece under the platter."

"Calder asks Henry what the rancher plans to eat."

"Beef and cream sauce." Shane slapped his thigh. "It's easy for some extra horseradish to fall into the cream sauce. Calder and Sweet understand each other. Revenge will be sweet."

Devin rolled her eyes. "Cutter's going to cough himself into next week."

"Next year would be to Calder's liking." Shane crossed his arms over his chest and tucked his hands beneath his armpits. "Calder exits the kitchen and returns to the boardwalk. He enters the café the moment Wayne Cutter receives his meal. Lingering near the entrance, he watches Cutter cut his meat, take his first bite . . . and turn as red as a live coal." Shane laughed out loud. "The man can't hold his horseradish."

"Poor Cutter." Devin sighed.

"Breathing like a steam engine, Cutter lunges for his water glass. In his haste, the delicate crystal goblet tips and spills, showering Miss Rose. Cutter coughs, chokes, and thumps his chest. His hired gun calls for more water."

"Across from Cutter, Rose Coltraine rises stiffly," Devin cut in. "Her full tafetta skirt is soaked clear through to her petticoats."

"Dare Calder rides to her rescue," Shane said.

"Miss Rose smiles apologetically. She'd thought he'd stood her up for dinner. Wayne had been kind enough to keep her company."

"Kind, my ass," Shane said. "The man's a weasel."

"Calder explains that a showdown at the Garter made him late," Devin said. "Rose's gaze darkens with concern as she looks him over from his black Stetson to his western boots."

"Calder tells her no one was hurt. He's corralled the two young guns, and they'll be gone by sunup."

"Rose thanks him for protecting the Garter."

"Calder protects what is his."

"What, exactly, is his?" Devin swiveled her chair so fast she slammed into his knees.

Shane rubbed his kneecaps. "Wayne Cutter recently signed over his half of the Garter to Dare Calder."

Devin shook her head. "No, he did not."

"He most certainly did," Shane insisted. "Gunslinger

justice. Cutter transferred the deed for his freedom. A small price to avoid jail."

Devin wanted to lock up both Shane and Calder and throw away the key. "I'm not happy with the outcome of this scene."

Shane patted her on the shoulder. "Trust me, it's all for the good of the book."

She had a bad feeling about this plot twist. If Shane persisted with this partnership, then she would force the courtship. "Once Wayne Cutter's coughing spell eases, he tips his white Stetson and walks red-faced from the café. The meal is ruined for Rose. When Calder offers a buggy ride and picnic under the stars, she agrees."

Shane snorted. "Calder's never been on a picnic in his life."

"There's a first time for everything." Devin declared, leaving no room for argument. "It's time for Rose and Calder to engage their hearts and souls—"

"And their sex organs."

She wanted to scream. "Is sex always on your mind?"

"Not so much on *my* mind as it is on Calder's."

She thumped Shane on his forehead with her palm. "You create Calder's thoughts. Courtship doesn't guarantee consummation."

Shane backed his chair beyond her reach. "Let's get them on a quilt at the picnic and see if Calder nibbles more than a chicken breast."

"An hour later, Dare Calder hands Miss Rose up into a buggy he's rented from the livery." Devin was eager to move the story forward. "A fancy rig with a black leather seat, packed with an old patchwork quilt, a hamper of food prepared by Henry Sweet, and pulled by a high-stepping pony. Once seated, Rose fluffs out the skirt on her pink gown, still damp from the goblet Wayne Cutter overturned in her lap."

"A snap of the whip and the buggy rolls out of town," Shane continued. "Where are they headed?"

"Someplace quiet."

"How about the banks of Bent Tree Creek, just south of Cutter's Bend, and northeast of Horse Collar Junction?" he suggested.

Devin stopped typing. "You've researched—"

"Nothing that heavy," he confessed. "I scanned *Scoundrel's Kiss* and learned the lay of the land."

"Then you're aware the road's rutted, more fit for a single rider than a fancy buggy."

"My plans went to bump and bounce." He wiggled his brows suggestively. "A lot of bump and sway in the buggy gives a bounce to Rose's bosom that even the pleats on her bodice can't hide."

Devin brushed her bangs off her forehead and massaged her temples. "Can't they just enjoy the cool evening air, the incredible sunset?"

"Not when Calder's groin goes giddyap with each jostle and jounce."

She groaned. "Back to the sex?"

"Did we ever leave it?"

"Let's get them to Bent Tree Creek," she said. "There Calder can wade in the water and cool his libido."

"Do you think Rose would hike up her skirts and join him?" he asked.

"Rose Coltraine wouldn't wet a corner of her petticoat if Calder suddenly went facedown in the water and floated with the current."

Shane narrowed his eyes. "That's harsh, Dev. Once at the creek, Calder will find a thick cushion of sweet-smelling grass so he can spread the quilt, whip out—"

"Whip out what?"

"The food, Dev, relax." He had the nerve to look offended. "There's cold fried chicken, old-fashioned potato salad, and fresh apple pie."

"Rose settles at the opposite edge of the patchwork quilt, a good three feet from Calder and the hamper," Devin directed. "She tucks her skirt tightly beneath her, and waits for Calder to unpack the food."

"Breast?"

"Excuse me?"

"Calder just offered Rose a piece of chicken," Shane said.

"Rose would prefer a drumstick."

"Calder adds potato salad to her plate. With her first bite, a touch of dressing smears at the corner of her mouth. Calder leans in—"

"And hands her a linen napkin," Devin inserted before Shane had Calder licking the dressing from Rose's lips.

Shane's brows drew together. "This picnic's for the ants."

"A whole colony would be preferable to Calder's company."

"The ants in Miss Coltraine's pantaloons will get more action than Calder."

The corner of Devin's eye began to twitch, as did the corners of Shane's mouth. "Calder won't suck the dressing from Rose's mouth if she'll agree to feed him," he said.

She lifted a brow. "Toss him scraps from across the quilt?"

"He's not a dog, Dev," he said with disgust. "Calder wants to lie across Rose's lap, his head cushioned at the juncture of her thighs, her heaving bosom—"

"There's no passion in her breast for Calder," Devin said.

Shane leaned back in his chair and stared up at the ceiling. "I'll give you a walk along the bank of the river if you allow Calder a deep, openmouthed kiss and a little fondling."

"Calder will pick wildflowers, and tell Rose she's as sweet-smelling as the bouquet. He will liken the stars in the heavens to the sparkle in her eyes."

Shane swore softly, and Devin smiled in victory. "Afterward, Calder folds the quilt into a tidy square before handing Rose into the buggy."

"Handing her up, can he grope her fanny?" he asked.

"Rose will empty the hamper over his head if he touches more than her elbow," Devin warned.

"One hell of a picnic. Maybe on the ride back to town—"

"Calder will lick no more than dust from his lips," she informed him.

Shane leaned forward. "Does Rose gain satisfaction by teasing Calder to full erection, straining both his button-fly and his self-control?"

Devin sniffed. "I've never considered Rose a tease."

"What do you consider her then?"

"A smart woman who won't bed a gone-tomorrow gunslinger."

Shane scratched his chin. "I bet if you consulted her, she'd tell you different."

Devin blinked. "Consult her? I created her!"

"Then cut her a little slack. Grant her a little pleasure."

"You'd like that, wouldn't you?"

"Not me, so much, but Calder could use the release."

Devin had heard enough. She saved the scene and

turned off the computer. She glanced at the Art Deco clock. "The concert, McNamara. It's time to get ready. I don't want to walk in late."

He rose slowly. "Bet I'm slicked down before you're gussied up."

"What's the bet?"

"Loser prepares breakfast for a week."

"Breakfast beyond pouring cereal in a bowl?"

"Breakfast cooked in a frying pan on the stove."

"Let me think about it." She slid back her chair and stood. Edging around the corner of her desk, she inched backward. Her gaze held his until she hit her bedroom door. "You're on!" She dashed inside and slammed the door, stripping off her clothes as she walked to her closet.

"Get a move on, Dev. Stagecoach is pulling out." Shane felt anything but relaxed as he pounded on Devin's bedroom door. He wasn't overly anxious to attend the concert, and Devin's prolonged primping had him chomping at the bit.

"Two minutes," she called to him.

"Any longer and you'll be flipping pancakes next week." He turned from her door and began to pace the room. Circling the coffee table, he cast a withering glance at the bouquet of carnations Skip Huddleston had sent. The flowers had begun to wilt. Shane took it upon himself to dump them in the trash. He fanned out the magazines on the tabletop, hoping Devin wouldn't miss her flowers.

"Sorry I took so long," Devin apologized as she entered the main room and advanced on Shane, "but I had to make a last-minute adjustment to my vest."

"An adjustment?" Her bare arms and deep cleavage distracted him from the russet suede. As did the wave of her unbound hair that curled about her slender shoulders and over the swells of her breasts. Although two gold clasps held the buffed calfskin across the valley of her breasts, the ends gaped just below her breastbone, revealing an expanse of creamy skin. Way too much skin.

Wrapped about her hand-span waist, a glitzy rhinestone belt was looped through stonewashed denims that hugged a sweet tush and a sleek length of leg. Devin tapped the toe of her navy cowboy boot impatiently. "I thought you were in an all-fired hurry to leave."

Shane caught his breath, but his pulse ran wild. His conservative writing partner had cut loose for the concert. So loose she was falling out of her vest. "The vest needs another clasp."

"It was designed for only one," she explained, her toe still tapping, "but I added a second."

"Add a zipper."

She blinked at him as if she were unable to comprehend his request. "Whatever for? It's quite fashionable—"

Shane never let her finish. Reaching out, he snagged the clasps with two fingers and drew her toward him. His knuckles curved inside the vest and slid between her breasts.

Her heart slammed against the side of his fingers, then beat as wildly as his own. "You're showing more breast than a chicken dinner. Close up the front or slip on a T-shirt." His soft tone was deadly serious.

Devin blew out a breath. "The designer intended the cropped vest to mold the female torso and skim the hipbones. I don't understand your concern. . . ."

He shook his head, as baffled as she by the dangerous rise of possessiveness that demanded that no other man see her in such revealing attire.

Memories of Jamie Jensen wearing skimpy vests and short, tight skirts shot across his mind. Throughout their relationship the singer had flaunted her body on-stage and off, yet Shane had never felt the heart-gripping jealousy that Devin provoked.

This woman was meant for his eyes alone.

She dipped her head and licked her lips. "Are you embarrassed by the way I look?"

His nostrils flared, his jaw tensed, and a muscle jerked in the hollow of his cheek. "You're over-exposed."

"It's a concert, McNamara, and I'm cutting loose. There will be other women wearing a lot less than I."

He dipped his head closer to hers. "Are you going for the music or the men?"

She didn't miss a beat. "For the music, of course."

"Care to borrow one of my T-shirts?" he asked.

She scanned his large frame. "It might run a little big."

"There's nothing wrong with long and baggy."

Disengaging his fingers from the clasps on her vest, he turned on his heel and headed for his bedroom, returning shortly with a choice of two shirts. He held up each one for her inspection. The first bore a picture of Wild Bill Hickok riding a buffalo, with the inscription *Wild Bill's Buffalo Saloon, Deadwood, South Dakota* beneath the animal's hooves. The second shirt held a sketch of a pink flamingo wearing sunglasses against a backdrop of palm trees with a teal ocean. *Flamingo Joe's Food and Spirits, Kingston, Jamaica* was emblazoned beneath its beak.

Devin selected Wild Bill's. "Give me two minutes," she said as she escaped to her bedroom.

"It was two minutes twenty minutes ago," Shane grumbled.

"I heard that." Devin had left the door cracked.

Shane caught the flash of her flesh as she divested herself of the russet suede vest and worked the T-shirt over her head. The shirt hung to midthigh. She was well covered.

Devin reentered the room. Stopping before Shane, she asked, "Better?"

His gazed rested on her left breast. "That's the happiest T-shirt in my closet. Nice hump on the buffalo."

Devin slugged him on the arm.

He then snagged her hand and led her toward the front door.

"Do you have the tickets?" she asked as they crossed the yard to his Porsche.

Shane patted the front pocket of his black western shirt. "Safe for the moment."

"Don't lose them, McNamara."

"Wouldn't think of it, Dev." Having given his word, he wiped all thoughts of trashing them from his mind.

The first notes of the concert filled the Florida Sports Park by the time Devin and Shane had found a parking space, then the entrance to the outdoor arena. The open-air facility, used for both concerts and sports activities, was filled to overflowing with Jamie Jensen fans. With wolf whistles, catcalls, camera flashes, and strobe lights, the crowd surged to its feet when Jamie and her band hit the stage with her smash hit single, "Fire in Her Heart."

"Hey, McNamara! Shane McNamara!" Just inside the entrance. Ross Hunter approached them. He slapped Shane on the back and nodded to Devin. "Jamie asked me to watch for you. You've private seating up by the stage." He scuffed the toe of his boot in the dirt. "I also have a peace pipe in my back pocket if you choose to smoke it."

Shane shook his head. "No peace pipe, Ross. Devin wanted to hear the concert, not me."

Ross shrugged. "I tried."

"A little too hard," Shane said. "Stand up to J.J. Let her see you as a man and not just her manager."

Ross nodded slowly. "Follow me." He motioned Devin and Shane down a long aisle toward the stage.

Around them, enormous television screens illuminated the action on the stage, and couples danced wherever they could find two feet of space. Shane held Devin close to his side until they located the two chairs placed between the bleachers and the stage, so close to Jamie and her band, Shane could see the whites of their eyes.

J.J. sang to him as if he were the only one at the concert. She smiled her sexiest smile as she pranced across the stage to the hip-swaying beat of "Hot Talk." Her voice sounded high and strained, not as whiskey-smooth as Shane remembered. On a resigned sigh, he settled in for the show.

Entranced by the onstage action, Devin didn't hear a young man request a dance until he forcibly tapped her shoulder.

"Dance, pretty lady?" He was more boy than man, perhaps all of nineteen, with a lazy smile and lady-killer blue eyes.

Devin glanced at Shane, whose gaze tracked Jamie Jensen's every move. He would neither notice nor care if she danced the night away. A strange sense of loss claimed her heart.

"Do you line dance?" She forced a smile.

"With the best of them." The young man held out his hand. "Lander Nyland."

She placed her hand in his. "Devin James."

They moved into the aisle and joined a long line of dancers. Catching the country beat, Lander tossed his head, rolled his shoulders, and rotated his hips in a suggestive manner. Across from him Devin kicked up her heels and allowed the music to sweep the sadness from her soul. When Jamie slowed the rhythm of the night, Lander pulled her into his arms and held her close. A little too close. If only her partner were Shane . . .

Where the hell had Devin disappeared to? Shane looked beyond the stage to the seat now vacated by his writing partner. He'd been staring at J.J. for nearly an hour, awaiting any lick of the flame that once had set his heart and loins on fire. While she'd ignited the crowd, he'd felt not a spark. Not one single flicker.

A freedom born of relief swelled in his chest. He'd stepped from her fire unscathed. He wanted to howl at the moon.

The howling could wait until he located Devin. He stood and scanned the crowd, soon locating her in the arms of a Friday-night cowboy. Jealousy burned in his belly. The young gun had no right to hold his woman so close. . . .

His woman. The thought tucked around his heart with comfortable ease. Shane didn't try to shake it. Didn't try to adjust what fit so perfectly.

All he knew was that he should be the one dancing with Devin. Not some strutting teenage stud. His determined stride ate up the aisle until he reached her.

"I'm cutting in," Shane informed Devin's partner.

"Think again, pal." The younger man wrapped his

arm about Devin's waist when the song ended and a second slow number began. "I've kept the lady company while you were watching the show."

"Dance with me, Dev." The need to hold her was strong.

The young gun grinned. "The lady's hesitation speaks for itself."

Crushed by the crowd, Shane dodged an elbow but caught a swaying hip. Jarred forward, he stood intimidatingly close to Devin's partner. He had the man by six inches and twenty pounds. His jaw clenched as he drew a fist. . . .

Devin covered his hand with her own. His reason returned with her touch. "One dance, McNamara."

"Why only one?"

"That's all you deserve, you big bully." She turned to the younger man and smiled. "Perhaps later . . ."

Lander shook his head. "I don't claim-jump."

"I don't belong to Shane. You've misunderstood—"

"Give it a rest," Shane said as he pulled her close. He met the younger man's gaze over the top of Devin's head. "Ride fast. Ride hard."

Her dancing partner blended into the crowd.

"You didn't have to scare him off," she said against his chest.

"The hell I didn't." Shane enfolded her fully against him.

Devin's soft curves molded perfectly to him. No other woman had ever seemed so right in his arms.

Their bodies flush, they moved together, intimately slowly. Seduced by the ballad, he rested his chin against her unbound hair. Stroking his hand down the elegant length of her spine, he flattened his palm at the small of her back. She, in turn, teased the hair at the nape of his neck, then rose on tiptoe until their belt buckles rubbed and their zippers aligned. They embraced more than danced.

Lost in the music, he dropped a light kiss on her smooth forehead, then closed his eyes when she brushed her lips along his stubbled jaw.

"Dev . . ." His voice died along with the music. Shane opened his eyes and swept the crowd. "Caught in the spotlight dance," he whispered near her ear.

Released from his arms, Devin discovered all eyes upon them, including Jamie Jensen's trademark gold stare. The singer's look bore the heartache of lost love.

Silence threatened to engulf the sports park until Ross Hunter walked onstage. Amid the speculative whispers of the crowd, Devin watched as Ross crossed to Jamie. He took her microphone and passed it to Lake Crawford. His hands on her shoulders, Ross turned Jamie to face him.

A heated discussion ensued. Before thousands, Jamie waved her arms, ranted and raved. Ross stood quietly until Jamie stomped her foot. He scowled then, apparently having heard his fill. He threw up his hands and turned to walk away. Halfway across the platform, he stopped and returned to Jamie. His face red, he pulled her close and kissed her in front of God and an audience of thousands. Jamie thumped his shoulders with both hands and tried to kick his shins. A good thirty seconds elapsed before she clutched the front of his shirt and kissed him back. Their kiss went on and on. The crowd roared its approval.

Devin stood with her mouth open, so taken aback she couldn't speak.

Beside her, Shane whooped the loudest of all.

She grabbed Shane's arm and pushed him forward. "Don't let Ross take Jamie from you."

"He's not taking her from me," Shane explained.

"She was always his. They belong together." He chucked her on her chin. "You can close your mouth now."

Jamie and Ross. The concept was slow to sink in. "I'm sure if you wanted her—"

He pressed a finger to her lips to silence her. "I don't want her, Dev. J.J. and I were over before we ever began."

"What about you joining her on tour?"

He shook his head. "Her tour was never in my plans."

"You're sure?" *Please, God, let him be sure.*

"Jamie was never the one," he said. "I've no regrets."

Devin sighed a happy sigh and turned back to the stage. Jamie and Ross had separated, but still held hands. Jamie wore a dazed expression, and Ross looked satisfied, as if he'd conquered the world.

Jamie took her microphone from Lake Crawford. "Let's end the evening smoking," she called to the crowd. "It's been a long time since I've sung "Tell It to the Wind," so you're going to have to sing along with me. Ready?"

The audience raised the roof with its excitement. Across the crowd, Devin watched as Jamie again sought Shane. She smiled and blew him a kiss. "Good-bye, Shane."

Ross Hunter gave him a thumbs-up.

"Good-bye, Jamie," Shane said softly. "Good luck, Ross."

Jamie began to sing, her voice now strong and on key. Devin had never heard her sound better. From the corner of her eye she studied Shane. He stood tall, his weight on his left hip, his hands jammed into his jeans pockets. His expression was thoughtful and relaxed, as if he were pleased over the outcome of the evening.

No more pleased, however, than Devin. Her heart was light, and she had the wild urge to play.

"Ready to leave?" Shane asked.

"Whenever you are."

"Let's beat the traffic out of the lot."

He took her hand and led her through the crowd that was now clapping and singing along with the band.

Once outside the gate, they crossed the parking lot in silence. Reaching the Porsche, he held open her car door.

"Full moon tonight." He leaned in alarmingly close. "A night meant for howling. Care to answer my call of the wild?"

A one-night howl? Her pulse picked up and her heart took flight. Anticipation heated her belly. She licked her lips. "I'll think about it."

"You have until we reach the cottage."

Thirty minutes later Devin stood beside Shane in the front yard of the cottage, and listened as he threw back his head and howled at the moon. His howl was deep and sexy, and coyote-wild. It was obvious the man had howled more than once in his life.

"Your turn," he said.

Her first attempt at howling was scratchy and no more than a long croak. Her second try sent shivers down her spine. She could howl.

She laughed and hugged herself.

He draped an arm about her shoulders as they walked toward the cottage. "Care to play with me, Dev?"

"What did you have in mind?"

"Let's start with stroke poker," he said, holding the door open for her. "Five-card draw, the winner strokes the loser."

Devin could barely breathe. "Maybe a few hands."

Shane wiggled his two, and she slapped them away. "Hands of cards, you idiot."

He pulled a deck from the blue athletic bag and joined her on the sofa. "Sit closer," he insisted.

Devin scooted across the cushions until their thighs touched. She felt his nearness as surely as she felt her own heartbeat.

Shane pulled the coffee table within arm's reach. He then shuffled the cards like a Las Vegas dealer. "Do you feel lucky?"

She couldn't lose at this game. If Shane weren't touching her, she would be touching him. Anticipation warmed her blood. She felt daring and alive and, for the first time in her life, not the least bit sensible. She rubbed her hands together. "Deal, McNamara."

With the first hand he drew three fives to her two of a kind. His smile was lazy and very male as he skimmed one finger over her cheekbone. He moved so slowly, his touch turned erotic. "So soft," he whispered.

The next hand she held three of a kind, only to have Shane draw four tens. He tipped up her chin with the pad of his finger and stroked the corner of her mouth. Her lips parted. "So sexy," he breathed against her mouth.

Aroused by his warm, moist breath, she fought the urge to kiss his finger. Her own fingers itched to touch him. Where was her winning hand?

Her one pair did not beat his flush. He captured the curve of her jaw in his palm, forcing her to look at him, before he ran one finger down her neck to the pulse point at the base of her throat. "So excited." Her heartbeat quickened just for him.

The next hand was the best she'd been dealt thus far. Devin thought she'd won with four of a kind, but Shane drew a straight flush. Did the man have cards up his sleeve?

Her cheeks heated as he looked her over, deciding where to touch her next. She nearly came out of her skin when his hand hovered over her left breast, then retreated to graze her breastbone.

"Can I deal?" she asked.

Shane handed over the cards. "Afraid I stacked the deck?"

"You've won every hand."

He shrugged. "Just lucky, I guess."

Her luck had to change. Unfortunately it didn't change with the next hand. Her straight did not beat his full house. Her mouth went dry and her stomach clenched as he brushed her breast, and her nipple puckered with his featherlight touch.

"Your body responds well to this game," he said, brushing her breast a second time.

"Cheater." Devin pulled back slightly. "One stroke, not two."

"The penalty for cheating allows you to stroke the cheater."

She lifted one brow. "I want to see the rule book."

His lips twitched. "There are no written rules for stroke poker."

"You make them up as you go along?"

"Only those rules that make you feel good."

Devin wanted to touch him. More important, she wanted him so hot and breathless he combusted with her touch.

"I'll wait for my winning hand."

He looked pained. "Then deal."

She lost to him again, his two pairs topping her one pair.

He took her hand in his and placed it over his heart. The beat was that of a runner, one headed for the finish line. His breathing had also grown heavier. Taking all the time in the world, he traced all five of her fingers from her knuckles to her nails.

Her breath caught. "You took five turns."

"I'll pay the penalty. Touch me five times."

She licked her lips. "You're going to have to wait for my winning hand."

He reached for the cards. "Let me stack the deck."

She swatted his hand away. "Patience, McNamara."

His mouth pinched. "I've run out."

The next hand restored Devin's faith in Lady Luck. Her royal flush beat Shane's straight. But where should she touch him?

His whole body visibly stiffened when she lifted her hand toward his forehead, then lowered it toward his shoulder. She played with him, making him anticipate her move as her hand fanned his chest and abdomen, yet never fully stroked.

Shane groaned. "You're killing me, Dev."

She felt strong and womanly and in control. She wanted to tease him further, but the pained look on his face forced her move. She leaned in so close their bodies brushed, a full brush of her breast against his chest, and her cheek against his chin.

Then with the boldest move of her entire life, Devin James cupped Shane McNamara's groin.

Her victory, however, was short-lived. He was on her in a heartbeat, pinning her between the cushions and his solid frame. He brushed his unshaven cheek against her hair and whispered, his voice husky as sin, "You bent the rules, Dev. Cupping isn't stroking. It's time to pay the penalty."

Chapter Ten

Shane made certain his penalties were pure pleasure. He eased onto his side and pulled her snug against him. He kissed her slowly. Anticipation of the long night ahead stretched like an aphrodisiac. They had time and each other, and nothing else mattered.

A soft sigh escaped Devin as he parted her lips and deepened the kiss. She shivered when his tongue rubbed hotly over hers. Heat twisted inside him, heavy and urgent. She tasted of mint and womanly promise. He savored her.

He nipped her chin, then raised his head. "I want you naked."

Propping himself on one elbow, he held her with his gaze as he stripped away Wild Bill, then her black satin bra. Rising slightly, Devin slid her fingers beneath his western shirt. A single jerk and the row of metal snaps split apart. His chest was now as bare as her breasts.

Her gaze swept the rounded muscles of his shoulder

as he leaned over her and unbuckled her belt. He then flicked the snap on her jeans with his thumb and pulled down the tab on her zipper. She arched her hips, and he stripped off her jeans.

Time was lost to sensation as her world went into soft focus. He was all teeth, tongue, strength, and restraint. He tasted of experience. Sucking her lower lip between his own, he grazed the soft inner flesh with his teeth. He drew her above and beyond herself, and into him.

With his hands on her hips, Shane drew Devin across his lap, and she straddled him. Cupping the fullness of her breasts on both sides, his long fingers teased her nipples to an aching stiffness. She clutched his shoulders and rocked against his groin, the satin crotch of her black panties riding the silver buttons on his fly. She was wet; she wanted him.

Backing onto his thighs, she then rose on her knees. She unbuttoned Shane's jeans, freeing him to work the Levi's over his thighs and down his calves, to slip on a condom. Her panties quickly joined his jeans.

"No Jockeys or boxers?" she asked as she again straddled his thighs.

"Briefs, but only with a tux."

She felt his warm hardness against her pubic bone, and traced its length and thickness. "Sweet mercy."

After stroking the warm underside of her breast, he caressed the concave curve of her stomach, then, with his palm on her pubic bone, slid one finger deep inside her. "Sweet, sweet mercy."

Heat flashed through Devin, and a soft sheen of perspiration broke across her chest as she molded her fingers over his hard pectorals, grazing the tiny erect male nipples. The fierce hammering of his heart echoed her own.

White-hot hunger coursed through both of them

and sizzled in the air around them. She rocked forward as he clutched her hips and drew her up and over him. He eased her down slowly. The melting heat of her body drove him deeper, and he filled her completely.

"So tight," he murmured against her lips before thrusting his tongue into her mouth.

Thick, swelling pleasure drove her rhythm as she moved her body forward and back, up and down, no longer certain where he began and she left off. Her pulse beat to his racing breath. Her hips showed the imprint of his fingers and thumbs.

Climax crept up on them in tingling waves bordering on acute pain. There were no thoughts, no words, nothing but pure emotion as her body went as rigid as his, then shuddered in release. As if in slow motion, her body finally collapsed. She rested her head in the hollow of his neck.

Brushing the damp strands of her hair off her forehead, Shane kissed her lightly and confessed, "I'm mighty smitten, Devin James."

She curled into his body, and he held her close.

The night tucked around them, hinting of warmth and promise and new love.

Morning dawned in shades of pale violet light. Devin felt so lazy and weak, she couldn't move. Her body had been well loved by an incredible lover. Her howl at the moon had released her inner animal. She and Shane had mated all night long. He'd allowed her one hour of sleep before she'd awakened to find him already inside her. She had climaxed with his first thrust.

"Dev, you awake?" Shane stirred beside her.

"Not wide-awake."

"Neither am I." His big body curved against her back as his hand slid over her hip and flattened on her belly.

Her stomach took that moment to growl.

"Hungry?" he asked.

"Mmm, breakfast in bed sounds good."

"We're on a couch we failed to make into a bed." She felt his muscles flex against her back as he stretched. "I never thought of the pullout."

She hadn't either. She'd been too taken with his kisses, hands, and erection to bother with something as trivial as pulling out the bed. She eased up on one elbow, naked and uncaring of her nudity. In the heat of the night, Shane's lack of modesty had rubbed off on her. She'd found happily-ever-after in her own skin.

"I owe you breakfast," she said on a yawn.

"Which I'll help you make."

"Do you cook?" she asked, rolling toward him.

He pressed his morning erection into her belly. "I'm always cooking."

"I've never been hungrier in my life."

"Start with me, and we'll end with Belgian waffles and fresh strawberries."

She nipped his shoulder, then licked the bite. "Don't let me start without you."

"I'll catch up." Shane sucked her lower lip into his mouth, and feasted until full.

Ninety minutes later Devin joined Shane in the kitchen; she was freshly showered and casually dressed in short linen overalls. Tide blue, and worn without a top, the overalls provided a tempting view of tan limbs and peekaboo breasts.

Overnight Devin had gone from tailored to casual. If he could just rid her of that tight-ass braid . . .

"Do we have the ingredients for waffles?" she asked as she slipped a chef-style apron over her head and tied the strings at the small of her back.

"Ingredients and a cookbook," he supplied. He scratched the front of his navy T-shirt, where a green horned toad wore a wicked smile, and *Horny Devil Lounge, Darwin, Australia* curved in red script above the lizard's hornlike spines. "I'm here to help."

He watched as she moved around the kitchen, so natural and at ease with the mixing bowl, spatula, and electric hand mixer. He liked this homey feeling of her cooking breakfast almost as much as he'd enjoyed last night's lovemaking on the sofa. Such a small space, yet so much action. Devin's body had bent like a gymnasts.

It was the best sex he'd ever had. Might ever have. Without fighting the emotions, he understood why. His heart had been involved. He'd felt not only the wild tug of lust, but also the gentle pull of love. He'd embraced the feelings as strongly as he'd embraced Devin James. Sensations of peace and perfection had wrapped themselves about his heart. He wanted Devin in his future.

She was the one.

"Crack the eggs?" she asked.

He did his best. Two of the three eggs missed the bowl and slimed the outer edge, and the one that made it into the bowl came with a lot of shell. He dumped the contents into the sink and started over. After one full carton of Grade-A eggs, he succeeded in his mission.

Devin came to stand beside him. Their bodies brushed and her hip rested near his thigh. He liked her close.

"What next?" he asked.

"Sifting the flour should be easy."

Easy, his ass. The flour puffed up in his face like a mushroom cloud. He made a grab for a hand towel to wipe off his face, and half the flour was dumped on the counter.

Devin cleaned up behind him. She bumped him out of the way with her hip and measured in the sugar, baking soda, and a touch of cinnamon. Dangling the measuring spoons from her fingers, she requested, "Rinse these off, please."

Shane threaded his fingers through hers and drew her hand to his mouth. He'd noticed that several granules of sugar had stuck to her wrist, and he licked the spot clean. Devin suddenly sounded short-winded.

After rinsing off the spoons he came up behind her. He leaned in, placing his hands on the counter on either side of her, and molded his body to hers. She pressed her bottom into his groin and wiggled just enough to make him hard. Shane groaned against her hair. She was soft and warm and cooking more than waffles.

"Want to fool around?" he whispered.

She shook her head. "The batter is almost ready to go into the waffle iron."

He pressed into her again. "I'm as hot as any waffle iron."

"Food first."

He kissed the side of her neck. "Come on, Dev. . . ."

She turned then, on both him and his erection. She jammed the beaters on the electric hand mixer into the snap above his zipper. "Stop working on top of me."

She was serious, and he jumped back. He immediately thanked his lucky stars the mixer hadn't been on, and hadn't beaten more than batter.

He moved several feet to her right, and watched as she poured the batter onto the waffle iron. The batter sizzled, and the scent of cinnamon filled the kitchen. His mouth watered.

"Can you slice the strawberries?" Devin asked as she set the timer on the waffle iron.

He cut the strawberries into fourths, and nicked his finger only twice. One of the nicks demanded a Band-Aid.

The kitchen was not his domain.

By the time he'd cleaned up his mess Devin had laid out two place settings on the breakfast bar and served the waffles. She added the strawberries and a sprinkle of powdered sugar, then heated up the maple syrup.

Shane sank onto a bar stool and ate his breakfast. Once he'd polished off two waffles, he watched Devin finish her meal. He liked the way she licked her lips, then her fingers, savoring every bite. As if slapped by the rubber spatula, he realized he wanted Devin James sitting across from him at breakfast every day until they both had thinning hair and false teeth. He'd like most of their breakfasts to be eaten in bed.

"I'm glad you lost the bet," he said.

"Don't get too cocky," she returned. "You're fixing lunch."

"Your choice: Mexican, Italian, or Chinese."

"No takeout," she insisted. "There's a barbecue beyond the hammock. You can grill hot dogs."

Her smile forced him to agree. This wasn't the time to tell Devin he had never barbecued. He'd better program Smokey the Bear on his speed dial before he lit the charcoal.

"Shane?" Devin touched his arm.

He returned from his thoughts and looked at her.

"You're fondling Mrs. Butterworth when you could be fondling me."

Fondling the syrup dispenser? He glanced down and

found his forefinger wrapped around Mrs. Butterworth's breast, his thumb over her buttocks. The corners of his lips twitched. "She's hot, Dev."

"Next time I won't heat the syrup in the microwave."

He set Mrs. Butterworth aside and reached for Devin. Curving his hand behind her head, he pulled her in for a kiss. She tasted of powdered sugar and strawberries. "Care to join me in the hot tub?" he breathed against her lips.

"Is it safe to go in the water right after eating?"

He grinned. "It's a hot tub, Dev. We sit and relax. There's no room to swim laps."

She blew out her cheeks. "I'm so full, I'll sink."

He kissed the tip of her nose. "I'll be your water wings."

Devin liked the idea of him holding her afloat. "Swimsuit or skin?"

"Definitely skin." His tongue darted in her ear, the moist tip as warm as the goose bumps he raised. "I want you sleek and slippery and slick with need."

Leaving their dishes in the sink, Shane led her to the lanai. His skilled fingers unclasped the straps on the bibbed front of her overalls, along with the two oversize ivory buttons on either side of her waist. His knuckles skimmed the outer curves of her breasts as the soft fabric shimmied over her hipbones and down her thighs.

She then assisted him, unzipping his cutoffs as he jerked the horned toad T-shirt over his head. She delighted in the slow slide of the denim over his lean hips and long legs.

One step to the left and he'd dropped his cutoffs atop her overalls. A kick to their shoes and two pairs skidded across the cement and collided near the sliding glass doors. There, the rubber rim of one running shoe kissed the ringed toe on her Italian leather sandal.

A second step forward and the solid width on his chest brushed against the swells of her breasts. His erection nudged her navel.

Advancing further, he backed her against the three-foot-high redwood siding. "One step up, a short stretch over the rim, and you'll be submerged in steam and me," he said.

Steam and Shane. She would luxuriate in both.

She took one step, and he was there to assist her. Sliding one hand beneath her left breast and the other beneath her right thigh, he helped her over the rim. The brush of his hair-roughened chest against her shoulder blades and the rub of his thigh high on her hip both tickled and tantalized. She nearly lost her footing when his fingers flexed and stretched beneath her bottom, and the callused tips brushed the wet warmth of her sex.

As the steam and bubbles rose in seductive welcome, he slid two fingers deep inside her. She arched back against him and tilted her head until their gazes locked. His gray eyes hazed with wanting. Wanting her. Her own need throbbed, a wild pulse felt in every cell of her body.

Amid the whirls and spraying jets, Shane stroked her deeply; when he withdrew she whimpered softly. As the water lapped their thighs, swirled over their bellies, sluiced higher, he bypassed the wooden bench and sank to his knees.

Devin followed him down, then jerked straight as one of the high-powered jets shot her left buttock. "I've been goosed!"

"Goosed now, gratified later." His lips twitched. "Initiation time, hotshot."

He cuffed her wrist and drew her down until she reclined against his body. Her shoulders rested on his chest; her bottom was cradled on his groin. He held her tightly. Possessively.

Anticipation left them with rapid heartbeats and heavy breathing. He brushed his jaw against her cheek and pressed a light kiss against her ear.

"I've never made love in a hot tub," she confessed.

"There's a lot to be said for slippery when wet."

A film of steam was all that separated them. When he kissed her, their lips strained to touch, postponing the inevitable moment when she would turn and face him, and he would mate fully with her mouth.

He kneaded her upper arms, squeezed her elbows, then drew her arms down tightly to her sides when she sought to change positions and straddle his thighs.

He held her from him and demanded she wait. "Let it build, Dev." His teeth grazed her shoulder blade. "Feel your blood get hot and your body go liquid. Sweat, swell, and rise on the steam."

As water sloshed between them, they flicked droplets from their cheeks and chins with the tips of their tongues, then joined their parted lips.

He slid his hands upward, a seductive climb over her ribs, stopping a fraction of an inch beneath her breasts. He lingered there for several heartbeats before stroking downward to palm her waist, hips, and buttocks. He absorbed her moan on a deeper kiss.

The encounter stretched beyond pleasure. They lived just beyond each other's reach, yet beneath each other's skin. Their kisses broke on her gasp of pleasure when Shane tilted her hips slightly forward and the first blast of the hot-tub jet shot between her thighs.

Sin and sensation. Unbearable pleasure.

Devin's body jerked back against Shane. She rolled

her head from side to side, and her breath hitched. "McNamara, should I—"

"Enjoy the jet?" He nuzzled her neck. "Go with the flow."

He repositioned her hips, and she quickly discovered the flow, a succession of erotic gushes directed at the center of her passion. Sweat and steam filmed her forehead. Her hips twisted as spasms claimed her belly with each frothy gush. She rocked against Shane's groin, finding his need as long and hard as the jet spray.

"I want you inside me, Shane."

Her sanity slipped as he slanted forward and streamlined into her. A burst of spray hit them where they joined. She climaxed, as did he, on his second thrust.

For a timeless moment she floated outside of herself, all limp and liquid. The sound of bubbles and the gentle slosh of water against the sides of the hot tub lulled her. She rested her head on Shane's shoulder and closed her eyes.

"Don't let me drown." She started to doze.

He kissed her temple. "We're both about to go under."

"I could use a nap."

He agreed. "Rest recharges the batteries."

She turned to face him. "I do like you charged."

"Give me thirty minutes, Dev, and I'll be up and running."

"Love bites." Shane stood bare-chested before the bathroom mirror, checking out the tiny teeth marks that scored his collarbone, ribs, and belly. His inner thigh. Devin James knew how to sample and taste. The swirl of her tongue . . . Flick, lick, suck, swirl. The woman had eaten more than one ice-cream cone in her lifetime; of that he was certain. He'd bet she could tie a cherry stem in a knot with just her tongue.

He closed his eyes, seeking his calm place where satisfaction soothed as warm as sunshine and Devin wore nothing but a sated smile. He loved her innocent exuberance. She was in his blood, his heart, his soul. He loved her.

"Oh, my Lord, I've scarred you for life!" Wrapped in nothing but a towel and a deep rose blush, Devin entered his bathroom, her hand over her heart.

"You've branded me, Dev. I'm all yours."

"I like that idea." She tugged on the terry cloth towel that wrapped his waist, and pulled him around to face her. "I'd like you even better if you'd start lunch."

He scrunched up his nose. "Ah, the barbecue. Why not just boil the hot dogs?"

She traced one finger along his jawline. "Nothing compares to meat cooked outdoors over a fire."

"I'll give it my best shot."

His best shot wasn't quite good enough. Lunch was a burned offering, at best. "Thought they'd plump when you cooked them," he said as he handed Devin a plate of franks that had sizzled to one-inch size.

She eyed the plate, "They look like cocktail weenies."

Shane wiped the sweat from his brow with the back of his hand. "The charcoal got a little hot. I saved the dogs, but the buns are toasted crumbs among the ashes."

It was obvious his skills did not stretch to grill master. Devin lifted a brow. "How much charcoal did you use?"

"A good portion of the bag." A twenty-pound bag.

"Six briquettes would have done the job."

"So I discovered."

He scuffed the toe of his running shoe across the

tile floor. The rubber squeaked and left a small black mark.

Black, the color of night, bad moods, and burned hot dogs. How hard should it have been to start a damn fire? A bag of charcoal, a book of matches, and one simple strike of the match.

Instead of a controlled flame, he'd built a bonfire on the grill and nearly cremated Oscar Mayer. The flames had jumped so high they'd singed his eyebrows. It was obvious he and the Boy Scouts had never sat at the same campfire. One bucket of water hadn't been nearly enough to put out the fire. He'd had to retrieve the garden hose and spray it down thoroughly.

"Sorry about the hot dogs," he apologized.

Devin surprised him by popping one in her mouth. "They're crunchy, but edible."

Shane sampled one. Edible, his ass. "They taste like charcoal."

He took the plate from Devin and upended it in the garbage. He left the kitchen, crossed to his desk, and snagged his car keys. "Give me thirty minutes," he said. "Lunch will be catered by Frank's Furters, the best deli dogs you've ever tasted."

Lunch was good, Devin had to agree as she polished off her second chili dog. She wiped her mouth, then took a sip of her root beer. "I've been thinking about *Calder's Rose*," she said.

Shane drank from her glass of root beer. "When have you had time to think about the book? Before your orgasm on the sofa bed or after the jet climax in the hot tub?"

"While you were out getting hot dogs," she said. "I think the final chapter should have Calder entering the Scarlet Garter dressed in a city suit, his hair slicked back, carrying a small bouquet of pansies. Though the catcalls from the bar don't please him, he knows Miss Rose will be delighted with his offering. Especially his heartfelt poem. His declaration of love."

Shane's breath left him all at once. "City suit? Pansies? A poem? Are you out of your mind? My readers would never recognize my gunslinger."

"Everyone can understand a proposal on bended knee."

"Calder's not getting hitched."

She licked her lips. "Rose can be quite persuasive. There's a two-story house on the outskirts of Cutter's Bend that's the perfect place to raise a family."

Shane's eyes narrowed. "Calder's a drifter. How's he going to support a wife and kids?"

"With Rose tending the Garter, Calder would never have to work. He could stay home and raise the children."

Shane ground his teeth. "Throwing himself on a picket fence would be less painful."

"Picket fence? Great idea. It would corral the kids."

He rose off the bar stool, stacked the plates, and collected the silverware. "Has Rose asked Calder if he even likes children?"

"He told her he'd like a dozen."

Shane dropped the dishes in the sink, and Devin was certain the plates hadn't survived the crash. "That ending doesn't work for me."

"Then give me an alternative, cowboy."

"Cowboy . . ." He let the word trail off. He looked her full in the face and a slow grin spread over his features. The lines around his lips and eyes looked rugged and sexy. "I prefer Shamus, ma'am, should you choose to call me again."

Devin thrilled to Shane's lazy Southern drawl. He

was definitely a creative lover. The look in his eyes challenged and enticed her to fall into any role she so desired. As long as she desired him.

There was no need for costumes or a change of décor. Seduced by his imagination, she slipped into character. A swish of her khaki drawstring skirt, a tug on her Pacific-blue crop top, and her clothes were transformed into a low-cut black satin gown. A stomp of her foot and a pair of braided leather sandals became fashionable high-button shoes.

Floor tiles shifted to a boardwalk of long wooden planks as Devin James sashayed into Shane McNamara's western fantasy. The sight of her trim ankles and a glimpse of her garter nearly brought him to his knees.

"Shamus . . . the preacher man?"

His brow lifted in interest as she described the man he had become.

"Your reputation proceeds you like ten miles of bad road. You're a hired gun, known far and wide for cleaning up dirty towns and keeping whole counties in line. Your saving grace is in the swiftness of your kill. Heard tell you even say a prayer over the dead man's grave."

Shane smiled his approval, which Devin returned. He then deepened his drawl and drew her into character. "Been told the Black Orchid's the best brothel this side of Amarillo. I'm looking for a woman name Divine."

"Once you find her?" she asked.

"She's known to relieve a man of his trail dust."

Divine. A fallen dove. Leave it to Shane to paint her as a lady of pleasure. If he wanted bawdy and brassy, she'd show him ill repute.

Without even touching each other they became

aroused, their heartbeats quickening, their skin growing hot. Imperceptibly he leaned toward her, heightening the tension, locking it between them.

"Look no farther." She licked her lips enticingly. "I'm Divine Lang. Should you care to join me, it'll cost you a month's wages."

He extracted a half-dollar from the pocket of his outback shorts. He flipped the coin in the air and caught it, then slapped it on the back of his hand. "Got a double eagle, ma'am. What will it buy?"

"Some wild turkey and oysters, a bottle of sweet mash whiskey and my passion." She tossed her head like the character Divine, a practiced gesture that drew a man's gaze to her long blond tresses.

"Praise be." Captivated by the thickness and length of her hair, he followed the silken wave over her shoulders and across her breasts. His breathing deepened. His nostrils flared. Yet he remained noncommittal.

"Interested?" She warmed beneath his heated gaze.

His lips twitched. "I'm like a smart horse trader, ma'am. I take a long, hard look at the horse's teeth and coat lest I make a rash decision."

"Don't expect me to whinny." Her hands on her hips, she speculated, "If your look is all that gets long and hard, preacher man, go spread your gospel elsewhere."

He threw back his head and laughed. "Fiesty little filly." Her indignation and spunk attracted him, as did her heaving bustline.

Intentionally slowly, he traced one long finger along her plunging neckline, then slipped the gold coin between her breasts. Lost to her warmth, he lingered, brushing the swells, his thumb coveting one nipple. He'd always had a fondness for blondes with pale pink areolae. This woman was a true blonde, as fair as they came.

A light came into her eyes that told him she liked his touch, and ached for more. Sexual surrender . . .

She set him back on his boot heels when she snared his wrist and stilled his fondling. For a charged moment her heart pounded as if there were a kicking mule inside her chest. She flirted with the idea of taking her leave. The man on the boardwalk raised the devil in her.

High-priced, she handpicked her gents, taking only the prosperous to her four-poster. She allowed no involvement beyond the hour spent in her bed. Tonight, however, the evening settled on her like a lover. Hot. Naked. Pulsing with expectancy.

The devil take her. She was more interested in pleasure than profit tonight.

Transposed over Shane's head, a dark, low-crowned hat shadowed his eyes, as silvery gray as the Mexican pesos that wrapped his headband. Instead of his *Vampire Beer, Great with a Stake* T-shirt, she saw a long dark coat parted over a black silk kerchief, a sun-faded chambray shirt, and a six-gun strapped to the thigh of his dark denims. Instead of his running shoes were scuffed boots with silver spurs as tarnished as his life.

He had the hard look of a man who'd faced-down death and won.

As he leveled his gaze on her, one corner of his mouth curled and a knowing smile appeared. The pulse at the base of her throat throbbed with the same longing now centered in his groin. A painful longing born of spending too many nights alone on his bedroll.

The prairie winds had whispered of the wanton Divine, and beneath the stars he'd prayed for one evening in her company.

He stroked one long finger over her silken cheek. Need darkened his eyes with sinful promise. "I'd pay a full year's wages to have you."

She ran her finger over his heavily shadowed jaw. "My room's on the second floor."

The construction of stairs enhanced their fantasy as they crossed the threshold between living room and bedroom. She glanced over her shoulder to be sure he followed. He had. She liked the way he moved. The man had some mighty fine swagger in his hips.

They climbed slowly. Once reaching the landing, they headed down a long hallway. He slowed his stride, tailoring it to her shorter one.

"Hear those bedsprings squeaking?" she asked.

He removed his hat and slapped it against his thigh. "Damn busy evening."

"After nine o'clock the crowd thickens," she informed him. "A line forms from the end of the bar to the bottom of the stairs. By midnight most of the men are as stiff as their shots of whiskey."

Her chamber was small, serviceable. Neither frills nor trinkets adorned it. The woman alone provided the allure.

In an imaginary motion, he shucked his duster and tossed it over a swing-arm floor lamp, momentarily converted to a wooden coatrack. His hat and gun belt followed. He leaned against the doorjamb and awaited her welcome.

"Whiskey, Shamus?" she asked.

He shook his head, wanting nothing more than to drink her in.

She slid her hands over her satin-smooth hips before clasping them demurely at the juncture of her thighs. Her pale hands, long-nailed and experienced, were known to stroke a man to bucking release. The thought of those fingertips plying their trade stirred more than his soul. His arousal jutted into his button-fly.

She licked her lips. "Confess your desire, preacher man."

He crossed to her then, leaned in, and rubbed his cheek against hers. "You're as pretty as a field of wild-flowers, and smell as fresh as morning. I rode clear across the state of Texas to find you. I won't settle for a quick roll in the hay. I'm looking for a wildfire burn. A night of slow, deep heat that creeps under a man's skin, kindles in memory, and keeps him warm through the bitter blast of winter."

The creamy curve of her jaw went slack against his dark whiskers. "I've never allowed a man to spend the entire night."

"You will tonight."

Tangible pleasure. . . . He stood close, and his erection pressed hard and hot against her belly. Rising on tiptoe, she tongued his ear. "Come save my soul, preacher man, 'cause my virginity's long been lost."

She blew in his ear, then nipped his lobe. She trailed openmouthed kisses along his neck and across his jaw, grazing the corner of his mouth and drawing on his lower lip.

"I can only imagine what you've seen and done, Miss Divine." he said alluding to their fantasy. "You've lived on a street of fallen women. You've made a living beneath many men, and spun a lot of spurs." He paused, bowed his head, then looked at her with reverence. "But you make me feel like the first."

Smoothing his hands up her arms and onto her shoulders, he gentled his grip slightly, so the pressure of his fingers would not bruise her. At the base of her throat he brushed his thumb over her pulse and caught the jump in her heartbeat and her blush of awareness. He liked her skittish.

Upward he moved along the slender column of her neck, then fanned his fingers until she threw her head back. He nuzzled the sweet, soft flesh just beneath her chin.

"By all that's holy." He swept a path of moist kisses beneath her ear, then grazed her jawline with his teeth.

Bracketing her face between his large hands, he brought her mouth to his, never breaking their gaze. Her eyelids fluttered as he teased the corners of her lips with featherlight kisses.

"Eyes wide open," he breathed over her slightly parted lips. "I want to see you wanting me."

No other man had ever sought her satisfaction.

Sexual excitement hummed in her blood. The scent of his wildness mixed with her orange-blossom toilet water. The fantasy, the intensity of his need, left her breathless.

He caught her expectant sigh on the tip of his tongue, then slanted his mouth and thrust deeper, rolling his tongue over hers.

She swayed, and he steadied her.

Her heart began a dull, hard beat. Desire grew from the bottom of her abdomen. She lifted his hand and pressed it to her breast, then rubbed against him suggestively. He guided her free hand to the buttons on his pants. She began to undo them, starting with the lowest button and working her way up.

He worked his way down. He kissed her breasts through the bodice of her dress and imagined the row of hooks and eyes he would soon disengage. Then, lifting his head, he eased the satin off her shoulders and watched it pool at her tightly cinched waist. The front clasp of her satin demicups became the lacing of her corset. He freed her of the silken ties, then parted the undergarment over her breasts. The swells rose high and firm without the foundation.

"Unnecessary entrapment." He tugged the corset/ bra free, then soothed the reddened indentations that marred her ribs.

A sigh escaped her lips. A tightness grew between her legs and coiled into her belly as he lowered the dress over her thighs. She stood before him, and he could almost imagine her wearing pale orchid garters, fashionable shoes, and an anxious smile instead of her white satin thong.

His throat went dry and he could barely swallow. Even in his sweetest dreams he hadn't envisioned her perfection. Flawless skin. Breasts as smooth and shapely and firm as her bottom. Her infinite length of leg.

"Natural as God intended," he said. "There's nothing soiled about you."

"Such conviction, preacher man." She smiled her first real smile while working the imaginary buttons on his shirt. It soon lay as open as the fly on his pants. She pulled the sun-faded chambray over wide shoulders, a well-developed chest, and a hard, flat stomach. Dense, curling hair made a wedge across his chest and drew a dark line down the center of his body. The line widened just beneath his navel. A tug at his waistline, and her lips followed his pants down corded thighs and sinewy calves.

She untied his running shoes so he could kick off his cowboy boots, thrust his denims/shorts aside. His breathing rough, he wove his fingers into her hair and eased her up his body. Above his calf her lips pleasured his inner thigh then his hipbone, and she flicked his navel with her tongue. She left love bites up the center of his torso, and sucked his nipples.

As his erection hardened, his heart softened. He wasn't supposed to have a heart in the romantic sense. He'd ridden life hard. His trail had no end. He had no dang business thinking like a lover. Yet right now he found it impossible to think otherwise.

He wanted to seduce her.

She wanted to bring him to his knees.

Slipping two fingers beneath his imaginary black silk kerchief, she tugged gently and led him naked to her bed. She envisioned it of weathered barn wood instead of scrolled brass. "Do unto me, preacher man, as I plan to do unto you."

She pulled him down behind her. They fell onto the mattress—feather tick—and sank into its comfort. The sweet curve of her nakedness molded his hard length. Enveloped by his male scent and the heat of his skin, she lost herself in his nearness.

Dismissing time, they entered a world of raw surrender. She sought the initiative and straddled him, only to be rolled beneath his body in one liquid turn. He then pulled on protection and settled between her thighs. He exuded the sheer power of bone and muscle and male need.

With agonizing slowness he nibbled on her sexy lower lip, the tender curve of her shoulder, the fragility of her collarbone, and the lushness of her breasts. His late-afternoon beard abraded her chest, then downward, her belly, and eventually her inner thighs. He laved away the redness, then returned to her mouth.

Lifting her hips with his hands, he brought her to him. His fingers thrust into the hollow at the base of her spine, and his thumbs pressed into her stomach. Beneath his strong body their hipbones meshed, his long legs and arms imprisoning her as his body bore down and his arousal rubbed, probed, and opened her slowly.

She accepted him with a throaty moan.

His penetration was as long as a Sunday sermon.

Something came alive in her. The force of the fantasy sensitized her skin. She shifted restlessly. A sheen of perspiration collected on her breasts.

Excitement ranged through his body in waves of surging possession. His features grew taut, straining in passion. His heartbeat thundered in his ears. Raw hunger burned him, and his chest heaved with labored breath.

He was in danger of losing control.

She rode the edge of discovery. Overheated, tense, anticipating, she lost the ability to discern which one of them initiated a movement. Each thrust pleasured her differently. She could no longer feel their borders. Her head spun with a passion so unnatural to her character that she felt transformed and yet possessed by a man who took her outside of herself and into him.

Their gazes locked; they maintained an almost cautious rhythm as his pleasure was transferred to her. His ability to draw out her desire, to divine her needs, seemed uncanny.

All at once the path of his life grew clear to him. Their separate pasts were shattered by a mutual orgasm. Darkness blazed and throbbed behind his eyes. Her moan of completion meant everything to him.

Through the window, moonlight cast them in silver shadows. Once their heartbeats stilled, silence settled on them like a second skin.

Replete, he rolled off her, then pulled her close. Satisfaction shone in his eyes. He stretched, flexed, and squeezed her shoulder gently.

Her eyes were soft, liquid. She curled into his big body, wonderfully tired. She wanted to exist only in the immediate memory of their lovemaking.

He kissed her almost lovingly, as if she'd given him the grandest gift, and he was thankful—eternally thankful—for the long night ahead. From this moment forth she'd always be on his conscious mind, always in his dreams. Her softness had left a mark on his heart.

At rooster's first crow, Shane, still the preacher man, blew a last bit of sunshine up her skirts.

After claiming her, he claimed his clothes.

While he dressed, she consciously took in the width of his chest, the firmness of his backside, the stretch of muscle as he buttoned his shirt and hiked up his denims, so she could recall the memory at any given time. She held every admiring glance he cast her way close to her heart.

Her silent tongue, as useless as a button on a fancy bonnet, forced her to nod her farewell as he tipped his low-crowned hat and strode out the door.

Wrapped in a sheet, a smile, and the scent of her man, she rolled onto her side and closed her eyes.

Their fantasy faded as she punched her pillow, and he retreated to the kitchen for a late-night snack.

Hours later, reality shimmered on rays of sunshine through the bedroom window of the writer's cottage, awakening Devin and Shane. The warmth spread across her bare bottom and his firm belly. She yawned and rubbed against his thigh, feeling as lazy as the morning. Contentment flowed. She'd been well loved.

"That was a good fantasy." She sighed into his shoulder.

"Damn fine fantasy." A smile played across his lips,

yet his eyes remained closed. "You can stretch my imagination any old time."

She raised herself on one elbow and studied his handsome, relaxed face. She wondered how many women the preacher man had ministered to.

"Divine's the only woman with whom Shamus shared communion." He had read her mind, and she was grateful for his answer. He was as in tune with her thoughts as he was with her body. She snuggled closer. . . .

Crunch. She rolled back and found cracker crumbs stuck to her thigh and hip. She brushed them onto the satin sheet. "Midnight munchies, McNamara?"

"You wore me out, woman." He dropped a kiss on her forehead. "I had to keep up my strength."

Her gaze skimmed his thick chest, tight abdomen, and the full length of his erection. "I won't kick you out of bed for eating crackers."

"Let me show my appreciation." He pressed his knee between her thighs and rubbed upward slowly, awaiting her response.

She put her hand on his knee. "Allow me to pleasure you."

Rising, she went to her bedroom and dressed just for him. For the first time yesterday, she'd discovered his gift of the classic black pumps when she'd opened the shoe box holding her mocha-brown flats.

She'd wear that gift for him now.

She returned shortly in her thigh-high nylons, rhinestone-studded heels, and her sexiest smile. When he moaned his appreciation, she sheathed him in Tangerine Tango, then later in Strawberry Sin. Shane could have glowed in the dark.

* * *

"Miss Rose, are you there?" Dare Calder called out. They were but voices now, mere traces of their former selves.

"I'm right here, Mr. Calder," came her reply from the far corner of the living room.

"Don't give up the ghost," he said. "I'll find a way to return us to the livin'."

Her breath rose raggedly. "I've faded, Mr. Calder. My voice will be gone by morning."

"I won't let you leave me," he insisted.

"You have no choice, sir. Devin and Shane have stolen our existence."

"Their fallin' in love made us weak."

"They are strong in their commitment. Vows will soon be pledged."

Calder swore. The oath nearly took his life.

"I'll . . . I'll miss you, Mr. Calder."

"You will?" he asked, startled by her confession.

"You've caused me frustration and embarrassment, but I've never wished you dead. For all our differences, I've grown quite fond of you."

"You have?" He'd never been more stunned, especially since he'd grown to favor her also.

"I wish we'd had more time. . . ."

"Don't count us dead and buried." He cleared his throat and forced out words he never thought to speak. "I need you, Rose."

"How so, sir?"

"I need you to remember me as . . . as . . ."

"A good man, Mr. Calder?"

"Would that be so impossible?" he asked.

"We've walked a long road together. Even when you ride out of town, I'll never forget you, sir."

She cared for him. No other woman had spoken with such sincerity.

His heart kicked, his chest swelled, and his breathing came easier. Warmth filled him, as did the newfound intimacy. Across the room, Rose Coltraine in her soft pink gown became visible. The scent of tea roses wafted on the air. No one had ever looked nor smelled so good to him.

Within seconds the toe of his boot came into focus, and he felt his body gain height and breadth once again. He rolled and lit a cigarette, then inhaled deeply. He'd missed his smoke.

Eee doggies! For the first time in his life he had a purpose. Rose and his fondness for her, however frail, would give the two of them strength to finish *Calder's Rose*. The book belonged to them; it was their story.

No one else could write the ending as it was intended to be written. He'd go down fightin' if need be.

He stroked his six-gun. It was time to take Shane and Devin hostage.

Chapter Eleven

"We haven't gotten out of bed in three days," Devin said on a yawn.

Shane hugged her close. "Let's make it a full week."

Devin shook her head. "It's time to face the world."

He dropped a kiss on her forehead. "You are my world, Devin James."

"Our world can't stop because of sex."

He pressed his groin against her thigh and rotated his hips. "Grinding halts work for me."

"You're easy, McNamara."

"Only when it comes to you, Dev."

She pushed herself to a sitting position, her back against two king-size pillows. "I'm going to shower—"

"So am I." He was out of bed and headed for the bathroom in two seconds flat.

She sat on the edge of the bed. "I'd planned to shower alone."

"Conservation, woman." He stood naked against the

doorjamb, tall and lean with a flat, firm belly and his morning erection. "Two in the shower saves on water."

She ran her fingers along her cheek and chin, now tender from his whisker burn. "Shave first; then we shower."

"Sandpaper." He rubbed his jaw. "I hate to rub you raw."

While Shane ran a razor over his jaw, Devin sat on a brass-legged stool before the vanity in his bathroom wearing his *Tusker Tavern, Mombasa, Kenya* T-shirt, while he wore nothing but the shaving lather on his face. She ran her gaze down his strong back and tight buttocks, savoring the sight of him. She could look at him forever. His strength, tempered with gentleness, made her blood hum. She wanted him, thick and deep inside her once again.

She met his gaze in the mirror, and he winked as if reading her mind. Her body pulsed in immediate response.

Having finished shaving, he patted his face dry, then approached her, all buff, shaven, and fully aroused. "Nice T-shirt. Care to tell me what's under the elephant's trunk?"

Devin looked down at the pale blue cotton shirt. Each of the mammal's gray ears fanned one of her breasts, and the ivory tusks split over her ribs. The trunk curved just below her navel. "Perhaps you'd like to explore, Great White Hunter?"

Being the hunter he was, he rid her of the T-shirt in one slick move. "Let's shower."

Together they stepped into the octagonal frosted-glass stall. Shane adjusted the water, then reached for Devin.

Blood rushed to her cheeks and her breath quickened in anticipation. Her skin throbbed beneath the pulsing spray. As water flowed over the hard angles and flat planes of his body, she encircled his neck and drew him close. Shane kissed the drops of water from her lips, then her breasts and abdomen.

His hands were slippery and her body soapy when he bent his knees, lifted her by the waist, and pushed her against the tiled wall. He rocked forward, holding her there, belly to belly, with his hips and thighs and rigid need.

"Wrap your legs around me," he said roughly.

She did as he requested, and with one thrust took him deeply. Their mouths hot, their bodies slick, they quickly found a rhythm that satisfied them both. The moment her spasm rocked his body, Shane stiffened and his back arched in a final wave of release.

He held her high against his chest until she could stand, then kicked open the stall door and released the steam. The mirrors in the bathroom hazed with moisture.

He grabbed a plush black towel from the rack and began to pat her dry. His kisses followed the velour, and Devin shuddered.

She leaned against the vanity. "McNamara . . ."

"Mmm-mm . . ." He nuzzled her neck.

"The . . . book."

He dipped his head, and laved her nipple. "Mmm-hmm . . ."

"Work . . . now."

He nipped her abdomen. "Work . . . later."

"Mmm-mm." He grazed her hipbone with his teeth, and she grew as hot as his mouth.

He placed an openmouthed kiss high on her inner thigh. "Time to write," he breathed against the juncture of her thighs as he slowly worked his way back up her body.

"Write?" She was wound so sexually tight, her stomach was in knots.

His gaze was as heated as her skin. "I want you sitting on a hot rock during our writing session, wanting me, and itching for the book to end."

Standing so close their bodies brushed, she stroked the curve of his buttock, his hip, the washboard scrub of his stomach, before curving her hand over his erection and squeezing. He swelled and lengthened. His Adam's apple worked, and his surprised moan rose from deep in his chest.

"Hot rock for two." Her fingers teased and toyed, and he pulsed against her palm before she released him.

She then snagged a clean *Kangaroo Brew, Perth, Australia* T-shirt from his closet and slipped it over her head. She smiled down at the brown kangaroo with a beer in its pouch. She loved Shane McNamara and his dozens of T-shirts.

After pulling on a pair of drawstring shorts, she walked out the bedroom door. Shane's frustrated howl followed her into the living room. His howl was deep and sexy, a pleading to mate. Smiling to herself, Devin chose to make him suffer for just a little while.

Two feet into the main room, Devin nearly tripped over her own feet. Her heart quit beating, and her breathing died on a final exhale.

Just beyond the sofa, the light from her monitor cast an eerie glow over her desk. Shadows jumped off the wall, shifting, snaking, seemingly alive. The scents of leather and roses teased the air. The room pulsed with another presence.

Movement behind her desk drew her gaze. Two people were silhouetted against the morning light, a man and a woman.

Her indrawn breath drew their attention.

The man immediately moved toward her. He looked like the Marlboro Man or a close cousin. His eyes were gray, and as cold and hard as those of any criminal. His hand rested on his six-gun.

The woman soon joined him. She stood to his left, somewhat shadowed by his size. She was blond and blue-eyed, soft and feminine, and utterly beautiful. From what Devin could see, she was dressed in an old-fashioned gown of palest pink, and wore gloves to match. One pointed-toed shoe peeked from beneath the hem of her gown.

The woman was as refined as the man was rough.

While the woman's gaze held a familiar fondness, the man's look aimed to kill.

Who were these people dressed in western garb, who now stood before her as if they owned the cottage or were about to take it over? As if they planned to stay . . .

Realization hit with a shiver and rash of goose bumps. Devin blinked, surely she had lost her mind. "*Rose Coltraine?*"

The woman broke into a radiant smile.

The man's scowl darkened to the point of being dangerous. "Stop blinkin', Miss James. We're no longer a figment of your imagination."

Devin ceased blinking. She covered her eyes with her hand, and peeked between her index and middle finger.

"Stop starin' at me from between your fingers," the man ordered.

Devin dropped her hand. "Shane," she croaked out. "I-I need—"

"Sex?" He strolled form the bedroom. "I'm your man."

"Keep your pants on. We have company," Devin informed him.

"And so we have . . ." His voice trailed off as he came to stand beside her, bare chested, his jeans zipped but unbuttoned. He stared at the two intruders with open interest.

Devin licked her lips. "Do you see what I see?"

He took his time in answering. "Uninvited guests? A costume party? I see a beautiful blonde in a saloon-style gown and a cowboy—"

"A gunslinger, mister." The man cut Shane a sharp look.

Shane stepped closer, his eyes narrowed on the man who could pass for his next of kin. The man's jaw tightened, and his nostrils flared. They faced each other as if for a shoot out, neither one moving.

Shane was the first to break eye contact. He shook his head, his expression one of utter disbelief. "Calder? *Dare Calder?*"

The man palmed his six-gun. "As you live and breathe."

Shane pushed Devin behind him. "Fictional characters don't have substance, yet you appear as tall and solid as any man."

"And twice as intimidatin'." Calder drew his six-gun and aimed it at Shane's stomach. "Care to sit a spell?"

It was an order, not a request. Devin balked; the gunslinger would not dictate her life. "Held hostage by our imaginations? No way in—"

Calder cocked his gun, the sound real enough.

Rose Coltraine stepped to his side; her skirt swayed and her petticoats rustled. She placed her gloved hand over his wrist. "You promised no violence, Mr. Calder."

"I haven't shot anyone . . . yet."

"Nor shall you, sir," she said.

Calder tipped back his Stetson. "As long as they co-operate"—he waived his six-gun at Devin and Shane—"no one will get hurt."

"Don't rile my gunslinger. I'm not certain what he's capable of doing while outside my mind," Shane whispered from the corner of his mouth as he took Devin's hand and led her to the sofa.

She had no plans to irritate Calder. Easing down beside Shane, she kept her eyes on the gunslinger and his revolver.

Beside her, Shane crossed his arms over his bare chest.

Calder tracked his every move. "Make yourself decent in front of womenfolk," he said as he shucked off his brown leather vest and tossed it to Shane.

As Shane slipped on the vest, Devin reached over and fingered the leather. It was soft and worn, and smelled of sunshine, trail dust, and wanted man. Devin half expected bounty hunter Art Noble to storm the room at any moment.

Clearing his throat, Shane stared directly at Calder. "I've known my imagination to run wild, but this stretches—"

"Beyond belief?" Calder lifted a brow, his expression smug.

Devin leaned forward, more fascinated than fearful. "Our characters have taken on lives of their own. How can that be?"

Rose Coltraine clasped her gloved hands together, all prim and proper. "I have always lived in your heart and mind, as Dare Calder has lived in Shane's," she calmly explained to Devin. "We were no more than a printed description in your books until your—"

"Fussin' and fightin' gave us life," Calder finished for her.

Devin lifted a brow. "Our anger, frustration, and jealousy brought you to life?"

"Damn straight," Calder said.

Shane blew out a breath. "You're a manifestation of our emotions."

"Our negative emotions," Devin said, as curious as Shane. "What of our passion? How has that affected you?"

"Damn near killed us," Calder said in a growl. "We've heard the bedsprings creakin'." He nodded to Shane. "I've inherited your lust for"—he glanced at Devin and Rose—"life."

Devin gaped, then recovered. "You're not Shane's child."

"He created me—that makes us family," Calder said matter-of-factly. "You and Miss Rose could pass for sisters."

Devin looked thoughtfully at Rose. She and the saloon proprietress were both slender and blond with blue eyes and—

Devin shook herself mentally. This was downright crazy!

"Coffee . . . I need coffee," Devin said.

"Make it the Kenya Believe It blend," Shane said.

Ignoring Calder's gun now leveled on her, Devin pushed off the sofa and padded barefoot to the kitchen. "Hot and black and—"

"So strong you'll waken from this dream?" Calder asked. "Ain't gonna happen, Miss James."

Devin brewed a full pot. After pouring it into a carafe, she grabbed four mugs and returned to the living room. She set the carafe and mugs on the coffee table, then asked, "Who would care for a cup?"

Rose politely declined, and Calder eyed the carafe with suspicion. He waited until Devin and Shane had taken their first sips before he agreed to a cup. His hand brushed Devin's when she handed him his mug. She found his skin warm and rough, and pulsing with life.

Dare Calder walked among the living, tall, domineering, and dangerous.

She watched him take his first sip of Plantation Kenya, then grimace. He set the mug on the corner of Devin's desk. "Too weak. Not to my likin'."

Devin had never brewed it so strong.

Biting down on her bottom lip, Devin backtracked to something Calder had said earlier. She needed clarification. "If our passion nearly destroyed you, how have you managed to survive?"

Calder looked at Rose, his gaze hot and appreciative. One corner of his mouth curled into a slow, sexy smile. In that instant the gunslinger's resemblance to Shane was uncanny.

When Rose dipped her head and blushed, Devin suddenly understood. It was written all over them. "You've grown fond of each other."

"Fond enough to finish the book we started," Calder informed her.

Devin gasped as a light went on in her head. "You're the mystery writers!"

Calder nodded. "Damn fine writin', I must say."

Devin covered her face and groaned. "I blamed Shane—"

"I blamed Devin—" Shane said simultaneously. "The boot print and shot glass—"

"The scent of roses, leather, and cigarette smoke," Devin continued, "all make sense now."

"You never suspected Rose and I had a hand in the writin'?" Calder smirked.

Devin sighed. "Not in my wildest dreams."

Silence held them in a cottage where fantasy now blended with reality.

Shane set his mug on the coffee table and looked Calder dead in the eye. "What do you want from us?"

"Your cooperation," Calder said.

Shane spread his hands wide. "Talk to me."

Calder proceeded to do just that. "You two can fill in the middle, but Miss Rose and I plan to write the final chapter of our book."

"Your book?" Devin asked.

"Our story, our book." Calder stood firm. "You and Shane forced Rose and me onto the same page, and we'll not be leavin' until we're satisfied with the outcome."

Rose twisted her gloved hands. "Mr. Calder and I have reached an understanding. We've agreed on how the story must end."

Calder twirled his six-gun, his smile wicked. "Virgin or pleasured woman?" He looked directly at Shane. "Are you a bettin' man?"

Devin's heart sank. The cards appeared stacked against Rose Coltraine.

Cutter's Bend

The sun set on Cutter's Bend, the shadows and stillness closing in on the boardwalk where Rose Coltraine and Dare Calder stood separated by their good-byes.

On Main Street, a horse blew out, a hoof clicked on a stone, and someone shifted in his saddle. The creak of a buckboard sounded rusty on the night air.

"You're leaving? So soon?" The small, aching sensation surprised Miss Rose as she plucked at the skirt on her twilight-pink gown.

303

Calder's mouth curved faintly. "I've never stayed so long."

Rose bit down on her bottom lip. "You've a business to oversee, Mr. Calder. Your partnership in the Garter should keep you in Cutter's Bend."

"The Garter belongs to you, Rose, not to me." He withdrew a folded document from the front pocket of his chambray shirt. "Here's the deed to the Garter, done up in your name."

Rose's hand shook as she unfolded the paper and read each word carefully. All was in order. From this day forth the Scarlet Garter belonged to her—only to her. "I don't know how to thank you, Mr. Calder," she said.

His gaze heated. "Someday you'll thank me with more than a handshake."

She blushed. "The town's growing, sir. Perhaps in a year or two you'd consider settling here."

"Count on it, Rose." He held her in his gaze. "While I'm gone, Marshal Morgan will make regular rounds at the Garter. He'll be checking on you for me."

"I don't need his protection. I've taken care of—"

He stepped toward her, so close his denims rustled her satin gown. "No argument, I want you safe."

She dipped her head. "I'll miss you, Mr. Calder."

"I'll hold a fond memory of you also, Miss Coltraine."

Calder shifted his stance, as restless as the breeze, and Rose knew he would soon take to his saddle.

"Might I kiss you?" he asked.

She glanced down the boardwalk. Numerous townspeople milled about, and several craned their necks, openly curious. "Here, sir, in public?"

"I want you branded mine." He then slid his hands into her hair and his tongue between her lips. He

304

burned his memory into her mouth and her mind.

A strange feeling gripped Dare, one he couldn't fight. Her softness, her inexperience and purity, left a mark on his heart. A permanent one. He knew, in that instant, that his trail would end at Rose Coltraine's door.

His body stirred and his blood thickened. He grew hard and heavy in a matter of heartbeats.

He felt Rose squirm against him. "Your gun belt has twisted." She broke the kiss and lowered her gaze. Her eyes widened and color rouged her cheeks. A ridge of man, not metal, probed her skirts.

She trembled, then sighed, suddenly wanting more from him than his good-byes.

It was difficult for Calder to walk away when he'd rather have stayed. Tipping his Stetson, he turned and stepped off the boardwalk. He grabbed the reins from the hitching post and mounted his mustang. He kicked him into a gallop. On the outskirts of town he slowed his mount, turned in the saddle, and caught a final glimpse of Rose Coltraine.

He'd left his heart in Cutter's Bend.

"Satisfied?" Dare Calder appeared arrogantly pleased with himself.

Shane heard Devin's sigh of relief, and knew his writing partner would breathe more easily now. He met Calder's cocky grin. "You treated Rose with the dignity she deserved."

"She's quite a lady," Calder agreed. "I wouldn't mind returnin' to Cutter's Bend someday."

"I feel a sequel in our future," Devin said.

Shane squeezed her knee. "Speaking of our future—"

"It's time to rope her in," Calder cut in.

"Rope who in?" Devin shifted on the sofa.

Shane knew exactly where Calder was headed, and he planned to head him off. "I'll take care of the roping on my own time."

Calder shook his head, determination etched on his rugged features. "You'll do it now before witnesses."

Shane glared at Calder. "Who's in charge here?"

"The man with the gun." Calder widened his stance.

Shane bent to his gunslinger's request. Clasping Devin's hand, he brought it to his lips and kissed her palm. She looked uncertain and confused until he popped the question. "Would you care to hang your toothbrush next to mine for the rest of our lives?"

"Hanging brushes for cleaning teeth?" Rose Coltraine laid her hand on Calder's forearm. "That doesn't sound like—"

"It ain't," Calder replied none too pleased. "The man's ploddin' like a plowhorse."

Shane blew out a breath. He hadn't planned on an audience to his proposal. He met Devin's gaze: her aqua eyes were clear and wide, and told the entire story. She loved him. No other woman had ever looked at him with so much trust and caring. His heart punched hard in his chest. "Marry me, Devin James."

She lifted a hand to stroke his cheek. "I will."

Two little words, warm with feeling, were all he needed to hear. "I love you, Dev."

"I love you, too."

Happiness stirred his soul. Slowly he smoothed his hand through her hair and brought his mouth down to meet her lips. She tucked herself into his body, her arms circling his neck and her breasts flattening against his chest.

In the far recesses of Shane's mind, he registered a

man's chuckle of approval and a woman's romantic sigh.

"Time to saddle up," drifted to him, only to be wiped away when Devin's tongue glanced his, teasing and tempting, and taking him beyond himself.

His kiss moved to her ear, her cheek, then back to her mouth, a slow, unhurried progression. Their lips brushed and clung in infinite kisses as he stroked the sweet curve of her shoulder, the elegant slide of her spine, before he cupped her rounded hip and pressed her closer to him. He was holding her so close, it almost seemed as if they were an extension of the same person.

"Shane?" His name on her lips lingered soft and warm. "Calder and Rose?"

Resting his forehead against hers, he kissed the tip of her nose, then turned to where Rose had recently wrung her hands and Calder had held them at gunpoint. The room stood empty, except for the faint scent of roses, old leather, and the mustiness of time.

"Where have they gone?" Devin asked.

Shane rubbed his palms over his eyes to be sure his vision was clear. He then rose, circled the living room, and peered into the bedrooms. "They've obviously disappeared," he informed Devin from the kitchen.

"Where would they go?" Her hand rested over her heart, her expression anxious and a little sad. "I feel like a mother who's lost her child."

Shane returned to the sofa. "Perhaps they're back where they belong, in our active consciousness."

Devin fingered the points on Calder's leather vest. "He forgot his vest."

"Calder will collect his vest when he returns for the sequel." Of that Shane was certain.

The telephone rang, disrupting further contemplation.

Devin crossed to her desk and hit the button for the speakerphone. "Writer's cottage."

"Devin, it's Victoria Patton." Their publicist's voice filled the room. "Is Shane nearby?"

Shane came to stand by Devin. He curved his arm around her shoulders and hugged her close. "I'm as close as skin, Vic."

"Skin . . ." Victoria paused. "You've apparently gotten a lot closer since we last spoke."

"Close enough to horse trade," Shane said. "The completed manuscript is ready on deadline for a justice of the peace."

There was another pause before Victoria said, "Congratulations! I'm so happy for you both."

"I'm happy too, Vic," Shane said, and realized how very much he meant it. For the first time in his life his spirit felt free, yet connected—to a sexy blonde with a tight-ass braid.

"How soon shall I schedule this wedding? Today, tomorrow, next week?" Vic asked.

Shane looked at Devin and lifted his brow. "Your call, Dev."

Devin's lips curved in a smile that would bring him to his knees for the rest of his life. "The sooner the better."

"This afternoon," Shane decided.

"We'll need you to stand up for us, Vic," Devin said.

"My pleasure. I'll get back to you with the time," Vic promised. "A wedding between coauthors." Shane could almost hear her rubbing her hands together. "This is a publicist's dream."

"No photographers today," Shane said, "but maybe tomorrow."

"I'll set up an interview or two," Vic added. "By the way, did the secretarial temp work out?"

"She's spreading a little joy in California," Devin responded with a grin. "Shane and I discovered we work best alone."

"I'm glad there will be no trouble completing the manuscript." Shane could hear the relief in Victoria's voice. "Any plans once the book is completed?"

"A long honeymoon," Shane said as he squeezed Devin's shoulders. "One that lasts a lifetime."

"Let me check with the courthouse and see what strings I can pull to get you married today," Vic said. "I'll get back to you shortly."

"You don't feel too rushed, do you?" Shane asked as he disconnected the speakerphone, then joined Devin on the sofa. He pulled her onto his lap and cuddled her close. "A girl plans her wedding from the day she takes her first step. She's writing wedding vows after her first date. She's cutting pictures of wedding dresses out of bridal magazines—"

Devin poked him in the ribs. "Not this girl. I was too busy writing short stories to plan a wedding."

Shane kissed her forehead. "I like your mind, Devin James."

"I like your body." Twisting on his lap, Devin straddled him. She curled her arms about his shoulders and settled snuggly on his thighs. He clutched her hips as she rocked against him.

"Happy trails, McNamara," she said against his mouth.

Shane let Devin take him for the ride of his life.

Improper English

KATIE MACALISTER

Sassy American Alexandra Freemar isn't about to put up with any flak from the uptight—albeit gorgeous—Scotland Yard inspector who accuses her of breaking and entering. She doesn't have time. She has two months in London to write the perfect romance novel—two months to prove that she can succeed as an author.

Luckily, reserved Englishmen are not her cup of tea. Yet one kiss tells her Alexander Block might not be quite as proper as she thought. Unfortunately, the gentleman isn't interested in a summer fling. And while Alix knows every imaginable euphemism for the male member, she soon realizes she has a lot to learn about love.

LYNSAY SANDS
THE LOVING DAYLIGHTS

Shy Jane Spyrus loves gadgets. She can build anything B.L.I.S.S. needs in its international fight against crime—although agents aren't exactly queuing up at her door. Some of them think her innovations are too . . . well, innovative. Like her shrink-wrap prophylactic constraints. But they just don't realize that item's potential.

Of course, you can't use wacky inventions to fix all your problems. Jane will have to team up with another *human being*—and Abel Andretti arrives just in time. He will help Jane find her kidnapped neighbor, stop the evil machinations of Dirk Ensecksi, and most of all he will show her how to love the daylights out of something without batteries.

- -